I0637678

The Return of Prince Malock

Book Two in the Prince Malock World

by Timothy L. Cerepaka

An Annulus Publishing Book

Annulus Publishing, Cherokee, Texas, 2014

Published by Annulus Publishing

Copyright © Timothy L. Cerepaka 2014. All rights reserved.

ISBN-13: 978-0692303252

ISBN-10: 0692303251

Cover by Elaina Lee of For the Muse Design
(http://www.forthemusedesign.com)

Acknowledgments

I would like to thank my uncle, James Wilhite, once again for helping me get this novel into publishable shape. I would also like to thank my family for supporting me while I wrote this novel.

Chapter One

WHEN SKIMIF—AN AQUARIAN farmer of seaweed, a highly profitable business in his hometown of Tunya, a small town located not far from the larger city of Nemo —opened his eyes, he at first saw only darkness, but then a brilliant light shone forth, almost blinding him in its intensity. Yet he couldn't close his eyes, couldn't even look away, and soon the brilliant light disappeared, replaced by the rays of the sun that illuminated a barren earth hundreds of miles below him.

Then cracks in the ground began to appear and soon they burst, unleashing tons and tons of water, more water than Skimif had ever seen in his life. He saw the water cover the entire surface of the planet, rapidly growing until all that was left was a gigantic continent and thousands, if not millions, of tiny islands scattered everywhere. Skimif blinked, and the next moment found himself standing in the middle of a huge jungle on the continent. He blinked again and saw a naked human lying curled on the ground before him. The human had brownish skin and appeared to be male. The human opened his eyes and looked around at his surroundings like a newborn baby seeing the world for the first time.

It took Skimif a moment to realize that he was seeing the human through his left eye. Through his right, he saw an aquarian—one who resembled a hammerhead shark, much like he did, except thinner—floating in the deep ocean, observing the world around her with the same expression that the human wore. Seeing both simultaneously made Skimif's head pound and his stomach churn, but he didn't throw up.

Then he was back in the sky again and he saw stars falling from the night sky, but they weren't stars at all. Instead, they were beings of all shapes and sizes. One being that flew past him was a woman who appeared to be made out of water; another was an octopus-like creature with a green humanoid head. There appeared to be hundreds of thousands of these beings, each one glowing as brightly as the next, as they soared toward the earth below.

And then Skimif was flying with them and he soon found himself standing in the middle of a desert, a barren plain that stretched for miles in every direction. But the plain was not entirely empty. The stars—the beings, the gods—had landed on the ground, but rather than co-mingling together, they took sides. Half of them stood on the north side of the desert, while the other half stood on the south side. And in between them were a handful of statues that looked just like humans and aquarians.

Another shift in reality found Skimif standing in the jungle from before, but things were different now. The trees burned with flames, while the jungle itself slapped away at the flames with thick wet vines.

Yet with every flame the trees succeeded in putting out, a dozen more would spring up in its place. Skimif looked up and saw two beings—one a being wreathed in fire, the other a man with green skin—in combat in the area, their every movement mimicked by the fire and trees below.

One more shift and Skimif found himself hovering over the surface of the Crystal Sea, but the Crystal Sea was not its usual smooth, calm self. Hundreds if not thousands of gallons of water arose from the ocean, growing larger and larger, while a nearby volcano shook with a shudder. Then the volcano exploded, sending plumes of smoke and flame and magma hurtling toward the water. The volcanic projectiles struck the walls of water, evaporating much of it while simultaneously creating a massive steam cloud. It looked like the volcano had won, but then the sea rose up again and fired toward the volcano, striking its base with enough force to crack it open.

As with before, Skimif noticed two beings. One was a woman whose body flowed like the ocean waves, while the other was a woman with lava for hair. The two females seemed to be in control of the sea and volcano, respectively, but before Skimif could see who would win, another blink transported him to the clouds above.

No; above the clouds. The whole world lay out before Skimif, like the fields of seaweed that he farmed. His eyes were drawn to the massive green continent directly below him, a continent that seemed to cover the entirety of the northern half of the world. Then he noticed huge cracks spreading through the continent's surface, which divided over and over again into smaller and smaller cracks until the whole thing exploded.

When the explosion cleared, the massive green continent was no more. In its place were hundreds of thousands of islands, some large, some small, but each completely independent of the others surrounding it. One thing all of the islands had in common, however, was the mass cries of pain and fear that seemed to reach up to the heavens themselves, as if the inhabitants of each island were crying out for the help of a higher power.

Then Skimif felt something behind him and he turned. He couldn't comprehend even half of what he was currently looking at. It appeared to be—and he couldn't even say this with one ounce of certainty—tendrils made of light reaching out from the darkness of the sky. They reached from beyond the sun, from beyond the stars, down into the planet below.

When Skimif turned to follow the tendrils, he found himself down in the world again, hovering over the sea. He was not alone, however. The gods from before—that had to be who they were, they couldn't be anyone else—also hovered above the waves that crashed below, but the waves were much more subdued now, as if they were tired and needed a nap. As earlier, the gods were separated into two groups: One in the north, one in the south.

But the gods looked different now. Though each side still had hundreds of gods, it was clear that both sides had lost a significant number of their fellow deities. Of those who were still alive, only perhaps a dozen altogether appeared uninjured. The rest looked like they had been through a war, with injuries ranging from the broken limbs to bashed skulls, as well as one god who was missing one whole arm and didn't seem to have grown it back yet.

A brilliant glowing line separated the two groups, which Skimif realized was one of the light tendrils from before. A god from each side approached the line, but it was reluctantly. The god from the northern side resembled a bald man with golden robes that shone brilliantly, like the afternoon sun, while the god from the south side resembled a strange octopus-like creature, with a green human-like head on top.

The two stopped just before either of them could cross the line. Then their right arms were jerked up, almost unnaturally so, and they shook hands, like they were putting aside their differences to become one. But it was clear that they hadn't forgiven each other. The two of them glared at each other and let go of the other's hand as soon as they could.

As soon as the two gods ceased their handshake, everything changed again. Everything moved quickly now. He saw all of history play out before him. Nations, empires, and kingdoms rose and fell; humans and aquarians alike discovered magic and its various uses; war spontaneously broke out between humans and aquarians or between humans and humans or aquarians and aquarians; the gods intervened occasionally; and then Skimif saw a massive city on the edge of the world, jutting out into the endless void beyond creation.

Then the light tendrils from before extended from the Void. They wrapped around the city's massive buildings and began to tear apart the city itself. The gods appeared to combat the tendrils, but they were knocked aside as easily as if they had been annoying insects. Even worse, the gods did not get up.

Then Skimif gasped and his eyes opened, but for real this time. His arms were tied down by something, he didn't know what, but he thrashed about to free himself anyway, biting at his bindings. His sharp teeth cut through the thin bindings and he swam up through the water until he was well above the tendrils that had sought to hold him down.

His heart beating fast, Skimif looked down and realized that he had only fallen asleep in his seaweed field. A quick glance at his arms and legs told him that he had simply gotten his limbs tangled in the seaweed, which meant that he had overreacted slightly.

It took Skimif a moment to remember how he had gotten there. He had been swimming through the field, looking for any weed-gobblers after hearing of an outbreak of them just north of Tunya, when he had lost consciousness for no reason. It took him even longer to remember what he had seen in his dream.

No, Skimif thought, shaking his head. *Not a dream. A vision. A vision of the future.*

Skimif could not be sure why, but he felt a stirring urge in the pit of his stomach to act on his vision. But he didn't know what to do until a single sentence escaped his lips, a sentence that he was certain had not come from his mind, a sentence he was equally certain was true:

"The Day of the Gods is coming."

Chapter Two

Four months later ...

PRINCE MALOCK LEANED AGAINST the railing of the top deck of the *Clockwork Heart*, his eyes scanning the distant horizon intently. Not that he could see much; with the sunrise still several hours away, it would be a while before Carnag, his homeland, came into view. Yet still Malock was the first one up early in the morning, before breakfast, hoping to be the very first passenger aboard the ship—technically the body of the Mechanical Goddess, although it looked and acted like a ship—to see his home.

His eyes flickered down to the deck below. A handful of automatons—the children of the Mechanical Goddess—milled around, swabbing the metal plating, cleaning the emergency boats hanging off the davits, and other such chores necessary to keep the ship in good shape. And although he could not see it, Malock knew that at least one automaton was clinging to the side of the ship, scraping off barnacles and other things that the Mechanical Goddess's body had collected over the past month. Why the automaton didn't wait until the *Clockwork Heart* stopped somewhere to perform that task, Malock didn't know.

Then again, Malock thought, glancing over his shoulder at the massive smokestacks that jutted from the center of the ship, *when has anyone ever said that the gods or their servants acted logically?*

The smokestacks sent columns of smoke into the air just then, though Malock didn't know if the Mechanical Goddess was trying to say something to him or if she was just blowing off smoke as part of the ship's engine. Malock didn't quite understand how the *Clockwork Heart* worked, even after Hanarova, the katabans who worked for the Goddess, had explained it to him. He had never seen a ship powered by smoke, much less one with an engine, and despite his distaste for the Mechanical Goddess, he was nonetheless fascinated by it.

The *Clockwork Heart* was so different from his old ship, the *Iron Wind,* which, due to the massive damage it had taken back on World's End, had to be left behind. Malock had sold the remains of the ship to a katabans who owned a ship salvaging company on World's End. The company owner had given Malock a hundred 'crimsonite,' apparently the currency used on that island, as payment. The bag of crimsonite was still in Malock's cabin on the ship, though he didn't think it would have a whole lot of value up north.

That's not to say that Malock sold the *Iron Wind* without thinking. It was a difficult decision to make, not helped in the least by his initial blatant refusal of the Mechanical Goddess's offer to take them back north. He only did it because he didn't have the funds to repair the old ship and because he recognized the value in having the protection of a goddess on the way up north. He was thankful that the Mechanical Goddess had not taken back her offer, although she did demand that Malock and his crew help out whenever she needed them to, though as far as Malock could tell the Goddess's automatons performed most of the work just fine on their own.

Of course, Malock had had a hell of a time convincing the rest of his crew to go along with it. Jenur Takren in particular had been against it, mostly because she still remembered how the Mechanical Goddess had nearly fed her to some of the other southern gods. The other members of the crew had been against it because they associated the Mechanical Goddess with the Tusked God, not an unfair association to make, seeing as the Tusked God had turned up on the Mechanical Goddess's island when they visited that island and almost succeeded in killing the entire crew.

Malock only succeeded in convincing the rest of them to come with him by pointing out how staying on World's End meant staying with the gods, many of whom made their homes there. If there was one thing Malock could say about his crew, it was that they hated, or at least heavily distrusted, the gods.

Well, except for a few. Arisha Frag, the former galley cook of the *Iron Wind*, had decided to remain behind on World's End. She said that she wanted to stay because of the city's beauty and majesty, as well as to bring her closer to the gods. Why she wanted to be closer to the gods when every other member of the crew wanted to be away from the gods, Malock didn't know. He just knew that he had allowed Frag and a few others who agreed with her to stay behind because he was not in the mood to argue with them about it.

He supposed they didn't trust the Mechanical Goddess, which was understandable. Many times throughout the voyage home he had thought that the Mechanical Goddess might just be up to her old tricks again, but so far she had not tried to feed him or any of his men to her siblings again. In fact, Malock had not seen any gods at all since they had left World's End, aside from the Mechanical Goddess herself. He wasn't sure, but he suspected the Goddess must have put him and his entire crew under her protection, which, according to the Treaty regulating the behavior and limitations of the gods, made it impossible for any other gods to kill or seriously injure him and his crew.

Whatever the reason, all Malock knew was that they were not more than a day or two away from Carnag, if even that much. They had passed the Dividing Line—the imaginary line separating the northern seas and its isles from the southern seas—a week ago, an astonishingly fast time whenever Malock thought about it. Then again, the *Clockwork Heart* was no ordinary ship, not in the least because it was actually the current body of a goddess.

Of course, they would have reached Carnag a few days sooner if they hadn't stopped by the island of Destan briefly. They had done that because Jenur Takren had wanted to go there and bury Kinker Dolan, a member of their crew who had died on World's End, who was originally from Destan. Malock wanted Jenur to stay, but she made it quite clear that she no longer saw herself as being under his authority anymore and that she would do as she pleased. She claimed that she had made a promise to Kinker prior to his death that she intended to keep, but she had not told Malock what that promise was.

Maybe she promised to bury him on his home island or something, Malock thought. *Suppose it doesn't matter. Jenur will be fine. She can take care of herself.*

"You're up early," said a familiar feminine voice behind him, one that was far too bright and cheery this early in the morning.

Knowing who it was, Malock turned around to face the source of the voice. "I could say the same about you, Hanarova."

Standing at the top of the stairs he had used to get up was a tall woman: Hanarova, the katabans servant of the Mechanical Goddess. Her green hair was much shorter than it had been when Malock had first seen her, having been cut to a more practical size for the voyage north. Nor did she wear her upside down flower dress; instead, she wore a bag-like shirt, very simple and practical, with a hole for the head and two for the arms. The shirt lacked a collar, being open at the top, although the shirt itself was covered with a doublet. A Monmouth cap covered her head, while her feet were bare upon the cold metal floor beneath her feet. If he had not seen her dressed like that every day for the past month, he would have had a hard time recognizing her.

"I have to be up early," said Hana. "You know, to supervise the automatons, make sure everything is running correctly, that sort of thing. I just thought you humans always slept in."

Malock frowned. "I've been getting up at this time every day for the past month and you just now noticed?"

"I've noticed," said Hana. "I was just wondering if you were going to give up at some point. What are you even looking for anyway?"

"Home," Malock said. "Isn't it obvious?"

Now it was Hana's turn to frown. "Right. 'Homesickness' is what you mortals call it, right? As a katabans, I've never understood how you mortals can get so attached to one place. We katabans never get attached to anywhere, even those of us who actually do own our own homes."

"Then I can't explain it to you," said Malock. "Nor do I need to. It's not necessary for you to understand."

"That I can agree with," said Hana. "By the way, the Mechanical Goddess says Carnag should be coming up soon, probably by the time the sun rises."

"How does she know that?" said Malock. "She's never been to Carnag before, has she?"

Hana smirked. "The Mechanical Goddess has a variety of instruments and devices she uses to figure out where everything is in relation to her. It's how we've managed to avoid running into any other ships on the way up north."

"Oh," said Malock, glancing starboard out into the open sea. "Now that you mention it, it is kind of strange how we've came so far without running into even a small fishing boat."

"The Mechanical Goddess isn't interested in being seen by mortals," said Hana. "Though I suppose when we reach Carnag she probably will be seen by some of your people."

Malock looked at the smokestacks that towered over him and Hana. "Then why did she decide to head up north at all? Surely she didn't do it because she wanted to help us."

"Her reasons for heading up north are entirely her own, Malock," said Hana. "Which is to say that she ordered me to keep it a secret from you and your crew. It's none of your business, as you mortals might say."

"That doesn't sound good," said Malock.

"Don't worry," said Hana. "She's not planning to start a war or kill mortals or anything. Remember, the southern gods can't even harm mortals when they go beyond the Dividing Line. The Mechanical Goddess simply has business to do up here, which is why she offered to take you and your crew back home. Two stones with one bird, you understand."

The *Clockwork Heart*'s smokestacks shot columns of thick smoke into the air, reminding Malock of the boot factories back on Carnag.

"All right," said Malock. "How long does she intend to stay up north?"

"As long as she has to," said Hana. "Which is another way of saying that it's none of your business."

"Right," said Malock. "As long as she is not kidnapping mortals to feed to her siblings, she can do what she likes around here."

The ship shuddered, almost throwing Malock off his feet. He gripped the railing to steady himself until the ship ceased shuddering. Hana smirked.

"Guess she didn't like your tone," Hana said. "I admit I'm not a big fan of it, either."

Malock stomped his boot against the deck, but all he succeeded in doing was banging his boot against the metal. "I honestly cannot wait until I am off this ship."

"The Mechanical Goddess says the feeling is mutual," said Hana. "She only tolerates you because she is trying to make up for almost killing you and your crew back on Stalf."

Malock frowned. "Why would she ...? Gah. The gods never make any sense."

"They don't need to make sense," said Hana. "By the way, breakfast is starting soon. The cooks are preparing it even as we speak."

At that, Malock's stomach rumbled. The food served aboard the *Clockwork Heart* was some of the best food that Malock had ever tasted, much better than the food he and the others had had to eat aboard the *Iron Wind* during its last month on the seas. He even thought he could already smell the bacon and eggs, even though the galley was below deck and there was no way he could smell whatever it was they were cooking below.

"That sounds good," said Malock. "I was getting hungry. How soon?"

"In a few minutes," said Hana. "I believe the rest of your crew is already awake and waiting for it in the dining room below deck."

"Then I should go and join them," said Malock. He walked past Hana, who moved out of the way, and was halfway down the stairs when he stopped and looked over his shoulder at her. "Hana, when Carnag comes into view, could you tell me? I want to see it."

Hana nodded. "Don't you worry about that. Everyone will know when Carnag comes into view. You don't have to worry about not seeing it."

Malock nodded his thanks, then continued walking down the stairs, thinking, *It's been a long time, but soon, we will be home. And then maybe life will go back to normal. Maybe we'll even forget all of what happened on World's End.*

That seemed very unlikely to Malock, but he decided to think positive for a change. He was getting tired of constant negativity.

Chapter Three

JENUR TAKREN CROUCHED AS low as she could on the roof of a store that sold fruit; specifically, it sold yarunda pears. She knew this because the owner had tried to sell her some when she was walking through the town earlier, but she had ignored his sales pitch because she didn't want him to see her face—not when she had spent the last two weeks keeping her entire existence a secret from the other Destanians.

Because once she did what she was going to do, she knew she would have little time to escape Destan.

Peering around the store's large, wooden pear-shaped sign, Jenur looked down into the streets below. Hundreds of people, members of every Tribe on Destan, crowded the streets of the town of Rimo. Blue streamers ran from rooftop to rooftop, while many of the buildings, houses, and stores in town had received a new coat of sea blue paint over the last couple of weeks in preparation for the Sea Festival. In particular, the Temple of Kano—the large stone building that dominated the southern end of Rimo—had been painted with images of Kano and the sea. The painting that stood out to her most was one featuring Kano standing before a massive wave, one hand held up like she was holding it back all on her own.

It was a beautiful work of art, one which Jenur thought rivaled the art of the Northern Artists, whose work she had seen on the island of Yura a year ago.

I shouldn't get distracted, Jenur thought, her eyes focusing on the front door of the Temple. *Otherwise, I might miss my chance and all of my work over the past two weeks will be for nothing.*

Just to be sure nothing would go wrong, Jenur decided to go over her plan once more. She had a few minutes to spare, after all, as Deber Noman was still in the Temple preparing for her grand appearance. Plus—though Jenur would never say this aloud, mostly because it would be bad luck to do so—she was not entirely sure the plan would work, even though she was convinced it was a good plan.

Her plan was simple. When Priestess Deber, the leader of the Destanians and also Head Priestess of Kano, walked out of the Temple, Jenur would take her blowgun and fire a poisonous dart into Deber's neck. The dart would be full of kenyo poison, a type of poison Jenur had used often in her days as a member of the Dark Tigers Guild. Assuming the dart hit in the right spot, Deber would be dead within minutes.

It sounded so simple in her mind, but as she looked out over the crowds, Jenur had her doubts. She had a steady hand, a good aim, and her blowgun—which she had snatched from a Nikon weapons dealer who had traveled all the way to Destan to sell his wares here—was of a very high quality. But Deber wouldn't be alone. She would be protected by the Priestly Guard, a group of Destanians from the

Warrior tribe whose sole duty was to protect Deber night and day. None of them knew about Jenur, true, but they would nonetheless defend their Priestess as if they did.

Even if Jenur succeeded, there was the problem of escape. Jenur didn't have a ship or even a boat of her own to make her getaway with. The remaining Priests would probably shut down all travel to and from the island, while the Priestly Guard would scour Rimo and every inch of Destan for the assassin. Even the average Destanians would likely help in the search. Jenur had been here long enough to know just how valuable Deber was to everyone who lived here, which just emphasized the need for her to make a quick escape after she performed the deadly deed.

But not all hope was lost because, amid the crowd of Destanians celebrating the Sea Festival, she spotted a handful of white, wide-brim hats. Those were the hats of a group of visiting Shikans who had come from the north to participate in the Sea Festival as tourists. Their ship, the *Easy Going*, was docked at the north end of the island, not far from Rimo. Jenur planned to sneak aboard their ship after assassinating Deber and hide there until the Shikans decided to leave. True, the Priestly Guard could demand that the Shikans let them search their ship, but she doubted they would succeed because these particular Shikans were, from what she had learned, very important and very rich businessmen and women, who likely had friends in the Shikan government who might not take kindly to having their friends treated like potential criminals. Most likely, the Shikans would leave Destan when Jenur killed Deber; after all, they probably wouldn't want to remain on the same island as as assassin.

Jenur checked her blowgun again just to make sure it was loaded. It was shaped like a rifle, except instead of using gun powder, the blowgun had an air pump that had at least as much strength as a normal gun. The only difference was that it was silent, which would be helpful for when she had to make her escape. When she gave it some thought, she supposed that made it more of an air gun than a blowgun, but Jenur was never one to quibble over semantics.

After making sure the blowgun was good, Jenur once more looked out into the streets. Still no sign of Deber just yet. She wondered what was taking the Priestess so long to show up.

She probably got caught up in killing another little boy, Jenur thought. *Or maybe she's ruining the life of another innocent old man. Just like Kinker.*

Jenur almost choked when she thought about her deceased friend, Kinker Dolan. When she had come to Destan a couple of weeks ago, she had brought Kinker's corpse with her. She had given him a burial at sea, partly because she wasn't sure what kind of burial rituals they performed on Destan and partly because she didn't want any of the Destanians to see Kinker's body. As far as she knew, all of the Destanians believed Kinker to be dead. If Kinker's body turned up on Destan, no doubt the Priestly Guard would have investigated it, which would have definitely messed up her plans.

Her hands started to hurt, causing her to look down at them. She was gripping the blowgun with too much intensity. Relaxing her grip, Jenur took a deep breath. She had already cried over Kinker's death before. In fact, she had spent most of the voyage from World's End mourning him. She could no longer mourn him, at least right now, because she had something important to do now, and she could not do it if she was constantly crying over Kinker's death.

Remember the promise you made to him, Jen, Jenur thought. *You didn't promise to cry about his death. You promised to kill Deber. And that is a promise you will deliver. You've killed people before, people way more important than Deber, and you can do it again.*

Of course, that confidence was tempered by the fact that Jenur had left the Dark Tigers Guild precisely because she was done killing people for money. She still knew all of the various assassination techniques that all Dark Tigers were taught (plus a few she had learned on her own), but that didn't mean she had to use them. That she was now trying to assassinate someone again—even if she wasn't doing it for money—caused her more than a little cognitive dissonance.

Doesn't matter, Jenur thought. *This is different. No one is paying me to kill Deber. I am doing this of my own free will. And once I do it, I will head back up north and never lay another finger on another human being ever again.*

That still did little to quell her own doubts, but Jenur ignored them because at that moment the large wooden doors to the Temple swung open. A bent over, old woman with the same dark skin color as Kinker walked out of the doorway, flanked on all sides by a group of tall, muscular men armed with leather armor and spears and swords. The old woman wore sea-blue robes, with tiny crystals embedded in the fabric that reflected the light of the sun. The crystals were stitched in such a way that they resembled raindrops, a dazzling effect if Jenur ever saw one.

The old woman walked with her head held high, like a queen, while the Priestly Guard walked with the kind of trained disciplined only soldiers displayed. Though the Priestly Guard kept their eyes ahead, Jenur knew that they were constantly aware of everything around them. The Priestly Guard would be the most difficult part because, while none of them were mages, every member knew a little bit of magic. And as the old saying went, a little bit of magic could go a long way.

Which meant that Jenur would have to be even quicker about this than she currently planned.

When Deber and her Priestly Guard emerged from the Temple, all of the people in the streets below stopped to look at them. As Deber and her Guard made their way down the street, the Destanians and visitors from other islands stepped back to allow her through. More than a few Destanians looked at the Priestess with awe and one man—who was clearly a cripple, as he had no feet and was sitting in a wagon being drawn by a young girl who might have been his daughter—reached out to touch the hem of Deber's robes as she passed, as if he thought she could heal him. He failed to do that because one of the Guard slapped his hand away, but the cripple still looked at Deber with the kind of reverence one normally reserved for the gods themselves.

If only he knew her true nature, Jenur thought, *then he might not be so eager to touch even the hem of her cloak.*

Jenur double-checked her blowgun again, just to be sure that it was loaded. Then she took aim as discreetly as she could, but then she realized that from her current position she couldn't hit Deber. Though Deber was by no means keeping her head down or even pretending to be humble, her Guard protected her on every side. While Jenur was no fan of the Priestly Guard, she was not interested in taking any of them down at the moment. Besides, she only had one dart and if she wasted it on one of the Guard, then all of her plans would be set back again.

Scowling, Jenur lowered her blowgun and made her way to the back of the roof. She decided she would find a better spot to shoot Deber. Besides, she knew where Deber was going anyway. All she needed to do was find a good spot to shoot from and she would be fine.

From what Jenur had gathered over the last two weeks, the main event of the Sea Festival was the slaughtering of a kakro shark on a giant wooden altar built in Rimo's town square. The shark was supposedly killed as a sacrifice to Kano, though why Deber and the Destanians thought Kano wanted animal sacrifice, Jenur didn't know. All she knew was that Deber would climb the altar alone, putting her well above the crowd, meaning it would be impossible for any of the Guards to protect her from a poison dart to the neck.

Jenur climbed down the ladder on the back of the building and dropped to the street softly. After a quick look around the area to make sure no one was around, Jenur made her way through the backstreets. Having spent the last couple of weeks exploring the town's layout, she knew the quickest way to get to the square from her current position.

Just as Jenur made her way down an alleyway that would cut the time needed to get her there in half, someone nearby said, "Hey, young woman. Where are you going?"

Jenur stopped, not because she wanted to, but because the voice was so familiar. It sounded just like Kinker's, but that couldn't be him. She looked around the small alleyway she stood in until she spotted Kinker standing in the doorway of the building to her right, a puzzled expression on his face. His beard, his skin, his nose ... it was all the same.

No. Jenur shook her head and looked more closely. The man wasn't Kinker. He looked a lot like Kinker, but when Jenur looked more closely, she realized there were several significant differences between him and Kinker. For one, the man's beard was not as white or long as Kinker's. His eyes were far less kind and his arms were larger, like he worked out more. He also wore a blue cotton shirt, but then, all of the old men in Destan seemed to wear that kind of shirt. It had some sort of significance for the Sea Festival, but for the life of her Jenur could not figure out what that significance was. It may have meant that the man was an organizer for the Festival, though again Jenur was not sure, mostly because it didn't seem like very important information for her to learn.

"Did you say something to me?" said Jenur.

The old man nodded. "I asked where are you going. Evidently the words of elders must always fall on the deaf ears of youth."

Jenur immediately decided she didn't like the old man, but she didn't have time to argue. She heard the sounds of the crowds following Deber to the town square and knew she had to get going, but the man looked so much like Kinker that she could not help but stand there and stare at him.

"I'm going to the town square," said Jenur, doing her best to seem as innocent and charming as she could. "Going to see the Sacrifice to Kano, like everyone else."

The old man frowned, making his resemblance to Kinker even more uncanny. "If that were so, then why are you not with the Procession? Where are your parents?"

Still smiling as pleasantly as she could, Jenur said, "I may not look it, but I'm actually a full-grown adult woman, so I don't need my parents. I'm fine on my own."

The old man peered at her more closely. "I don't think I've ever seen you around here before, girl. Are you visiting for the Sea Festival?"

"Yes," said Jenur. "I came from Nikos. It was a long voyage."

"You still haven't told me why you aren't with the Procession, though," said the old man. "You look like you know your way around this town, even though you're a foreigner."

Jenur bit her lower lip. Whoever this old man was, he was too smart. She had to think of an excuse quick.

"Well, this isn't the first time I've been down here," said Jenur. "I actually have family down here. My cousin used to show me around town all the time, taught me all the best shortcuts."

"Who is your cousin?" said the old man. "I don't know of any family in Destan that has relatives in Nikos. Besides, you don't sound like a Nikon. Your voice is too high-pitched, even for a Nikon woman."

"Not all Nikons are the same," said Jenur. "As for my family, well, that's none of your business. I don't even know why I am standing here talking to you. I'm just wasting time."

"What is your name?" said the old man.

"Tell me your name first," said Jenur.

The old man stroked his beard, not out of habit, but apparently out of anger. "You are very disrespectful toward your elders, young lady. But very well; my name is Rint."

He said that as if his first name was the only form of identification he needed.

"My name is Gaharna Vicin," said Jenur. It was a false name she had used during her Dark Tiger days and she had never forgotten it. "By the way, why aren't you following the Procession? Aren't you interested in seeing the Sacrifice?"

Rint averted his eyes for just a moment before he looked at her again and said, "Oh, I've seen the Sacrifice enough times over my life, I think. I am working here in this shop, so I am taking advantage of the Procession to clean up and get ready for the aftermath of the Sacrifice. Usually people come by here to buy my wares after the Sacrifice, so it's a good way to make a lot of money."

Jenur immediately knew Rint was lying because she noticed how carefully he worded his excuse. But for the life of her she could not figure out why he was lying to her, nor did she have time to find out because the sounds of the Procession were getting fainter and fainter and she really needed to leave right away.

"Right," said Jenur. "Well, nice meeting you, Rint. If you will excuse me, I really have to go. I don't want to miss the Sacrifice for anything in the world."

Even before the words left her mouth, Jenur was on her way out of the alleyway, not even looking at Rint. She heard Rint calling her name, but she didn't stop and look. She picked up the pace, hoping she would get to the town square before anyone else.

In just a few minutes, Jenur found herself standing in the town square, having made it there before the Procession. The large wooden altar—which towered above every other building in the town, dwarfed only by the Temple of Kano itself—had the large, striped kakro shark already lying on it. The shark was apparently already dead because it didn't seem to be moving or breathing, but Jenur figured that it would only count as a sacrifice after Deber spilled its blood.

After making sure no one was watching, Jenur found another store, this one selling fishing equipment, and climbed it easily. Just as she got behind the store's sign, the head of the Procession appeared at the other end of the square. Soon the entire town square was filled with the festival-goers, who took their places around the altar as Deber and her Guard made their way to the back of the altar, where Deber would take a set of stairs all the way to the top.

While the festival-goers talked and chattered, Jenur examined the sign she hid behind more closely. It had no holes in it, but that didn't discourage her. She pulled out her knife and began digging out a hole in the wooden sign just as Deber started speaking.

"Greetings, my fellow Destanians," said Priestess Deber, her voice old yet regal. "I am so pleased to see how many of you have made it to the Sea Festival this year. And I am equally pleased to see that we have many visitors this year, some from Shika, some from Nikos, but all are welcomed just as if they were our own brothers and sisters. For many of you visitors, this will be the first time you witness the Sacrifice, which I can assure you will be a wonderful sight that you will remember forever."

The crowd whooped and cheered. Jenur finished cutting the hole out and peered through it. Deber stood on the top of the altar, a shiny golden knife in her right hand. At her feet lay the kakro shark, its dead eyes glinting in the sunlight. Jenur calculated the distance between the store and the altar and figured that she should be able to hit Deber from this distance and make her escape by the time the Guard realized where the dart had come from.

"Now then," said Deber as she fished out a piece of paper from her robes. "As we do every year at the Sea Festival, I shall recite the names of the men and women we lost during this year's murder season. It is a way to remember those who, through no fault of their own, lost their lives to the worst time of year around this island. We will also remember the lives of those who died heroically, giving their own lives to save the lives of others who were at the mercy of the sea."

Deber sounded so broke and emotional, but Jenur didn't know if she should believe that or not. The Priestess might very well be sad about the deaths of those who had died during murder season. Or she might have been pretending. Jenur didn't know or care. She just stuck the blowgun through the hole, making sure to aim directly for Deber's neck.

"Thankfully, this year we only lost ten people to the sea, the lowest death count on record since we began keeping count fifty years ago," said Deber. "Praise be to Kano for sparing so many of us! Now first on the list is Kinker Dolan, a fisherman who belonged to the Hook tribe. He is survived only by his older brother, who most of you know is a valued member of our community. Kinker died toward the start of murder season, his body swept away by the massive waves when he rowed out onto the sea in his tiny little fishing boat. May Kano rest his goodly soul."

Goodly soul? Jenur thought. *This coming from the woman who threatened to ruin his life if he told everyone her secrets?*

"I knew Kinker before his death," said Deber. "Though we were never the closest of friends, I nonetheless respected him for his work as a fisherman. He was a mentor to many younger members of the Hook tribe, and when his death was learned of, they mourned him all day and all night for a full week."

Jenur stopped aiming the blowgun for a moment to stare at the back of the sign in disbelief. It had never occurred to her that Kinker might have had friends on Destan who would have mourned his death (well, technically he didn't actually die until much later, but that was beside the point). It had never occurred to her to search out these friends of his and tell them about his final moments. Nor had it occurred to her that Kinker might have been a respected member of his community. For that matter, she didn't know that he had had an older brother. She knew that his parents had passed away years ago, but that didn't explain why Kinker had never mentioned his older brother to her.

I'll probably never get to meet him, Jenur thought, shaking her head and readjusting her blowgun's aim. *But I wish I could. I bet he's probably as nice as Kinker.*

Deber held up the paper and said, "The second person to die during murder season was—"

Her voice was suddenly cut off. The Priestess dropped the paper, which fluttered down into the crowd of spectators below, and she grasped her neck. Deber let out a strangled gasp and foam started forming in her mouth. A moment later, the Priestess fell backwards onto the altar with a definitive *thump* against the wood.

The crowd was silent for perhaps a full thirty seconds as everyone stared at the altar. Jenur blinked several times and double-checked her blowgun. The dart was still inside it. She hadn't accidentally fired it or anything. But Deber had clearly been hit with a poison dart of some sort.

Then someone in the crowd shouted, "By the gods, Priestess Deber is dead!"

As if on cue, the entire crowd started rioting. People surged forward, as if to make sure that Deber was all right, but the Priestly Guard held them back, using their swords and spears to keep the crowds at a distance. At the same time, the other Priests and Priestesses climbed up to the top of the altar and surrounded Deber's body like a flock of birds, perhaps inspecting it to find out how she had died.

Jenur recovered well before any of the crowd did. She pulled her blowgun out of its hole and looked around at the nearby rooftops, wondering who else could possibly have done it. As far as she knew, there were no other assassins gunning for Deber's life. But if Deber was indeed dead—and Jenur had no reason to believe otherwise—then that meant that there was indeed another assassin.

Based on the fact that Deber had reached for the right side of her neck, that meant that the assassin was somewhere to Jenur's left. Jenur peered around the left side of the sign, scanning the roofs of nearby buildings until she spotted the flutter of a black cape disappearing over the edge of a house at least two houses away.

Jenur didn't even think. She just dashed to the end of the roof and jumped from rooftop to rooftop as quickly as she could to catch up with the caped assassin. She didn't worry about being seen by anyone; after all, the crowd was still rioting, too busy mourning the death of their beloved Priestess to pay attention to whoever was on the rooftops.

She landed on the third building's rooftop, where she had seen the cape, and immediately ran to the back of the roof. She found a ladder leading down into the alleyway, which she quickly climbed down with the dexterity of a monkey. Upon reaching the street, she looked up and down it, trying to spot any clues as to the assassin's whereabouts, but she could not spot anyone or anything in the alley, save for a cat that was digging through a pile of fish bones someone had apparently tossed out of their house.

But that didn't mean she was going to give up. Jenur had no interest in avenging Deber's death, but she did have an interest in finding out who else held a grudge against Deber besides her. Was it one of Kinker's friends? Or did Deber have other enemies that Jenur didn't know about?

Based purely on intuition, Jenur ran to the right. Then again, it wasn't entirely non-rational. She had spotted footprints in the dirty streets; light prints, barely visible even in the daylight, but there nonetheless. They led away from the square toward the town's outer walls. Whoever the assassin was, he or she was attempting to make a break for it. And Jenur was going to catch them, wherever they may go.

She turned down a few alleys, making her wonder how such a small town could have so many alleyways before the footprints ended in a dead end. It was a tall stone wall, with buildings on either side. Jenur looked the wall up and down, frowning. She didn't see how the assassin could have gotten away. The wall was too tall to climb over and, being made of stone, was completely smooth and there were no ladders the assassin could have used to climb over. Then again, she could easily have lost him at some other point, making this whole thing moot.

Then Jenur heard the scraping of a shoe against the stone street and whirled around. Her heart failed her at the sight she beheld: A tall aquarian, his webbed hands poking out of black robes, wearing a tiger mask. Jenur didn't know his identity, but she did know one thing: He was a Dark Tiger. And the Dark Tigers wanted her dead.

Chapter Four

BREAKFAST IN THE *CLOCKWORK Heart* was different from breakfast on the *Iron Wind*. On the *Iron Wind*, each member of the crew had gotten only one fish, if even that much, and a little bit of water. Further, none of the sailors had had silverware, plates, bowls, or anything else to use to help eat. They had used their hands and their fingers. Even Malock didn't have that much silverware; he had had perhaps one spoon to himself, and it was not a very fancy one, either, from what he could recall of it (he had lost it the day they sold the *Iron Wind* to the salvaging company back on World's End).

On the *Clockwork Heart*, however, the entire crew was allowed to eat together in the dining room, which was located on the second lower deck. While the dining room was nowhere near as nice as the dining room back home in Carnag Hall, it was much better than the one they had had back on the *Iron Wind*. A long wooden table, with dozens of chairs on every side, ran the length of the room, with a beautiful white tablecloth that somehow seemed to keep itself clean despite the messy sailors eating at it. Dozens of different dishes—

ranging from scrambled eggs to bacon to fried kenyo and many other kinds of food that Malock had never seen before—had been placed on the table by the automaton cooks, who were very good at what they did, if the taste of the food was any indication.

Furthermore, every sailor had their own set of silverware to eat with. Not that anyone really bothered with the silverware. Most of the sailors just ate with their hands, as usual. This despite Malock's best attempts to teach them how to use silverware over the past month. He had given up when it became clear that his men didn't see the point in using silverware for any dishes except those that couldn't be easily handled with hands, such as lime fish soup, for example. Thus, Malock was often the only member of the crew at mealtimes who bothered with the forks and knives and spoons set before the hungry sailors, though of course none of his men ever gave him a hard time for it.

So it was this morning that Malock sat near the far right end of the table, quietly eating his breakfast, while the rest of the crew talked and ate noisily. Most of the talk centered around what they all planned to do when they got home. Now Malock had offered to give them all good paying jobs in the Carnagian Navy for their work on the *Iron Wind*, but sadly only a few had taken up his offer. The rest, it seemed, had different dreams they wanted to pursue (such as Ranof, the ship's former doctor, who was talking about returning to medicine when he returned home).

Not that Malock held that against them. His crew had been heavily traumatized by the voyage to the end of the world. In fact, he was surprised when he saw how energetic and excited they all were to get home. He knew that his crew had to be tough—they were sailors, after all, not exactly the kind of profession that made room for weak people—but it still took him aback every time he overheard his men talking about their future.

I guess they are all much stronger than I gave them credit for, Malock. *I suppose if you spend three months on a cramped ship sailing in the most dangerous seas in the world, while coming face to face with gods and pirates and other things and surviving, you should be able to handle a little trauma.*

Sitting beside Malock was Banika Koiro, the former boatswain of the *Iron Wind* as well as Malock's first mate. The middle-aged woman was as difficult to read as ever, even as she ate her food more quickly than Malock. On their first day on the voyage back home, Banika had told Malock that she was going to join the crew of another ship as soon as they reached Carnag, even though Malock had offered to give her an entire ship to captain of her own. She said that she was much happier working as the first mate of someone else, even though Malock knew that she could easily take up the mantle of captain again if she wanted or had to.

Oh, well, Malock thought, glancing at her as he ate some of his eggs. *Then again, I doubt my father would approve of giving the former captain of the* Grinf's Justice *her own ship again, even though its sinking wasn't actually her fault. Maybe they'll make her a captain of a squad of Justice Enforcers or something.*

That was another thing Malock was looking forward to seeing again: His parents. He had not been in contact with them at all during the voyage to World's End. The only current information he knew about them was that the Gray Pirates—who, prior to their destruction, had been the most notorious and wanted pirate crew in all of the Northern Isles—had stolen his mother's crown sometime after he left Carnag. He had been unable to retrieve the crown, however, because he didn't know where the Pirates had hidden it. He could just imagine his mother—dressed in her royal crimson robes, her long gray hair hanging below her shoulders—cursing Garnal Gray, the Captain of the Gray Pirates, as she sent out servants to find the crown again.

But what would Malock actually say to his parents? That he didn't know. He would definitely have to tell them about his voyage to World's End, but a part of him was reluctant to do so. Whenever he wondered about his reluctance, he realized the answer: Vashnas.

During the voyage to World's End, Malock had developed a relationship with an aquarian woman named Vashnas, who had claimed to be the only mortal to reach World's End and return alive again. But she hadn't been entirely honest about that and her true identity and origin had eventually led to her being killed by the sea goddess Kano. And that had hit Malock hard.

He shook his head. *What does it matter? I can tell them about Vashnas. Can't I?*

His thoughts were interrupted when the speaker—a strange machine if Malock ever saw one, which allowed a person's voice to be heard even if that person was not in the room—in the top right corner of the room suddenly blared. It was so loud that it drowned out the laughter and talk of all of the other sailors, causing them to look at it in surprise.

"Attention all passengers of the *Clockwork Heart*," a voice over the speaker—probably Hana's, though due to the distorted nature of it Malock had a hard time telling for sure—said. "The island of Carnag has just been spotted on the horizon. According to the navigational instruments that are too complicated for your mortal minds to understand, we should reach the island within the next couple of hours or so. I suggest you get your bags ready so you can depart the ship the minute we land there. Thank you!"

The speaker turned off with a clipping sound. Almost as soon as it did, Malock stood up and held up his glass of water, causing the rest of the crew to look at him.

"Men," said Malock, using his most authoritative captain voice. "You heard the voice. In just a couple of hours, we will finally reach our island home. We will see our friends and family and loved ones again. I just wanted to take this opportunity to tell you all that I am proud of all of you and also to mourn in silence those who died before they could see their homes again."

With that, the entire room went completely silent as each sailor put on a face of mourning, which was easy to do considering how many sailors they had lost since leaving for World's End. Malock brought his glass close to his chest and tilted his head down, thinking of Vashnas and Kinker more than anyone else.

And despite his best efforts, his thoughts strayed to the gods, to Kano, to Tinkar, to the Mechanical Goddess, and to every other deity he and his crew had run into on their voyage south. And though he did not mean to do it, his grip tightened around the thin glass cup and his hand shook just enough to cause the water to slosh onto his shirt, though none of his men noticed.

The next couple of hours were spent finishing up breakfast and packing up their things. Packing was not a difficult or time-consuming task; actually, it went by quickly, as the majority of the sailors had few possessions with them and those few who had brought along their possessions had only very small objects, such as good luck charms, that were easy to carry in one's pocket. Not even Malock had much. Aside from the clothes he wore and the bag of crimsonite he had received for trading in the *Iron Wind*, Malock had nothing, at least nothing on the ship.

When we get home, however, I will have more things than I will know what to do with, Malock thought as he made his way from his cabin near the bow of the ship to the hatch leading to the top deck. *I will have my bed and my closet full of clothes and all of that other stuff I left behind. I might actually be able to make myself look like a real prince again.*

That thought caused Malock to stop in the hallway and stare at his own reflection in one of the many mirrors that, for whatever reason, had been placed in the hallways of the ship's lower decks. Although the *Clockwork Heart* also contained bathrooms (making him wonder just what the ship didn't have) and he had taken advantage of those to clean up, he still didn't look quite as princely as he used to. His hair was still messy and he had a lot of scars over his face. His clothes looked nice, but they were clearly designed for practicality and already looked quite dirty and worn, looking absolutely nothing like the royal robes and doublet he would wear once he returned home. His boots, too, were simpler than the kind he originally wore, lacking the gold stitching and the embedded gemstones in the toes, but he had to admit that they were far more comfortable than the kind he was expected to wear as royalty.

Shaking his head and smiling, Malock continued on his way down to the hatch. Along the way, the other members of the crew exited their rooms and joined him. Soon the rest of the crew was following Malock down the hallway to the stairs that would take them top deck. Malock could feel the excitement that the crew was generating or maybe he was just so excited himself that he was attributing it to the others. Either way, all Malock knew was that he could not wait to see his home again.

So Malock was surprised when he climbed the steps leading out of the hatch and emerged onto the top deck just in time to see a dozen or so of the largest battleships he had ever seen surrounding the *Clockwork Heart*. The battleships flew the Carnagian flag, a red flag with the Hammer of Grinf sticking out of a boot stitched in gold on it, helping Malock to identify the fleet as the Carnagian Navy. Each ship was armed with at least a dozen cannons, all aimed at the now-still *Clockwork Heart*. None of them were close enough for Malock to see their crews; however, he knew that each ship had to have at least a hundred men aboard, not counting the dozen or so mages that were standard to every ship. The ships had blocked off every conceivable exit, making escape impossible.

Malock looked up at the highest deck as Hana made her way down the steps, looking totally unconcerned at the fleet of battleships threatening to sink them any minute. By now the rest of the crew of the *Iron Wind* had emerged from the hatch and they were all looking at the Carnagian Navy fleet with unease and even fear.

Malock met Hana at the bottom of the stairs just as she was stepping off them. "Where did these ships come from?"

Hana looked at him in surprise. "Oh, Malock, there you are. I was just looking for you."

"You didn't answer the question," said Malock. "How long have those ships been there?"

"Oh, they appeared a few minutes ago," said Hana. "I probably should have told you, but it was like they materialized out of nowhere a few minutes ago. Very strange."

That didn't sound strange to Malock. He knew that every ship in the Carnagian Navy had at least one auramancer on board at all times. Most likely the Navy ships had been invisible, a common tactic used by the ships that patrolled the waters around Carnag. It was supposed to discourage pirates or attacks from other nations, because if you couldn't see the enemy's defenses, then mounting on attack on them would be far too risky.

"I was just coming to get you," said Hana. "The Mechanical Goddess wants you to call them off before they try to sink her."

"The Mechanical Goddess is afraid of the cannons of a bunch of mortals?" said Malock.

TIMOTHY L. CEREPAKA

"No," said Hana. "Actually, those pathetic little guns probably can't even dent the ship's hull. It's just that the Mechanical Goddess isn't much interested in fighting a fleet of mortals, particularly in the north. She doesn't want to drag Grinf into this."

"I see," said Malock. "Well, I—"

At that moment, a loud voice—probably amplified by audimancy based on its volume—rang out from across the waters, coming from the ship directly in front of the *Clockwork Heart*. "This is Admiral Koroz Haner, First Admiral of the Carnagian Navy and Captain of the *Dividing Blade*, speaking. I demand that the Captain of your ... whatever that thing is, come out and identify himself and which island his, er, 'ship' represents or I will order the fleet to sink your vessel to the bottom of the sea. This is not a warning."

"They must seriously think we're a threat," said Banika, appearing out of nowhere at Malock's shoulder, "if Haner is leading this fleet."

"Indeed," said Malock. "Hana, take me up to the wheelhouse. I want to use the speaker to tell them who we are."

"Follow me," said Hana as she turned around and began climbing the stairs again, with Malock and Banika following.

The 'wheelhouse,' as Malock called it, was different from most wheelhouses that Malock had ever been in. It didn't actually have any wheels in it, but several buttons, levers, and switches of various sizes and kinds. Malock had only been up here a few times since they had left World's End, which is why he looked around the room with interest as Hana walked over to the speaker on the other side of the room. Thick glass windows on every side gave Malock an excellent view of the Carnagian Navy and the surrounding seas. And although he could not be sure, he thought he saw Carnag somewhere in the distance just beyond the *Dividing Blade*, though it could have just been his imagination.

"Here you go," said Hana, handing him a small device attached to a cord of some sort. "Just hold it up to your mouth, speak into it, and everyone in the area should be able to hear your beautiful voice."

Malock took the small device gingerly, as he had never handled it before, and looked at it. It was about the same size as his wallet and was black, with a strange net-like mesh of a soft yet firm substance fitted over a hole. He held the device up to his mouth and looked at Hana, who nodded encouragingly, while Banika simply stood nearby as usual, her arms crossed over her chest.

Taking a deep breath, Malock spoke into the device, "Attention Carnagian Navy fleet. This is Prince Tojas Malock, Crown Prince of the House of Carnag, son of King Halock and Queen Markinia, and former Captain of the *Iron Wind*, speaking. I order the entire fleet to pull back and to not engage in combat the ship upon which I and the rest of my crew are passengers. Do *not* open fire on the ship. I repeat, do *not*."

He was not sure they listened at first, but then Haner's voice roared across the sea again, slightly muffled by the glass windows of the wheelhouse.

"Prince Malock? How can we be sure that that is you?" said Haner. "That is not the *Iron Wind*, which was a schooner, or any of the other four ships which were part of the initial fleet that Prince

Malock led to World's End. That is ... well, I have no idea what that is, but it's definitely not a proud ship of the Carnagian Navy, that's for sure. Prove that you are who you say you are or I will have my men sink the ship to the bottom of the sea."

Malock looked at Banika. "How do I prove it's me?"

Banika held out her hand. "Give me the speaker. I'll handle this."

Uncertain, Malock handed Banika the speaker anyway. She held the small device up to her mouth like she did this sort of thing every day and spoke into it, saying, "Admiral Koroz Haner, this is Banika Koiro, the boatswain and first mate of the *Iron Wind*, as well as former Captain of the Carnagian Navy flagship, the *Grinf's Justice*. I can confirm that the person who you spoke to briefly was indeed Prince Tojas Malock, son of Queen Markinia and King Halock, and that you would be wise to lower your weapons and order your men to stand down."

She clicked the speaker off. As soon as she did, Haner's voice boomed again. "Banika? I can't believe it. I thought you were dead, you old hag you! Great to hear your voice again. All right, I believe you. Men, lower the cannons. It's all right. Our prince has finally returned."

Banika clicked the speaker on and spoke into it again. "Oh, and Haner? Could you please bring the *Dividing Blade* as close to the ship as possible? We have many men and women who would like to be on an a Carnagian ship again."

"Certainly," said Haner's voice again. "We'll pull right up next to you and let the crew board. We have plenty of room for your people.

Just hang tight for a few minutes. We'll be there very soon."

"Thank you," said Banika, before clicking the speaker off and handing it back to Malock. "There you go, Captain. We're perfectly safe."

Malock gave the speaker back to Hana as he looked at Banika in surprise. "How did you manage to convince him that you were you?"

"Haner and I have been friends for a long time," said Banika. "He would recognize my voice anywhere. And he knows I would never betray the Carnagian Navy or the Royal Family, so he naturally assumed that I was telling the truth."

"I didn't know that," said Malock. "Did you two work together on a ship once or something?"

"Our story is long," said Banika with a shrug. "I suggest we go down and await the arrival of the *Dividing Blade*, Captain. The rest of the crew of the *Iron Wind* is no doubt already awaiting it."

"Of course," said Malock. "Let's go."

Admiral Koroz Haner was a tall man; not quite as tall as Bifor Kamon—the mage who had tried to kill Malock—had been, but the Carnagian Navy Admiral nonetheless towered over Malock, Banika, and every other member of the crews of both the *Iron Wind* and the *Dividing Blade*. This made it slightly awkward when—the minute he stepped foot on the deck of the *Clockwork Heart* and spotted Malock —he got down on his hands and knees and said, in a pleading voice, "Forgive me, Your Majesty, for not believing your words immediately. I did not recognize this ship and under the circumstances I thought you might be a mimic trying to pull a fast one on us. If I am to be punished, let it be swift."

Malock, having forgotten just how servile Haner could be, scratched the back of his head and said, "It's not a problem, Admiral. You were just doing your job, which is to protect Carnag and its seas from unknown or enemy vessels. I would expect no less from you. You may stand."

Haner stood up. His short black hair was hidden underneath his large red cap, while five gold stars were stitched into the shoulders of his uniform. He stood erect and tall, like a true trained sailor of the Carnagian Navy, and the gold laces of his boots shone brightly in the sun's rays. The only difference between how he looked now and how Malock remembered him being was a minor scar just above Haner's right eye; otherwise, the Admiral looked exactly the same as he did four months ago when Malock first set sail for World's End.

"Thank you for your mercy, Prince Malock," said Haner, his voice far less mournful now. "It would have been more just for you to punish me, but I am thankful that I was not."

Malock nodded. "Well, we all make mistakes. I just want to get onto the ship and go home."

"Of course, Your Majesty," said Haner. Then he looked at Banika and broke into a smile. "Banika, how have you been? You look exhausted."

Banika shrugged. "I survived. That's about all I can say."

"Yes, you did," said Haner, nodding. "Of course you did. You're

Banika Koiro, one of the best sailors the Carnagian Navy has ever seen. Besides, you know I would be angry if you had died without telling me, eh?"

"That's true," said Banika. "I couldn't make you angry, now could I?"

Haner chuckled. "But enough joking. Sir," he said, addressing Malock again, "what, exactly, is this ... ship? I've never seen anything like it."

"Long story," said Malock. "All I ask of you is to let her leave when we have boarded the *Dividing Blade*. She's not a threat, however intimidating she may look."

"Are you sure, sir?" said Haner. "I'm not arguing with you, but to me, she looks quite a bit like a monster ready to kill."

Malock glanced over his shoulder at the tall smokestacks. "As I said, she is not a threat to us. She won't stay any longer than she has to. She's not interested in attacking us."

Haner gave him a questioning look. "You talk about the ship as though she were a real person."

An explosive blast of smoke shot out from the smokestacks. Haner jumped, almost tripping over his fancy boots, while the crews of the *Dividing Blade* and the *Iron Wind* looked up at it in surprise. One sailor from the *Dividing Blade*'s crew—who had come with Haner to help the crew of the *Iron Wind* board the *Dividing Blade*— almost fell overboard, but was thankfully caught by Ranof before he could do so.

"Let's just say you might want to moderate your choice of words around this ship, Admiral," said Malock. "She's not tolerant of perceived insults, to put it one way."

Haner didn't seem to hear him. He was looking up at the smokestacks with fear in his eyes. "A ship that can breathe fire? What kind of madness is this?"

At that moment, the entirety of the *Clockwork Heart* shuddered. Malock and Banika—used to the movements of the ship—kept their standing, but Haner didn't. He actually fell flat on his bottom, but got back to his feet as soon as the ship remained motionless. The few members of the *Dividing Blade*'s crew that had come with him were in varying states of composure, with one desperately clinging to the bulwarks of the *Clockwork Heart* like he was clinging for his life.

"As I said, you might want to moderate your choice of words, Admiral," said Malock. "The ship can be fairly passive aggressive."

"I see that," said Haner as Banika helped him to his feet. Then he looked at Banika and said, "Banika, you will have to tell me all about your voyage to World's End sometime. If you got a ship like this, then it must have been ... fascinating, to put it lightly."

He said that last sentence while glancing nervously at the smokestacks of the *Clockwork Heart*. Luckily for him, the Mechanical Goddess didn't seem to sense any disrespect in his voice, though even after traveling with her for a month, Malock could not always interpret her silence—or lack thereof—very accurately.

"I will tell you all about it later," said Banika. "But first, you should tell us all about what has happened on Carnag while we were away."

"That's right," said Haner, snapping his fingers. "Prince Malock, the villainous pirate captain Garnal Gray, of the Gray Pirates, stole your mother's—"

"I know," Malock cut him off. "We ran into Garnal on our way to World's End. She said she'd stolen my mother's crown, but I didn't know if she was telling the truth."

"Oh," said Haner, scratching the back of his head. "Wait, you actually spoke with her? How did you survive? Garnal Gray is supposed to be the most violent, deranged, and least sociable pirate in all of the Northern Isles."

"That is very true," said Malock. "But that's a story for later. Anything else happen while I was away?"

"Besides that, not much," said Haner with a shrug. "Trade with other lands is booming, construction on a new boot factory in southwest Harnos was completed just the other day, your father bought four new merchant ships to add to the Royal Family's fleet from the Royal Family of Nikos, and your marriage to Princess Raya Kabadi is—"

"My marriage to *who?*" said Malock, looking at Haner in surprise.

Haner suddenly looked up at the smokestacks again. "I don't believe I have ever seen a ship that breathes flame before. Even the legendary Pyro Pirates never—"

Malock grabbed Haner's jacket collar and forced the Admiral to look at him. "You mentioned Princess Kabadi."

"I-I did?" said Haner with the falsest innocent voice Malock had ever heard before. "You must have heard me say something else, Your

Majesty."

Malock shook his head. "No way. Why would you, the Admiral of the Carnagian Navy, mention the name of the Princess of Shika to me? What does Kabadi have to do with anything?"

Haner bit his lower lip, looking like he wished he was anywhere else. "Oh, fine. Your parents were supposed to break the news to you, but I guess the cat is out of the bag now. Your Majesty, exactly one month from today, you will be married to Princess Raya Kabadi, the Princess of Shika."

Malock let go of Haner's collar and said, "Impossible. Ridiculous. You're joking."

"It's no joke, sir," said Haner, readjusting his collar. "The marriage has been in the planning stages for months, although it hasn't been publicly announced yet. Only a very few people in the Carnagian and Shikan governments know about it. Hell, I only know about it because King Halock accidentally mentioned it to me when we were discussing ways to improve the Navy's efficiency about two weeks ago. King Halock threatened to fire me if I told anyone before he did."

Malock sighed heavily. "I'll explain to my father, Admiral, so you don't have to worry about losing your job. But I can't believe it. When did they decide this? Why didn't they consult me?"

"I don't know all the details, sir," said Haner. "I just know that your parents have been discussing the terms of the marriage with King Fabadi of Shika for months now. I have no idea whether Princess Kabadi knows it. I only know that it's a part of the peace treaty that your parents have been negotiating with King Fabadi over the last year."

"This is ridiculous," said Malock. "I just got back. I'm not getting married in a month. When I get back home, I'll tell my parents exactly what I think about their plans."

"I wouldn't do that if I were you, Your Majesty," said Haner. "Your parents were very adamant about it. They might get angry at you if you go against their wishes."

Malock thought about seeing the fury on Kano's face after she had slain Vashnas, and said, "I no longer fear my parents' fury, Admiral. Nor should you or anyone else."

Haner shrugged as if to say *It's your funeral.* "Do you wish to return to Carnag now?"

"Of course," said Malock as he redoubled the grip on his shoulder bag. "I have all of my possessions in this bag. I want to go directly to Carnag Hall as soon as possible."

"Yes, Your Majesty," said Haner, bowing. "Follow me onto the *Dividing Blade.* We will head back to Carnag immediately."

As it turned out, Malock and Banika were the only members of the *Iron Wind*'s crew to have yet to board the *Dividing Blade.* They followed Haner onto the ramp that connected the *Dividing Blade* to the *Clockwork Heart*, but stopped halfway when Hana's voice floated down from above. Malock turned in time to see Hana on the very top deck, leaning over the railing, waving at him like he was her best friend.

"Bye, bye, Mal!" said Hana, her voice far louder than it should.

"I'll miss you and the rest of your smelly crew when you're gone!"

"Your Majesty," said Haner, who was also looking up at the katabans, "may I ask who—"

"No, Admiral," said Malock, whirling around and continuing back onto the *Dividing Blade* as Banika followed him silently, "you may not ask who she is. Better for us all to forget her."

"Yes, sir," said Haner as he caught up with Malock, though he kept glancing over his shoulder at Hana just the same.

Chapter Five

TWO LONG, CURVED, HOOK-LIKE blades appeared in the Dark Tiger's hands as he dashed toward Jenur. Jenur didn't stand around defenseless, however. She drew her own knife out of her left pocket and leaped over the Dark Tiger's head as he passed underneath her. She landed behind him and swiped at the assassin, but he was faster than she, moving out of the way and allowing her blade to slice harmlessly through the air.

The Dark Tiger swung both curved blades down on her outstretched arm, but Jenur pulled it back just in time. The Tiger twisted his swords in midair, but Jenur jumped back, successfully avoiding having her head taken off her shoulders.

Sweat running down the back of her neck, Jenur raised her blade and dashed at the Dark Tiger. He held up both of his hook blades as if to block her attack, but that wasn't what Jenur was doing. She drew another knife out of her right pocket and hurled it directly at his now-exposed abdomen, sure that it would be a direct hit.

But to her surprise, a resounding metal *clang* echoed when the knife hit the Dark Tiger's abdomen, confirming that he wore body armor. The second knife fell to the ground as the Tiger looked at it in surprise, which Jenur realized was exactly the opportunity she was looking for.

Moving as fast as she could, Jenur ran at the Dark Tiger and slammed her elbow into his masked face. The Dark Tiger let out a groan as he dropped his blades and fell to his back, but Jenur wasn't done yet. She pinned him to the ground, straddling his body, and placed her knife at his throat, positioning it in the way that would make his throat bleed profusely if he moved it. The Dark Tiger, to his credit, seemed to realize that, as he stopped struggling and now lay there, his head lying to the right, looking at her sideways with his right eye.

"I don't know who you are, but you're pretty good for a Tiger," said Jenur, panting and wiping her sweaty hair off her forehead. "Almost got me. Now tell me who hired you to kill Priestess Deber."

The Dark Tiger was now looking at her with puzzled eyes, as if he was not sure what he was seeing. His gray eyes looked extremely familiar, but Jenur didn't know why, nor did she see any reason to dwell on that thought. She wasn't going to lower her defense, no matter what the Dark Tiger did.

Then he spoke in a voice that she instantly recognized. "Jenur? Is that you?"

Jenur's grip on her blade faltered. "Dad?"

"It's me," said the Dark Tiger in a voice that Jenur would always remember. "If you don't believe me, you can unmask me if you want."

Jenur didn't even think about it. With her free hand she reached over, grabbed his mask, and then ripped it off. She tossed the tiger mask aside as she looked at the face of her father, the Dark Tiger known as Quro the Thinker.

It had only been four months since Jenur had seen her father, but that didn't stop her from examining his face like she hadn't seen it in years. As always, his skin was a light blue, with a bunch of small tentacles hanging off his chin like a beard. His eyes were as gray as a storm cloud and the scar on his forehead was as prominent as always.

"I can't believe it," said Jenur. "What are you doing here?"

"I was about to ask you the same question," said Quro. "We—I— thought you were dead, Jenur. How did you even get here?"

Jenur removed her blade from her father's neck and stood up. Quro got to his feet, but slowly, and looked her in the eyes like he couldn't get enough of her.

Jenur looked away as she sheathed her knife. "So you were the one hired to kill Deber, huh?"

"That is the job I was given," said Quro. "But don't change the subject. When you ran away from the Dark Tigers and joined Prince Malock's fleet heading to World's End, I didn't think I'd ever see you again."

Jenur returned her gaze to Quro. "How did you know—"

"I tracked you down," said Quro. "I found the pirate crew that took you off Ruwa and made their captain tell me where you went. I spent a week in Carnag trying to find you, only to learn that a young woman who looked and acted very much like you had gotten a job as a deckhand on board one of Prince's Malock's sailing ships."

"Oh," said Jenur. She felt stupid for not expecting him to do that. "You didn't have to—"

"How could I not?" Quro said. "You are my one and only daughter. I would be a terrible father if I just let you run away without finding out where you ran to, at the very least."

"Did Wirm let you do that?" said Jenur. "I didn't think he would be okay with that."

"He wasn't," Quro admitted. "I searched for you without asking for Wirm's permission first. He flogged me when I got back to Ruwa and docked me half of my pay from my last assignment. But that is nothing compared to how I feel now, having found you and knowing that you are indeed alive. If I worshiped the gods, I might just praise them right now."

"Stop it," said Jenur, trying not to show her embarrassment. "Okay, okay, I get it. You were really worried for me. No need to go on."

"But how did you survive?" said Quro. "No one ever comes back from the southern seas alive. Was the voyage a success after all?"

Jenur shook her head, trying to come up with something to say. "Dad, it's none of your business. We really shouldn't have run into each other at all. You know the Rules. If a Dark Tiger runs across a former member of the Guild, then he's supposed to kill her. And if that Dark Tiger doesn't kill the traitor, then he'll get killed."

"I know the Rules all right, Jen," said Quro. "And I don't care. Much as I respect Nijok Wirm and the Rules of the Guild, I will not kill my own daughter just to satisfy them."

"What will you do when you return and Wirm asks you how the assignment went?" said Jenur. "You'll have to tell him then. Won't you?"

"Not necessarily," said Quro. "I do not need to tell him I ran into you. And he trusts me so much that I doubt he would ever think to ask me if I happened to run into my daughter who he also believes is dead."

In Jenur's mind eye, the powerful leader of the Dark Tigers loomed before her, causing her to shudder. "Wirm has his way of knowing when people lie to him. Remember that time when he punished Ruzyo for hiding money from him, which came as a complete surprise to the rest of us?"

"I am sure I can fool him," said Quro. "You don't have to worry. Even if Wirm does find out that we met, I would never tell him where you are."

"Because he would just track me down on his own, right?" said Jenur. "Look, Dad, it's wonderful seeing you again, but you do realize we're both screwed now, right? I was hoping to kill Deber myself without anyone seeing—"

"Hold on," said Quro, looking at her with that same stern look he had used on her whenever she had said something silly as a child. "*You* were planning to assassinate Deber? Who hired you?"

"No one, Dad," said Jenur with a sigh. "I was trying to avenge a friend whose life the old witch ruined. Money had nothing to do with it."

Quro tilted his head to the side. "Revenge? I didn't know you were into that."

"I'm not," said Jenur. "It's just that Deber really ruined my friend's life and I was going to teach her a lesson."

"Just who is this friend you keep talking about?" said Quro. "He must have been very special for you to try to kill someone for him."

Jenur tried not to think of Kinker because she knew that if she did she wouldn't be able to make it through the rest of the conversation coherently. "Look, it doesn't really matter. Who hired you to kill Deber?"

"The Rules of the Guild state very clearly that I, as a member of the Guild, am not allowed to disclose the identity of our clients to people outside the Guild," said Quro. "That includes you."

"I thought you said you were going to break the Rules for your daughter," said Jenur.

"Only the Rule about killing former members," said Quro. "Just because I see no reason to follow some Rules doesn't mean I see no reason to follow any of them."

Jenur rubbed her forehead. "All right. Whatever. Look, we probably shouldn't be standing here talking about this because the Priestly Guard is most likely looking for Deber's assassin, which is you. We can talk about this later, in a safer place."

"I want to discuss it now," said Quro. "Where were you? What happened on the voyage to World's End? And where is the rest of your crew?"

"I said later," said Jenur. "Look, can you get me off Destan? Do you have a boat or something we could take?"

"I do have a boat," Quro admitted. "But before we leave, I must collect the rest of my payment from my client. He already paid me half up front and promised me the rest after I completed the job."

Quro brushed past Jenur, who turned to follow him. Quro picked up his tiger mask and dusted it off as Jenur said, "So will I get to see your client?"

"I suppose it's unavoidable at this point," said Quro. "I'd rather you not, but I don't want you wandering around Rimo by yourself when the Priestly Guard are likely searching every inch of the town for me."

Jenur wanted to say she could take care of herself, but Quro was already climbing the nearest building. With a shrug, Jenur followed after him and soon both were on the rooftops of Rimo, making their way from building to building, keeping as low as they could to avoid being seen by the Priestly Guard or anyone else.

As it turned out, Quro's client had agreed to meet with Quro on the outskirts of Rimo, well away from the rioting crowds and the Priestly Guard. The place they had agreed to meet was an old building that might have once been used as a storage shed of some type for fish; at least, that's what Jenur assumed because when she and Quro entered it (using the back entrance where no one could see them entering) her nose was assaulted by the heavy scent of rotting fish. Quro didn't seem to mind it, though that may have been because he was an aquarian.

The building was dark, with no light at all except for the few weak rays that streamed in from the windows above. Jenur squinted in the darkness, seeing no one, until a light flared before her, startling her for a moment before the bright light died down. Her eyes adjusted to the change in light, allowing her to see an elderly man in the center of the room. He was sitting on an old wooden chair, like he had been expecting Quro to be here, an old lamp in his hand, the light of which cast a shadow over his face.

The elderly man frowned. "Quro, who is this young woman? I don't remember you having a partner."

"Her identity is not important," said Quro. "She is—"

"Wait," said Jenur, squinting more closely at the elderly man. "I think I've seen you before. Didn't we meet before?"

The elderly man's face was shrouded in shadow, but then he raised his lamp higher up to his face, revealing his features. Even while frowning, he resembled Kinker to a startling degree. "Yes, I think I recognize you. The liar who gave me a false name so I couldn't identify her. Gaharna Vicin, I think, was the name you gave me."

Quro looked at Jenur in surprise. "Jen, you already know Rint Dolan?"

"Dolan?" said Jenur, returning the surprised look. "That was Kinker's last name. Are you—"

"Hold on," said Rint, holding up his free hand. "How do you know Kinker? Quro, just who is this young woman?"

"How did you know I was lying to you earlier?" said Jenur. "I didn't leave any clues."

Before Rint could answer, Quro said, "Let's start over. I think we all have a lot of questions and none of them are going to be answered if we only ask them. First, Rint: The five hundred coins. Where are they?"

Rint Dolan scowled, but bent over the chair and lifted up a medium-sized bag that jingled when he held it. "Right here, as promised."

Rint threw the bag, which landed at Quro's feet. Jenur's father immediately knelt and opened the bag. He stuck his hand in it and moved it around inside, making more jingling noises. He pulled out one of the coins, examined it from every angle, and dropped it back into the bag. He then closed the bag and stood up.

"Thank you, Mr. Dolan," said Quro. "This looks to be the right amount."

"I made sure to count every coin," said Rint. "I do not swindle anyone, especially people as highly skilled in the art of assassination as you are."

Quro hefted the bag over his shoulder as Rint turned his eyes onto Jenur. Unlike Kinker, Rint looked at her with a disdain that seemed to emanate from him like light from the sun.

"Now tell me your story, young woman," said Rint. "How do you know my younger brother? And why did you hide your real identity from me?"

"First off, my name is Jenur Takren," said Jenur. "I gave you a false name because I didn't know if I could trust you or not. I didn't want anyone around here to know who I was."

"Why?" said Rint. "Were you up to no good?"

"Well, I was planning to kill Deber myself," said Jenur. She gestured at Quro and said, "But then Dad here got to her first. So I guess it doesn't really matter now whether you know my real name or not."

"You still haven't explained how you know Kinker," said Rint. "Kinker died during murder season months ago. I didn't see him die myself, but I found his boat missing and knew that it was the only logical explanation."

"That's the thing," said Jenur. "He didn't die. In fact, he survived and ended up on my ship. We worked together and became good friends."

Rint clutched his chest. "Impossible. Where is he now?"

Jenur lowered her eyes. "He's dead."

"What?" said Rint. "But you said—"

"He survived murder season," said Jenur, looking back up at Rint. "But he died after that."

Before Rint could ask any more questions, Jenur briefly described the voyage to World's End, largely focusing on Kinker. Rint interrupted only to ask the occasional question when she was unclear, but otherwise he listened intently to her whole story. Even Quro listened, though unlike Rint he never asked her any questions.

"I gave him a burial at sea when we returned to the north," Jenur finished. "So Kinks' body is right now in the Crystal Sea. I didn't know what else to do with him."

Rint stroked his short gray beard. "I cannot believe it. I don't know if I believe even half of what you just told me."

"I didn't see Kinker's death myself," said Jenur. "Malock was the only one to witness Vashnas's murder of him. But I saw Kinker's body, so there was no way I couldn't I believe him."

Even Quro looked stricken. "There are more gods than just the ones in the Northern Pantheon? And they like to eat mortals?"

"I don't understand all of it myself," said Jenur. "But it's the truth. Thankfully they can't kill us up here."

"Who cares if all of the gods like to eat us or not?" said Rint, pointing at Jenur. "I believe you, Jenur. You described Kinker exactly like how I remember him. I was skeptical at first, but only someone who knew him as well as I did could have described him the way you did."

"He was brave," said Jenur. "One of the bravest members of the crew, even though he wasn't originally a part of it. He—"

"But he still died," said Rint, sinking his face into his hands. "And I didn't even get a chance to see his corpse."

Jenur frowned. "I'm sorry. It's just that I didn't know that Kinker had an older brother. He never mentioned you."

Rint lifted his face up and scowled at her. "He didn't?"

"Nope," said Jenur. "He told me about his mother and father, but not about you."

Rint sighed. "Not surprising, I guess. Kinker and I have always gotten along, but he and I ... well, we weren't that close. Not as close as some siblings, anyway."

"What do you mean?" said Jenur. "Why?"

"Oh, mostly sibling rivalry things," said Rint. "We always tried to outdo each other, first for our mother's affection, and then in every other area of life where we could compete. We never harmed each other, but I admit that more than once our competitiveness got us in trouble."

Jenur had a hard time imagining Kinker as being highly competitive. "Really?"

"Truly," said Rint. "Once, when Kinker and I were in our twenties, our father told us to go fishing. We were supposed to bring back ten pounds of fish each, so Kinker and I made a competition out of it. Whoever caught ten pounds of fish faster would be the winner."

"How did that go wrong?" said Jenur.

Rint raised his free hand and said, "Well, when you're trying to reel in every little bite as quickly as you can and trying to unhook every fish you caught without hesitation, you do earn more than a few cuts along the hands."

Rint's hand was scarred, mostly along the fingers and palm. It looked disgusting, but after everything Jenur had seen on her voyage to World's End, she didn't feel too freaked out by it.

"Our parents were quite angry with us when they saw us come back with out cut-up hands," said Rint. "And that is probably the least painful thing we did to ourselves in our efforts to compete with each other."

"Oh," said Jenur. "Why did you hire Dad to kill Deber?"

"Because the old hag ruined my brother's life," said Rint. "If you knew Kinker, then you know what Deber made him do. He told me about it, but begged me not to tell anyone else what he did. He didn't want to be hated and despised. I agreed to keep it a secret, for his sake, even though the story filled me with rage when I first heard it."

His hands shook when he spoke, as though he were trying to restrain his anger even now. "So when Kinker was swept away in the waves of the Crystal Sea, I could not take it any longer. It took me a while, but I eventually got into contact with the Dark Tigers, which is how Quro here got involved in all of this."

Quro shrugged. "He offered us a lot of money. Which is the only reason Wirm agreed to let me go. We were surprised that anyone down this far south even had that kind of money."

"I saved up," said Rint. "That's how you get anything good when you're too poor to afford it otherwise."

"I see," said Jenur. "Well, what are we going to do now? The Priestly Guard are still looking for my Dad."

"They do not know that I hired him," said Rint. "Nor will they. I made sure to keep this deal a secret. They will never know about it. Deber's position will be replaced by one of the other Priests and eventually everyone will forget her. You two will leave Destan and I will return to my normal life as a fisherman."

"What a delightful little plan you've got there," said a voice above them. "Absolutely stunning and very simple. Of course, it's destined for failure. But you already knew that, didn't you?"

Jenur, Quro, and Rint looked up at the ceiling, Rint raising his lantern to illuminate it. Squatting on the rafters, ragged brown robes hanging off his limbs, was a man who looked very much like a monkey. His brown hair was wild all along his head and he grinned widely, his pale teeth reflecting the light of Rint's lantern. He looked quite at home in the rafters, like he'd lived up there his whole life.

"Who in the gods' many names are you?" said Rint. "And where did you come from?"

The little monkey man smirked and scratched the back of his neck. "My name is Ramufa the Nimble-Fingered. I am a famous freelancer, well-known throughout all of the Northern Isles for my quick fingers and affordable rates."

He flexed his fingers as he said that as if to emphasize his point.

Jenur looked at Quro. "Ever heard of him?"

"I think so," said Quro. "I seem to recall a man known as the Nimble-Fingered being known mostly in the northeast, but—"

"But nothing," said Ramufa, who was now doing a handstand, as if he could not contain his excitement. "The point is, I have found you and know all three of your names and faces. Quro the Thinker, Jenur Takren, and Rint Dolan. I have no idea who any of you are, of course, but it doesn't matter. I'm sure the Priestly Guard will recognize you all right away."

All three of them froze.

"The Priestly Guard?" said Rint. "Don't tell me you're working for the Priests."

Ramufa's grin widened even more as he returned to his sitting position. "Of course I am. They are paying me quite handsomely to find out who killed Deber. And what do you know, I did it. Those thousand coins will be mine to keep very soon."

"But that makes no sense," said Rint. "How did they know I had hired Quro to kill Deber? There's no way they could have predicted it. I didn't talk about it with anyone."

"I'm just a freelancer," said Ramufa with an exaggerated shrug. "They didn't tell me how they knew. They just asked me to hang around in this town until something happened. I was going to be paid five hundred coins, but now that I've actually caught the killer, I think I will get double that, maybe even triple if I hand you over too, Rint Dolan."

"What if we stop you before you hand Rint over to the Priests?" said Quro as he dropped his payment down to the floor and drew his hook blades out of his robes. "Jenur was a Dark Tiger and I am currently one. You don't want to mess with the Dark Tigers."

"Oh, that would have me trembling in my boots if I wore any," said Ramufa, raising his bare left foot and wiggling it in the air. "No, no. You see, I'm not a mere freelancer. I am also an initiate of the Thief's Way, trained by Master Hollech himself in fact. Which is to say that I have already disarmed both of you in the time it took me to explain that to you."

Jenur immediately patted her clothes in the spots where she kept her knives, but felt nothing. She looked at Quro, who was doing the same thing. He still had his hook blades, but two hands suddenly appeared out of the shadows and snatched the blades out of Quro's hands. Before Quro could react, the hands disappeared into the shadows. Above, Ramufa now held both of Quro's weapons in his hands.

"You Dark Tigers love your little toys, but without them, you are quite weak and defenseless," said Ramufa, turning the blades over in his hands. "And neither of you know a bit of magic, do you? Of course you don't. Heathens generally do not have access to magic because you heathens choose to shun the gods rather than embrace them."

"Then we'll run," said Jenur, turning to face the door that she and Quro had come through. "We'll get out of here before any of the Priestly Guard get here. If we move fast—"

Without warning, the door smashed inwards, causing Jenur to stagger back as a dozen members of the Priestly Guard streamed through the now open door, their swords and spears slashing through the air. She and Quro backed up to the center of the room, where Rint still stood, looking in disbelief as the members of the Priestly Guard circled the three of them.

Ramufa snickered. "What was that you were saying about moving fast, now?"

The lead Guard—a tall man with thick arms and short blonde hair—stepped forward, his shield and sword held at the ready. He glanced up at the rafters and said, "Good job, Ramufa. I didn't think you could do it, but you proved me wrong."

"As long as I am paid, I will be very happy," said Ramufa.

The lead Guard then turned his attention to Jenur and the others. He wore a blue leather helmet, which looked brand new, as if he had just gotten it the other day. "Which one of you killed Priestess Deber?"

"That is none of your business," said Jenur, folding her arms.

The lead Guard looked at her as if he considered what she just said an admission of guilt on her part. "I guess we'll just have to take all three of you in, then. Priestess Wesol will see you."

"Not unless we fight," said Jenur as she instinctively reached for her knife before remembering that it wasn't there.

"Don't worry, guardsmen," said Ramufa from above. "I already disarmed them. They are about as harmful as a teething puppy now."

Jenur was about to say that she could still fight, but Quro placed a hand on her shoulder and said, "Jen, don't."

Jenur looked up at him. "What? Why not?"

"We can't beat them," said Quro. "It would be foolish for us to fight them now. We would do better to let them arrest us."

Jenur's shoulders sagged, even though she still felt the desire to fight burning within her. "But we can't give up."

"I would listen to the aquarian, girl," said the lead Guard. "He knows that you can't defeat us. Especially with the old man at your side, who looks like he's about to faint any minute now."

Rint did look shaken and afraid. Sweat trailed down the side of his face and his lantern shook in his hand. If a fight were to break out now, Jenur had no doubt that he would be the first to die.

So Jenur shrugged Quro's hand off her shoulder and said to the lead Guard, "All right. You win. Just do what you're going to do to us and get it over with quick."

"As we will," said the lead Guard. "Men, arrest all three of them. Make sure they are chained together; more importantly, make sure they cannot escape."

Half of the Priestly Guard moved forward, pulling out chains and handcuffs to bind Jenur, Quro, and Rint with. Jenur reluctantly allowed them to bind her, but secretly, her mind was racing, looking for any way out of this situation at all. But she could not, for the life of her, think of a way to save not only her own life, but those of Quro and Rint as well.

So it was that Jenur allowed the Guard to lead her out of the smelly storage building, her spirit not yet broken, but very fragile.

Chapter Six

MOTHER, FATHER, I AM *not* getting married to Princess Raya Kabadi."

That was perhaps not the best thing for Malock to say to his parents—King Halock, who in his middle-age looked a lot like how Malock always thought he would when he got older, and Queen Markinia, who wore a silver crown that he recognized as belonging to Grandmother before her death, perhaps meant to replace the crown that the Gray Pirates stole—upon entering the throne room of Carnag Hall for the first time in several months, but he could think of no better way to begin the discussion. Besides, he didn't see any reason to beat around the bush, not when he was going to get married without his consent.

He stood with his arms crossed over his chest, looking up at them as they sat on their ornately carved thrones made of ruby and gold. Behind them loomed a large statue of Grinf, the God of Justice, Metal, and Fire, and also the patron god of Carnag and the Carnagian

Royal Family. As always, the statue of Grinf looked angry, like he was just about to smite a mortal who had committed some grievous crime against justice, and with his hammer held high above his head, he looked like he could easily carry out his threat, if he wanted to.

Both Father and Mother looked like he had socked them in the face. It pained him to see them so shocked, but he didn't see any reason to moderate his tone. He wanted answers, direct answers, and he could only get them if he spoke bluntly and without care as to what they thought or how they felt.

Then Father said, "Admiral Haner told you, didn't he?"

"Not on purpose," said Malock. "I ordered him to, so it's not his fault."

Father sighed. "I knew I couldn't trust that blabbermouth. I'm surprised he hasn't spilled all of the Navy's secrets to all of our enemies yet."

"Don't change the subject," said Malock. "He told me that I am going to be married to Princess Raya. When did I agree to this?"

Mother adjusted her new crown, which didn't seem to fit her head nearly as well as Grandmother's, and said, "You never did, but surely you know that this is how we do things in Carnag. Everyone does arranged marriage, except for the lowliest of peasants who can't afford to marry their filthy sons and daughters off. I don't know why you thought you were going to be the exception."

"It's not that," said Malock. "It's being married to Princess Raya, specifically, that bothers me. I had always assumed I would marry the daughter of some Carnagian nobleman or something. Not a dirty

Shikan, especially not a Shikan like Raya."

"Tojas, why don't we discuss this some other time?" said Father, rubbing his hands together like he always did when he was nervous. "You have had a long voyage and your mother and I are very much interested in hearing about how it all went."

"Lots of people died, I lost a lot of ships, and I learned a lot of things I wished I didn't," Malock said. "That's the short version. And again, you're changing the subject."

"We're not trying to change the subject," said Father. "We're just trying to find out what happened. You were gone for four months, after all."

"Yes, I know that," said Malock. "And yet you still promised to marry me to Raya even though you didn't know when or if I was going to return alive?"

"We had faith that you would," said Mother. "We asked Grinf day and night to protect you and bring you home safely. And it appears that he heard our prayers, praise be to His Most Justness."

Malock almost laughed, but he didn't. He just said, "But why? Haner mentioned something about our marriage being part of the peace negotiations that we've been doing with the Shikans over the last year or so."

"It's true," said Mother. "King Fabadi is just as interested in ending the longstanding hostilities between Carnag and Shika as we are. We decided that marrying you, our only son, to Princess Raya, Fabadi's only daughter, would be a good sign to both the Shikans and Carnagians that we are serious about putting our differences behind us."

Malock didn't think so. "Haner also told me that the marriage is next month. There's no way you could have planned for that unless you knew I was going to be coming back today."

"Haner obviously didn't give you all the facts," said Mother with a sigh. "Typical Haner. Well, we put the date of the wedding exactly one month after your return. Since you got back home today—the seventh day of the sixth month—that means that you will be married on the seventh day of the seventh month. If you had returned on today's date last month, the marriage would be today."

Malock threw up his hands. "Can't you at least postpone it? I'm still recovering from my voyage to World's End. I need time to rest and heal and get back into the groove of things."

"We can't do that," said Father, shaking his head. "We promised to King Fabadi—on Grinf's Most Just name no less—that we would marry you to Raya exactly one month after you returned. You know how serious oaths sworn on Grinf's name are."

Malock took a deep breath for a moment, trying to calm himself down. "But the age difference between me and Raya ... I mean, I'm thirty and she's what, twenty?"

"Twenty-one, actually," said Mother. "Her birthday was just last month and we sent her a beautiful set of new boots custom designed to fit her feet exactly. Just another way of spreading the good will that is so important for peace negotiations."

"Age is not an issue, Tojas," said Father. "You should know that. As much as I understand your shock, there is nothing you can say that will change anything. The marriage is going to happen whether you like it or not."

"Besides," said Mother, "Raya's not at all a bad girl. She's very smart, one of the most educated and intellectual princesses in all of the Northern Isles."

"She's also cold and unfriendly," said Malock. "Not to mention rude and self-centered. We'll be miserable together."

"You only say that because she didn't react well to your flirtations with her at the Northern Summit," Father pointed out. "Regardless, your happiness and her happiness do not matter very much in the grand scheme of things. The future of Carnag and Shika is what matters; nothing more."

"But—"

Father shook his head rapidly. "No buts. I know it sounds harsh, but this is a lesson I have always tried to instill in you, Tojas. You must sometimes sacrifice your own happiness for the good of your nation. When you take over the throne someday as King, then you will understand what I mean."

Malock wracked his brain for any argument he could use to convince them, but no matter how hard he thought, he couldn't think of anything that would work. He was well aware of the seriousness of oaths made in the name of a god and he was also aware of what King Fabadi might do if his parents called off the arrangement. Father's argument—that he should sacrifice his happiness for the good of Carnag—made the most sense of all, even though Malock wished it didn't. That didn't mean he was going to give up and accept it just yet, though.

As he thought about this, his gaze wandered up to the large statue of Grinf that towered over the three of them. It glinted slightly in the sunlight streaming in from the tall windows, making it look almost golden, which gave Malock an idea he hadn't considered before.

Looking back at Father and Mother, Malock pointed at the Grinf statue and said, "Did you consult Grinf about this issue before agreeing to it?"

In unison, Father and Mother looked embarrassed. Father scratched his chin, while Mother once again played with her ill-fitting crown. Malock wondered briefly why Mother didn't have the crown re-sized, but he dismissed the thought as unimportant for the moment.

"Oh, well," said Father with a gulp. "You see, we have been so busy over the last few months we just didn't have time—"

"My own parents, the ones who taught me through example and words the importance of seeking the approval of the gods before doing anything important, making up excuses for not consulting Grinf?" said Malock. "I am more than a little shocked at that, to be honest."

"We meant to," said Mother. "But we just didn't think Grinf would like to be disturbed over something that is really rather trivial in comparison to other matters that he no doubt deals with on a daily basis."

"But this marriage is huge," said Malock. "Shika and Carnag have been enemies for centuries precisely because Nimiko—Shika's patron god, the God of Light himself—and Grinf have been enemies. I would think that my marriage to one of Nimiko's followers would be a big deal to Grinf."

In reality, Malock didn't believe a word of his own argument. Based on his experience with the gods, he doubted very much that any of them cared who married who and for what reason. He had learned the hard way that the gods, even the northern gods, were not nearly as involved or interested in the lives of their followers as he had originally assumed. His parents, however, didn't know that and he didn't intend to tell them that because he was still processing that information himself.

Father bowed his head. "Yes, you are absolutely right. We should have consulted Grinf before we did this. We were foolish not to. I just hope there is still time to do that."

"There probably is," said Mother, although she didn't sound convinced of her own words. "Let's summon High Priest Madar and have him contact Grinf for us."

"That's a good idea," said Father.

He grabbed the rope hanging next to his throne and pulled down on it. A loud bell rang throughout Carnag Hall just then, which would summon whichever servant was just outside the throne room.

A moment later, the doors at the end of the throne room creaked open and the young face of one of the servant boys appeared through the crack. "Yes, Your Majesty?"

"Go and retrieve High Priest Madar," said Father in his commanding, kingly voice. "Bring him directly to the throne room as quickly as possible. Tell him that the Carnagian Royal Family requires his expertise immediately."

The servant boy nodded, said, "Yes, sir, Your Majesty," and disappeared as he closed the doors.

Ten minutes later, High Priest Madar stood in the throne room with Malock and his parents. Madar was an old man, probably in his eighties (although Malock did not know the High Priest's age for certain). He wore the flowing crimson robes of the Grinfian Priesthood, with the gold conical hat that always looked a bit like a boot to Malock.

When he entered the throne room and spotted Malock, the High Priest smiled and said, "Why, hello there, Prince Malock. I have heard of your return from World's End. How did the voyage go?"

In spite of Malock's current feelings, he had to admit it was hard to stay angry at Madar. The High Priest had always been kind and gentle to him, especially when Malock was a young boy. He had been one of Malock's teachers during the Prince's teenage years, which was when they grew especially close, as it was Madar who had taught Malock the most about the gods.

So Malock said to Madar, "It didn't go as well as I'd hoped, but I came back alive, so I guess that's what matters in the end."

"Yes, of course," said Madar. He turned his gaze onto Father and said, "Lord Halock, what have you summoned me for?"

"We wish to speak with Grinf," said Father. "We want to ask him for his blessing of the coming union between Tojas and Princess Raya."

"Oh," said Madar. "Of course. Allow me to get the fire going in the furnace. It may take a few minutes."

The statue of Grinf that stood behind the thrones had been built on top of a large furnace that was usually cold and empty. In order to access it, Malock had to move the thrones (Father offered to summon the servants, but Malock said he could do it on his own) out of the way, allowing Madar to access the furnace. The old man thanked Malock and then set to work on the furnace, using his pyromancy to begin heating the statue.

For safety reasons, Malock and his parents had to stand back several feet away from the statue and Madar; thus, Malock couldn't see exactly what Madar was doing, as the High Priest's back was to him and he was kneeling before the furnace. He had seen Madar do this before, however, so he had an idea of what the High Priest was up to.

A few minutes later, Madar stood up and stepped back. The furnace was now burning hot and brightly, the flames roaring within it. The statue of Grinf began to glow as the heat from the furnace entered its hollow metal skeleton. In spite of the heat of the flames, the statue was never in danger of melting, perhaps because Madar controlled the flames. The temperature in the room rose, making Malock sweat slightly, but he was used to that so he didn't complain about it.

"Lord Grinf the Most Just," said Madar as he raised his hands. "Protector of the Carnagian Royal Family, Defender of the Defenseless, and Judge of the World, your always humble and ever-willing servants, King Halock and Queen Markinia, wish to speak with you and ask for your divine approval of the marriage of their son, Prince Tojas Malock, to the Princess of Shika, Princess Raya Kabadi."

The flames continued to burn. And unless Malock was mistaken, the temperature seemed to be on the rise, too. He looked at his parents, who were sweating at least as much as he was.

Even Madar had to wipe the sweat off his forehead, and as he spoke his voice became more and more strained, as if he was having a hard time breathing. "Lord Grinf the Most Just, if you would but give us one sign in the flames that I could interpret to understand your will—just one sign is all I ask—then we, your loyal and faithful servants, would be satisfied."

Now the flames were actually rising out of the furnace, licking at the feet of the Grinf statue. Malock didn't know if that was a good thing or a bad thing. In all of his years of seeing Madar contact Grinf, he could not remember seeing the flames rise that high. And based on the expressions of his parents' faces, neither could they.

Madar actually had to step back, but he still kept speaking. "Lord Grinf the Most Just, I still cannot read the flames. Would you please tell us what you want us to—"

Abruptly, the flames exploded over the statue of Grinf, completely covering it in flames. The fire was so violent that it sent Madar staggering back. He tripped over his robes and fell down the steps until he landed flat on his back. Father moved to help him, but a powerful heat wave shot out from the flames, forcing all three members of the Royal Family back. The entire throne room felt like a furnace now, but Malock didn't even try to run away. He just watched as the flames slowly lowered, revealing a sight he had never seen before.

Standing in the statue's place was a tall, muscular man whose skin was the same dark shade as Malock's. His gold eyes shone in the flames, while his red armor flickered and burned just like the fire at his feet. In his left hand he carried a large hammer that seemed to be made of gold, while his right hand burned like a fire. Though he was bald, it did not take away from his fierceness; in fact, it added to it. The fire continued to burn at his feet, even shooting up to his knees occasionally, but he didn't seem at all bothered by it.

"This cannot be," said Father, furiously wiping the sweat off his brow. "This has never happened before, no, not even once ..."

Grinf—the real Grinf—looked over them all with the dispassionate eyes of a judge. He was still the same size as the statue, making him seem gigantic. Malock didn't know what to do, so he just stood there, hoping that Grinf wasn't going to harm any of them.

Grinf pointed his hammer at Madar. "Justice has called. And justice will be served."

"Wh-What are you talking about, Lord Grinf?" said Madar, sweat drops literally rolling down his face. "What do you mean?"

"I mean that I have come to exact justice on those who deserve it," said Grinf. "Two people in this room have committed crimes that they must be punished for. They are you, High Priest Madar, and you, Prince Tojas Malock."

"What?" said Madar. "What crimes have I committed? I have never so much as harmed a child in my entire life. You must be mistaken, Lord Grinf."

The fire in Grinf's eyes expanded. "You dare accuse me of being mistaken? I am the God of Justice. I cannot be mistaken when it comes to matters of justice."

"Lord Grinf," said Father. Malock hadn't realized it until now, but Father had already taken several steps back from the God of Justice, perhaps to avoid getting burned. "Would you tell us what you mean when you say that Madar and Tojas committed crimes?"

Grinf shifted his gaze upward. The temperature around Malock rose perceptibly, making him want to take off his shirt, but he refrained from doing so. The god kept his hammer pointed at Madar, who was so frightened that he looked paralyzed.

"The crimes committed by the two mortals are simple," said Grinf. "Madar has deceived the entire Royal Family for decades by pretending to be able to divine my will through interpretation of the flames of this furnace for his own selfish purposes. I have overlooked this deception until now only because I have been dealing with far worse crimes, but I can no longer tolerate it."

Without warning, Madar got to his feet hastily and made a mad dash toward the exit. He could not run very fast, however, and did not get very far, before Grinf ripped off his two shoulder armor pieces and hurled them at the fleeing Priest. The shoulder pieces morphed in midair until they resembled shoes, which clamped onto Madar's feet, causing the old Priest to scream and dance in agony in his shoes.

"With your feet, you lead others down your own path of deception and selfishness," said Grinf. "So dance, dance away until you can no longer feel your feet or breathe the air around you."

Madar's shoes clinked and clanged against the floor. Mother and Father looked away, while Malock just stared at the screaming old man in disbelief. He wanted to help Madar, but he was too shocked by Grinf's actions to do anything except stand there and stare. Madar shrieked and screamed until he tripped and fell flat on his face, but he kept shaking his legs and feet as though he couldn't stop dancing.

Then Malock shook his head and shouted, "Grinf, stop it! You've punish him enough."

Grinf didn't appear to hear Malock, but a moment later, he snapped his fingers. The burning metal shoes clinging to Madar's feet flew off, morphing back into shoulder pads that returned to their position on Grinf's shoulders. He patted them into place for a moment before turning his gaze onto Malock.

"As for you, Prince Tojas Malock, I shall punish you for the crime you committed against Jenur Takren," said Grinf. He raised his hammer and pointed at Malock. "For accusing her of a crime she didn't commit—and worse, nearly handing her over to be punished in place of the actual criminal—your face shall be distorted forever."

This time, Malock didn't wait to see what Grinf was going to do. He turned and ran, almost knocking over Father in the process. He ran for the doors, but before he could reach them, a pillar of fire shot out of the floor in front of him, causing Malock to skid to a halt. He had just enough time to see Grinf's massive form towering over him before one of Grinf's hands wrapped around his face. And before Malock could scream, Grinf's hand exploded with fire, spreading it all over Malock's face.

There was no way Malock could even begin to describe the pain, feeling the fire eat away at his flesh. He couldn't even think. All he saw and felt and smelled and tasted and heard ... was flame.

And then Grinf pushed him back. Malock fell flat on his back and grabbed his face, but immediately let go when the pain in his face burned. He couldn't see anything, couldn't feel anything except the dull, burning pain that did not lessen even slightly. He heard his parents yelling and running toward him and the next moment he thought he saw them standing over him, but his eyes burned so badly that he couldn't be sure what he was seeing.

"Tojas, my son!" said Mother. "Can you speak?"

Malock didn't dare open his mouth, largely because he didn't trust his lips and tongue to work. He just nodded to show that he was listening, but he had to cut that movement short because it caused him so much pain that he wanted to scream.

"Lord Grinf," said Father, his voice quivering. "I ... I would never think to question your goodness, but—"

"But nothing," came Grinf's voice like the fire of the furnace. "Justice has been served."

"Will Tojas ... will he die?" said Mother, sounding close to tears now.

"No," said Grinf. "He will live. I made sure not to leave him with any lethal injuries. But his face will never be quite as handsome as it once was. Nor will the burning pain ever truly leave his face."

"What ... what will you do now?" said Father. "The wedding ... the marriage ..."

"What does love have to do with justice?" said Grinf. "Do as you please. I care not whether you marry your son to one of Nimiko's followers or not. I have other, far more important problems to attend to than to worry about such an insignificant event in the lives of two mortals."

"Thank you for your blessing, Lord Grinf," said Father. "Thank you."

Malock wasn't sure how that was supposed to be a blessing. His vision was clearing now and he raised his head just in time to see Grinf disappear in a burst of flame. He tried to throw a curse at the God of Justice, but his lips and tongue were uncooperative, so he only managed some gargled gibberish as Father shouted for the servants to fetch a panamancer and as Mother held his head in her lap. He hoped Grinf understood the message anyway.

Chapter Seven

THOUGH JENUR'S ARMS AND legs were bound, she had no pillow to rest her head on, no blanket to cover her body, and no knife with which she could free herself, Jenur wouldn't have minded it so much if maybe the entire prison didn't smell so bad. That, and the complete lack of light, made the entire situation far worse than it should have been.

Earlier, the three of them had been paraded through Rimo, their faces shown and their names shouted for all to hear, by the Priestly Guard. This caused most of the people to come out and yell and sneer at them; one older woman even threw a piece of a rotten ikadori peach at Jenur's head (which she managed to dodge, thankfully).

After that, the three of them were taken to the Temple of Kano, which apparently also doubled as a prison because the basement had three separate cells into which they were shoved. The Guard had also made sure to bound their arms and legs with tight ropes that dug into their skin. Jenur had tried to make a break for it at that point, but she had been overpowered by one of the Guards, which earned her tighter rope than what Quro and Rint got.

The head of the Guard had said that Priestess Wesol would be coming down soon to talk to them. He didn't say what she was going to talk to them about, though, and Jenur had no time to ask because the head Guard and the five other Guards he had brought with him left. While Jenur was glad they weren't being executed immediately, it did make her wonder how long it was until they actually were executed.

Not that she spoke much about it to Rint or Quro. Rint was too busy grumbling and complaining about being found and bound, while Quro's silence indicated to her that he was presently thinking. In all the years Jenur had known her dad, she knew better than to disturb him when he was thinking unless she had a very good reason for doing so. He was not known as the Thinker for nothing, after all. It was his wits that had allowed him to survive and succeed as a Dark Tiger and he was no doubt using those same wits to figure a way out of this situation.

Not to imply that Jenur was just going to sit by and let him do all of the thinking, of course. She, too, was thinking hard about how to escape this place, about how to break free of their bonds. Dozens of ideas came to mind, but as all of them involved her using her knife—which, thanks to Ramufa, she didn't have anymore—she shot down each one as it came. This frustrated her more than anything, as she disliked not having the answer immediately.

Just then, Jenur heard a creaking sound above, which she realized was the sound of the door opening. The door then slammed shut and the sounds of heavy feet began coming down the steps one at a time.

As the feet got closer, the dungeon itself became brighter, probably because of the lantern the person—whoever it was—was using.

Then a woman appeared, stepping down the stairs that led down from the Temple to the dungeon. Like most of the Destanian women that Jenur had seen, the woman had short, dark hair that was a clear sign of her age; which was to say, she was quite young (though probably older than Jenur herself). She wore the same blue robes that all of the Priests did, but it did little to hide her bulk. While she wasn't exactly overweight, she was larger than Jenur and it was easy to notice, especially in the face, which was quite chubby and round.

The Priestess stopped before Jenur's cell and raised her lamp to shine a light on her. Jenur squinted when the light hit her eyes, but she couldn't cover them due to her hands being tied behind her back.

Then the Priestess made her way down the line to the next cell, where Quro was. Jenur couldn't see her, but she heard the Priestess make a sound of disgust and then more footsteps until she stopped, probably in front of Rint's cell. More footsteps again and then the Priestess was standing in view of Jenur, holding her lamp up, perhaps so she could see them all equally or maybe so they could see her or perhaps both.

"My name is Priestess Wesol," said the Priestess. "I am the new head Priestess, having been given this noble duty by my fellow Priests after Deber's unfortunate assassination at the hands of this aquarian assassin."

She spoke in a monotone, which unnerved Jenur more than she'd like to admit.

"That is not all I am or have done," said Wesol, "but it is all you need to know."

"Why haven't you killed us?" came Quro's voice from the cell next to Jenur's. "You know who we are. You know what we did. You have no reason to spare us."

Jenur wished her dad would shut up, but to her surprise, Wesol said, "That is true. By all rights, I should order the Priestly Guard to drag your blasphemous behinds out into the town square and have you all beheaded for the entire island to see. Especially Rint, who as the mastermind behind the assassination deserves death more than either of you."

"Do it," said Rint's bitter voice. "Take me away and execute me. I don't care. Deber is dead and my brother is avenged. I have nothing else to live for."

"Straight to the point as always, Rint," said Wesol. "But I would rather not do that, at least not right away. You see, I've never been much of a fan of execution, whether public or private. I have no great love for any of you, but as a devoted Kanonite, I have always upheld the belief that killing other people—even criminals—is wrong."

"Is that why you let Deber sacrifice those innocent children to Kano?" said Rint, his voice laced with anger now. "Is that why you didn't dethrone the witch after she forced my brother to perform an awful deed?"

Wesol frowned, though she looked slightly nervous. "I have no idea what you are talking about, Rint. Priestess Deber never sacrificed anyone to Kano, much less innocent children. You must be mistaken."

"I'm not mistaken," said Rint. "Kinker told me all about it. Deber was an insane, evil witch who loved to kill and torture others. She was drunk with power and you know it."

"We are getting off topic," said Wesol. "Deber is dead now. Whatever she did is done and there is no point in worrying about it."

"Easy for you to say," said Rint. "You're not a family member of those children she killed."

Ignoring that, Wesol continued. "On the other hand, I have also always believed that justice must be served. I cannot simply let you three walk free, as the people would no doubt riot if they saw that. I therefore must punish you in some way without compromising my principles or inciting the wrath of the mob."

"Now I get it," said Quro, speaking up suddenly. "You know I am a member of the Dark Tigers. If I don't return to our base in a timely manner, Wirm will no doubt send someone down here to investigate. And if he finds out you killed me, then he will have you killed. The Grand Tiger is not forgiving towards those who harm his Tigers. Your own survival is your only interest, isn't it? You don't want him to kill you, so you're trying to think of a way to punish us without getting Wirm angry at you."

Wesol's eyes focused on the floor, like she was trying to hide something. "Even if that is true, it does not change the simple fact that justice must be served. Though I am not a follower of Grinf, even I recognize that criminals must be punished for their crimes against society. Do you not agree?"

"I agree," said Rint. "And I don't care. Punish me as you see fit. I have nothing to lose."

"So I have devised a method in which to punish you three while avoiding killing you needlessly," said Wesol. "It is quite simple, but should suffice. It will be a grand public spectacle so that everyone can see justice being served."

"What is it?" said Jenur. "Are you going to flog us?"

"Flogging would be ineffective," said Wesol. "Instead, I am going to send you three into the Aratan, which is just north of Rimo."

"The ... Aratan?" said Rint. His voice quavered when he said that word. "That's absolutely monstrous. We'll never survive that."

"What's the Aratan?" said Quro. "I've never heard of it. What's so bad about it?"

"The Aratan is the largest—and only—jungle on Destan," said Wesol. "It is largely uninhabited, in part due to the dangerous wildlife and flora that live within it."

"She is making a huge understatement," said Rint. "Monsters live there, big beasts capable of rending humans limb from limb with no difficulty at all. No one who has ever entered there has ever come out alive."

Jenur looked at Wesol in alarm. "You said you weren't going to kill us."

"And I'm not," said Wesol, her expression half-hidden in the shadows cast by the flickering lamp. "If you die, it will be at the hands of the monsters or because of the plants or because of something else. Not because of any orders I gave."

"A technicality, that's all it is," said Rint. "You're just as bad as Deber. Why, I bet you helped her kill some of those kids, didn't you? Admit it. You're a vicious killer who thinks Kano likes human sacrifice."

"You have no idea if she doesn't," said Wesol a little too quickly. "But that is beside the point. I am only doing what I believe is the best way to achieve justice while not compromising my principles. Besides, the Aratan will be far more merciful to you than I or the Priestly Guard."

"Don't try and pretend that you're better than Deber," said Rint. "You're not. You don't have any principles to compromise. The whole Priesthood is that way, all the way to the top. And that includes you."

"I don't have to stand around and take this abuse from a senile old man," said Wesol, wiping the sweat off her forehead. "Besides, I thought you would be happy about this. You might, after all, survive."

"You know we won't," said Rint. "No one has ever survived the Aratan. That place claims more lives every year than the Crystal Sea does during murder season."

"Not my problem," said Wesol. "Now I must leave and tell the Priestly Guard to take you out of town. The Sea Festival is still ongoing and every minute I spend down here talking to you murderers is another minute that is not spent on glorifying Kano and making money off the few tourists who choose to come down here this time of year. Good day."

With that, Wesol turned and began walking up the stairs. Jenur watched her go, the dungeon getting darker and darker the farther the Priestess walked until she heard the door open and close above. Without the light of the lamp, darkness claimed the dungeon once more.

"We have to get out of here," said Rint. "You two are Dark Tigers. Surely you've been in this kind of situation before?"

"We certainly have," said Quro. "Jenur, remember that time you and I were captured by that tribe of cannibal crustacean aquarians that live on Riuja, just south of Ruwa?"

"Yeah," said Jenur. "I remember. They wanted to eat you and rape me, right?"

"Correct," said Quro. "And you remember how we got out of that one, don't you?"

Jenur frowned, thinking hard. The specific episode Quro mentioned had taken place a while ago, back when she was fifteen, and she honestly hadn't thought much about it since then, mostly because the memories she associated with it were too unpleasant. "They were taking us to their sanctuary, where they were going to sacrifice you to their god and then take their turns with me, right?"

"Once again, correct," said Quro. "The crustaceans were followers of the obscure god Qunum, God of Crustaceans. We managed to escape by using the pepper powder pellets we had on us. Tossed them into their eyes, which disoriented them long enough for us to make our escape."

"I remember," said Jenur. "But what does that have to do with

91

our current situation? I don't have any pepper powder pellets and you probably don't, either."

"You're right," said Quro. "I don't. Ramufa stole them off me. He stole almost everything I could use as a weapon. Not sure how he found most of it, but he did."

Rint's voice came just then, sounding slightly confused. "*Almost* everything? What did he not—"

A snapping sound interrupted Rint, followed by someone getting to their feet. A moment later, a nearby door—which, based on the direction the sound was coming from, had to be Quro's cell door—groaned open. Then Jenur heard movement in front of her cell, heard someone fiddling with the lock, and then the door opened and the sound of someone's feet walking along the floor of her cell. Then she felt two slimy hands—Quro's hands, she realized—touch her hair and move down to her back, where her hands were tied together. She didn't know what he was doing, but when she heard the same snapping sound from before, Jenur immediately pulled her hands up in front of her and rubbed her wrists as Quro snapped the ropes binding her legs. Before she could ask him what he had done, Quro was gone, his feet slapping against the floor as he walked to Rint's cell.

After getting the blood circulating through her limbs again, Jenur got to her feet and walked out the open door. It was still too dark to see anything, but she heard a couple of snaps and then heard two sets of feet exiting Rint's cell. She sensed that Quro and Rint were nearby, though she could not see where they were.

"That was amazing, Quro," said Rint. "How did you do that?"

"Dragon shark scales," came Quro's voice. "Always carry some on me. I concealed them in my shirt sleeves, so it was easy for me to slip one out and use it to snap the ropes tying me down."

"But how did you snap the lock on your jail cell door?" said Rint. "Do you have a lock pick on you or something?"

"No," said Quro. "Dragon shark scales can also cut through most forms of metal. Very useful for making a quick escape, as I just demonstrated."

"That is some tool you've got there," said Rint. "Now what do we do?"

"We escape," said Quro. "We get out of Rimo, take my boat, and get out of here."

"Leave Destan?" said Rint with some hesitation. "But Destan is my home."

"And you will be killed if you stay here any longer," Jenur said. "You know that will happen. If you come with us, you will be safe."

"But where will I go?" said Rint. "What will I do? I've never even left Destan before. I don't know anything about the rest of the Northern Isles."

"That, you will have to figure out for yourself," said Quro. "I wish I could have gotten my full payment, but I guess you can pay me back another time. For now, we must go."

Chapter Eight

AFTER GRINF LEFT, MALOCK was not sure what happened. His face continued to burn, continued to hurt, and the pain was so awful that he couldn't even think or process much of what was happening around him. He heard his parents talking, felt someone's soft hands touch his face, felt someone lift him up and take him away, but none of it made any sense from his perspective. He could not put it all together in a coherent way. It all felt like a series of disconnected events that made no sense to him, so after a while he gave up trying to make sense of it.

It was only later—how much later, he could not say—that he opened his eyes and found himself lying in his bed in his room in Carnag Hall. He recognized the red silk sheets and the soft yet firm mattress under his back. It took him a moment to realize that he was also in his pajamas, even though he could not remember changing his clothes. He supposed that his servants must have changed him before he went to bed.

His face still burned. It wasn't nearly as bad as before, but he could not dismiss it very easily. He reached up and touched his face, which felt rough and course. The skin had healed, but he figured he must look terrible now. He had seen the faces of burn victims before and they had never looked good to him at all, even those burn victims who had once been beautiful or handsome. He shuddered to think of what he looked like now.

Nonetheless, he had a morbid desire to see his face anyway. He sat up in his bed, but before he could do anything, a soft dark hand reached over and grabbed his upper left arm as a woman's soft voice said, "Prince Malock, you shouldn't be up. You should be resting."

Instinctively, Malock jerked his arm from the woman's grasp and looked to his left. An older woman was sitting on a chair next to his bed, wearing robes of purest white, with the symbol of the goddess of Atikos—a bandage wrapped around a bleeding arm—stitched into the chest area. She had hair that was as white as the robes, almost bleached white, and in her other hand carried a short wooden wand.

"Friyu?" said Malock. His voice was slightly distorted through his lips. "Is that you?"

"Yes, it's me," said Friyu, nodding. "When you got burned, I was summoned by your parents to try to heal you with my panamancy. I did my best, but I was unable to restore your face to its original appearance."

"Did you try everything?"

"I tried all of the best burn healing spells that I know," said Friyu. "But whatever burned your face must have used a form of magic that I've never encountered before because none of my spells worked on it. Not a single one."

Malock remembered what Grinf had said earlier about his face being distorted 'forever.' At the time, he thought it was just hyperbole on Grinf's part, but if what Friyu said was true, then he had to assume that the God of Justice had been quite literal when he said 'forever.'

"Give me a mirror," said Malock.

"Your Majesty—"

"Right now," said Malock, using his most commanding tone. "I want to see my face."

Friyu shrugged and picked up a small hand mirror from the bed-stand next to Malock's bed. She handed the mirror to Malock, which the Prince took and gazed into. He almost retched at the face he saw.

The melted-looking cheeks, the half-shut eyelids, the distorted nose, the ends of his hair that were crisped black ... it was all hideous. A strong desire to hurl the mirror across the room overcame him just then, but as this happened to be his mirror that he had received as a present from his parents years ago, he just thrust it back into Friyu's hands and looked away, covering his face with his own hands as he did so.

"I am ugly," said Malock. "Worse than ugly; I am hideous."

"It's okay, Prince Malock," said Friyu in a soothing tone. "You're still alive and breathing, aren't you?"

"But I'm still ugly," said Malock, not bothering to look at her. "Just look at me. Once I was the handsomest Prince in all of the Northern Isles. Now I am the ugliest."

"Surely you're not as ugly as Prince Hanfu of Kikasa," said Friyu. "You still have your strapping body and princely physique."

"What is the use of having the perfect body if your face looks like melted cheese?" said Malock. "Where are my parents?"

"They were in the throne room, last I checked," said Friyu. "They were yelling at Madar. Something about him deceiving them for years or something. All I know is that Madar didn't look like he was in much of a position to defend himself."

A memory of Madar dancing with the burning shoes on his feet appeared in Malock's mind, making the Prince shudder in horror. He shook his head and then raised his face out of his hands. He looked at Friyu and said, "How long was I out?"

"A few hours," said Friyu. "You woke up awfully quickly, far more quickly than I thought you would."

"Good," said Malock. "I thought I had been asleep for days."

Friyu hesitated, then said, "If I may ask, Your Majesty, how, exactly, did your face get burned? What kind of magic caused it? Was it an accident?"

Malock almost said "Grinf did it," but then he thought better. He didn't think Friyu would understand why Grinf punished him. She was at least as loyal to Grinf as his parents were, despite her affiliation with Atikos, and he was in no mood to explain to her why Grinf punished him anyway.

So he said, "It was an accident. That's all you need to know about it right now."

Friyu looked a little disappointed, but she said, "Okay. I understand. It must have been very traumatic, whatever it was. I'm just worried about the long-term effects the burn will have on your face."

"I said, don't worry about it," said Malock. "Okay? It was an accident and it won't happen again." *Unless Grinf happens to remember some other 'crime' I committed at some point in the past, of course.*

"If you say so," said Friyu. "But really, if you could tell me exactly how you were burned, then I might be able to—"

"I said it's none of your business," said Malock, looking at her hard. "It's done and over with. You have nothing to worry about. You can't heal me anyway, even if you knew how it was done. It's just not important."

Friyu went quiet, but Malock didn't care if his tone was harsh. He was still distressed from having his face burned and was not interested in possibly endangering someone else's life by cursing Grinf. Besides, what was the point in telling her about it? She wouldn't believe it. After all, like most humans, Friyu probably—no, definitely, otherwise her magic wouldn't work—believed that the gods were good, that they were just, and that they never made mistakes or acted in reprehensible ways. Malock only wished he could be that naïve.

But he realized that he shouldn't have used such a harsh tone on her. Friyu had served the Carnagian Royal Family for years. In fact, she had been the one to deliver Malock when he had been born. She was probably the best panamancer in the entire island, and maybe even the best in all of the Northern Isles. To treat her with such disrespect was not a good thing.

So Malock took a deep breath and then spoke in a gentler voice. "Look, I was just ... I'm dead tired. I just got back from a four month voyage to the end of the world and now my face is burned and everything is just very confusing for me right now. I hope you weren't offended."

Friyu looked surprised, as if she had not expected him to apologize. "Oh, of course not, Your Majesty. I understand. I've had to help burn victims before and it is always traumatizing. Most do recover, of course, but they are never the same afterward."

Malock lay back down in his bed, trying to ignore his burning face but failing, as usual. "I think you've done all you can, Friyu. You may leave. I'll just rest in here for a while."

"If you say so, Your Majesty," said Friyu as she stood up. "I will be back in a few hours to check your progress."

Malock nodded as Friyu made her way across the room to the door. Just as she laid her hand on the doorknob, the door burst open and a familiar thin man jumped into the room. He wore extremely garish clothing; a bright blue doublet, with orange and red pants that were extremely baggy. On his head was a cap with a bell attached to it and in his hands was a pad of paper and a quill. Malock groaned internally when he saw the man.

"Darfna?" said Friyu in shock as she stepped back. "What are you doing here?"

Darfna put the tip of his quill to his mouth, as if contemplating the deepest mysteries of the gods, and then said, "Why, Doctor Friyu, I am here to see His Majesty Prince Malock. I have been commissioned by King Halock to write a play based off of Prince Malock's voyage to World's End. After all, that is the job of the official playwright/chronicler/historian of the Carnagian Royal Family, isn't it?"

"I thought you were visiting your family in Harnos," said Friyu. "When did you get back?"

"The minute I heard the rumors of Prince Malock's return, of course," said Darfna. "Rumors run faster than the God of Speed himself in Carnag. I naturally couldn't sit around and talk with my family, not when I knew that the King would undoubtedly want me to write a play based off the adventures of his only and beloved son."

Malock tried to sink a little deeper under his blankets, but Darfna must have noticed the movement because the playwright turned to face Malock's bed and said, "Prince Malock! I am so glad to see you are awake. Your father the King asked me to interview you and learn as much as possible about your voyage to the south. So why don't I draw a chair and sit next to you and you tell me everything you can remember?"

Malock pulled his blankets up close over his face. "Later. I'm tired and would like to rest right now."

Darfna held out his quill and notepad like he was begging for Malock's mercy. "I understand that, Your Majesty, but you don't understand. We have our most vivid memories of our adventures only after we've experienced them. If I let you rest, why, you might forget all the good details. And that would not be a good thing."

"It's fine," said Malock. "I'll remember everything. You don't have to worry about it."

"But I do," said Darfna, closing his eyes and pulling his quill and paper up to his chest. "The right detail is what makes a story come alive. Without that detail, oh, it doesn't matter how exciting or true the story is. It will be dead, mere words on a page."

Malock sighed. "Why don't you go interview the members of the crew of my ship instead? They all saw and experienced a lot of the same things that I did. They could give you details even I don't know."

"I really must agree with Prince Malock," said Friyu. "He has been through a variety of traumatic experiences, many I cannot even imagine, and then he got his face burned just hours after returning home—"

Darfna gasped. "He did? I mean, I am very sorry to hear about that, Your Majesty. Please describe to me in detail the circumstances leading up to your face being burned and the event itself so I may use it as a scene in the play."

"No," said Malock flatly. "As the Crown Prince of Carnag, I order both of you to leave. Do not even think about disturbing me while I rest, at least not until tomorrow."

Darfna almost dropped his quill and notepad. "Tomorrow? But —"

"No buts," said Malock. "If you do not leave me alone, then I will summon the guards and have them throw you in the dungeon for a week."

Darfna's shoulder slumped. "All right, Your Majesty." Then he smiled. "But first thing tomorrow morning, we will have a long, detailed interview in which you will describe to me the exact conditions you faced on the ship known as the *Iron Wind*, as well as all of the wonderful and terrible sights you saw on World's End, in extreme, vivid detail that will leave no room for the audience's imagi —"

"Out!" Malock shouted.

That worked. Darfna immediately retreated from the room, with Friyu following. Friyu closed the door behind her on the way out, giving Malock one last look before she closed it completely.

Now that he was alone, Malock sighed. He lowered the covers down from his face, as the silk felt strange against his burned skin. He had forgotten just how annoying Darfna could be. The playwright may have been a genius whose work was respected among the actors and writers of the Northern Isles, but he was far too eccentric and invasive for Malock's tastes. It was, in fact, the reason that Malock had not taken Darfna with him to World's End, as he didn't think he could tolerate the playwright for that long.

Malock turned on his side and closed his eyes. He really was tired. He hadn't realized it, but it was true. He had been so busy over the past few days that he hadn't paid much attention to his body, which was getting slower and slower every hour. He fully intended to take advantage of this time in order to get a good night's sleep.

But for some reason his mind wandered back to Princess Raya. He punched his pillow when he remembered her. What were his parents thinking, marrying him to Raya? They seemed to have forgotten that he and her had two entirely different personalities. There was no way they could ever work together. Raya was cold, calculating, highly intellectual, and not much of a fan of parties, whereas Malock—at least before going to World's End—had always held the belief that a life spent partying was a life well spent.

We will probably kill each other on our wedding night, rather than consummate our 'love,' Malock thought.

Yes, Malock understood the political reasoning behind it. In fact, in the months leading up to his vision from Kano summoning him to World's End, he had worked with his father to forge a new alliance with the Shikans, mostly as practice for when Malock would be come king. Yet neither his father nor King Fabadi, the King of Shika, had even once mentioned to Malock that they were planning an arranged marriage of any sort. Nor had Raya said anything to him about it, though he supposed that wasn't shocking, as Raya had only interacted with him insofar as her royal duties dictated that she had to, and no more. He wondered if the arranged marriage had come as a shock to her, too.

Probably, he thought, disgruntled. *I don't know King Fabadi very well, but I imagine he must have agreed to the marriage without consulting Raya first. Old bastard.*

Malock wasn't necessarily against marriage, per se. In his view, marriage was a good thing. He had always intended on marrying someone at some point, but he had also believed in enjoying yourself while you could. That was why he had maintained several illicit relationships with women of varying character throughout his youth. He felt it had given him a lot of experience, although he was aware of the reputation he had gained as a result of his 'frolicking,' as he liked to think of it.

But Raya? A Shikan? If you had asked him who his future wife was going to be, he certainly wouldn't have answered Raya. In fact, in all likelihood he would have named Vashnas as his ... as his wife.

Vashnas. Again, his mind replayed her death like a picture book. He saw Kano thrust her arm down Vashnas's throat, draining the fluid from Vashnas's body; saw Vashnas turn into dust; and it was all so real that it made his throat choke up. When Vash died, Malock had intended to stay away from romance for a while. Yet here his parents had not only chosen a wife for him, but were already preparing the wedding even as he lay there thinking about it.

If Vashnas was still alive, how would she react to this news? Malock thought. *I doubt she'd be very happy. Maybe she would have done what she did to Kinker and try to kill Raya.*

His mind a confused muddle, Malock forced himself to stop thinking about this subject. He closed his eyes even more tightly than before and did his best to drift to sleep, though this was not easy, for images of Vashnas and Raya swam before his eyes, however much he tried not to think about either.

Chapter Nine

PRINCESS RAYA KABADI, THE Princess of Shika, turned a page in her thick volume, *The History of Heathenism in the Northern Isles,* by the famous aquarian historian Arax, and squinted at the first line of text. The print in this book was tiny due to the tome's thick size, which had forced her to wear her glasses so she could make it out. Nonetheless, she was already halfway through the book and she hoped to finish at least two more chapters before going to bed tonight. It didn't bother her that the length of the average chapter in this book was forty pages; that just meant she would have more material to read.

The walls, floor, and ceiling—being made out of brightstone, a particular stone that was only found on Shika—glowed softly in the darkness, giving her enough light to read by even without her lamp. Her eyelids grew heavier with each passing minute, however, not helped by the soft recliner she sat in. She figured she would have to go to bed soon, even though she wanted to read more of this book.

Just then, a knock at Raya's room door snapped her out of her concentration. Annoyed, Raya looked up from her thick book and said, "Who is it?"

"It is I," said a familiar voice on the other side of the door. "One of your faithful servants. I have urgent news to report to you, Princess, news that you need to know right away."

Frowning, Raya picked up a bookmark and stuck it securely in the spot she was reading before saying, "Enter."

The door opened and the servant entered, a short, middle-aged man without a hair on his large head. Raya had trouble remembering his name, even though she saw him daily. She supposed it wasn't important.

"What's the news?" said Raya. "You know how I dislike being disturbed while I read."

The servant clapped his hands together excitedly. "I know, Princess, but your father King Fabadi just recently received a message from King Halock, the King of Carnag, and he told me to tell you that Prince Tojas Malock has returned from his voyage."

Raya—who had been lazing in her chair, as she usually did when she was reading—sat up straight. "Impossible. Prince Malock died during his voyage to World's End, didn't he?"

"It appears not, Your Majesty," said the servant. "According to the letter King Fabadi received a few minutes ago, Prince Malock and the remaining members of his crew arrived in Port Blasan, the capital of Carnag, earlier today, on a mysterious ship that no one has ever seen before. Prince Malock suffered a burn to the face when he returned, but is in otherwise good condition and is ready for the wedding, which will be exactly one month from today."

Raya grimaced. "So the marriage is going through after all, then."

"It would appear so," said the servant. "Let me just congratulate you, Princess Raya, on your upcoming marriage. I know this is a bit soon, but I have always been a loyal servant to the Family of Shika and I simply wish to let you know that I wish you the very best of—"

"Get out," said Raya.

"Excuse me, Your Majesty?" said the servant.

Raya pointed at the open door. "Leave me be, unless you have some more urgent news to share."

"Of course, of course, Your Majesty," said the servant as he backed out out of the room. "As your ever loyal servant, I know better than to argue with you even when I don't completely understand your orders. Why, just the other day—"

Raya snapped her fingers and the door immediately slammed in the servant's face.

I knew that learning some psychimancy was a good idea, Raya thought as she closed her book and placed it on the nightstand next to her chair.

Raya then stood up and walked over to the massive bookcase lining the back wall of her room. She walked down the line of books, which consisted of various classics and ancient writings on a variety subjects ranging from the nature of the gods to the history of Shika and everything in between, until she found the book she was looking for: An unassuming, thin yellow book, titled *The History of the Six Pillars of Magic,* by someone named Rundya, withered with use, that was almost lost between the thick volumes on either side of it.

She reached up and pulled the book forward until she heard a small 'click.' Then, to her left, a small section of the bookshelf slid away, revealing a secret door that was locked. Raya found the key to the lock behind the yellow book, unlocked the door, and opened it. She found herself staring into darkness, but it was not complete darkness, for at the very bottom of the stairs, a dull light shone. The light gave her enough to see by, ensuring that she would not trip accidentally on her way down.

Raising the hem of her dress just above her ankles so it wouldn't tangle up her feet as she walked, Raya made her way down the stairs. Every step was done carefully, even though she had no desire to hide her arrival from the prisoner below. It was a steep, old staircase, much older than the other parts of the Castle if the lack of brightstone was any indication, though who made it and why, Raya didn't know, as she had only discovered its existence a year ago and could find no mention of it in the Castle Library. Even her father didn't know about it; at least, if he did, he never spoke of it to her.

She finally reached the bottom of the staircase, where she found a tall, thick wooden door standing before her. It was not perfectly flush with the doorway, however, as light streamed through the cracks in the sides, top, and bottom. She pulled out her key ring and unlocked the door, which opened quietly, as she had personally oiled the hinges herself not long after she discovered the room's existence in order to decrease the likelihood of someone hearing it. She then pushed the door open and stepped inside.

The room was little more than a dungeon, though different from the ones that lay deep beneath Castle Shika. The ceiling was low, made of an old type of stone that had been popular from an earlier era of Shikan history. Raya theorized that the room may have been part of an older castle, possibly from the Primordia Era based on the needlessly intricate design triangular carvings in the floor and ceiling, though when she spotted faded paintings on the walls—some of which featured gods such as Nimiko or Grinf, while at least one was clearly a rough map of the Northern Isles—she had her doubts.

A single wooden chair sat against the wall to her right, while an empty plate with bread crumbs and juice leftover from soup sat in the center of the room, along with a cup of water that was only half-drunk. A line of crumbs trailed all the way to the back of the small room, where an old man sat, his wrists and ankles chained to the wall behind him. His head was bowed, but that didn't mean he was asleep. A brief memory of being struck by his powers flashed through her mind, making her take a cautious step forward as she closed the door behind her.

"What do you want?" said the old man, without looking up at her. "Come to taunt me again?"

Raya shook her head. "Taunting you would give me nothing except a perverse sense of pleasure, and unlike some people, I prefer intellectual pleasure over vengeful pleasure."

The old man looked up. He was almost completely bald, save for the gray, greasy ponytail hanging from the back of his head. His body continuously glowed, the source of the room's light, but over the past months since Raya had caught him, the man's light had weakened considerably, though it was still brighter than any light Raya could make. His skin was as dark as a Carnagian's, but the clothes he wore—a simple white shirt and brown trousers—were more akin to the style of a Shikan peasant, which made sense, seeing as he was very important to the Shikans.

"Don't play with me, mortal," said the man. "I have lived for countless centuries and in that time I have seen the true nature of mortals. I know how thoughtlessly cruel you can be and I know that the only reason you haven't killed me yet is because you can't."

Raya squinted slightly to protect her eyes from the man's glow. "I find that funny. A *god* telling a *mortal* how cruel we have been. I suppose you've forgotten about all of the countless ways in which the gods have treated us mortals cruelly and unfairly. Then again, I suppose you would already be quite familiar with that, wouldn't you, Nimiko?

The God of Light pointed a shaky finger at her. "You ungrateful little mortal. We gods have protected and served humanity since the dawn of time, and yet you treat me—the patron of your nation—like a mere slave."

"Oh, I'm perfectly aware of what you gods have done for us," said Raya. "I am also aware of what you gods *haven't* done for us; namely, aid us in any significant way without ulterior motives."

"You have no idea what we gods have done for you mortals," said Nimiko. "If you did, you would be on your hands and knees right now, pleading for my forgiveness of the crimes you have committed against me."

Raya smiled. "Maybe I would. But I probably wouldn't."

Nimiko tugged at his chains. "The only reason you speak bravely is because I am incapacitated by these infernal chains. Just what are they made of, anyway?"

"Void metal," said Raya. "The only known substance in the world that can bind a god. Surely you would have realized that by now; then again, you are the God of Light, not the God of Intelligence."

Nimiko's face went pale. "Void metal? Where did you get that? The gods have banned the substance from the Northern Isles. No mortal has it. Even we gods have only a little."

"Found it down here in this chamber," said Raya, gesturing at the room in which they stood. "I theorized they might be Void metal because, despite their obvious age, they showed no signs of rust or decay. I only recognized their age because they are woven in a style that is no longer used nowadays."

"Even so, I will be free someday," said Nimiko. "The other gods will notice my absence and will come to my rescue or at least send one of their servants to free me. What do you think will happen to you then? No mortal has ever survived the wrath of the gods. You certainly will not be the first."

"I know," said Raya. "But I doubt they will. After all, light is still working in the world. You are still maintaining it. Considering that you have been my captive for a few months now, I imagine the other gods simply don't know or care and won't care unless you die. From what research I've done, I've figured that you gods just don't care very much for each other unless something really bad happens to one of you."

Nimiko looked at her like she had lost her mind. "I have seen many arrogant mortals in my life, but few have shown the same kind of arrogance you do."

"I'll take that as a compliment," said Raya.

Nimiko frowned. "Why did you even come down here? Did you get bored and wish to torment me?"

"No," said Raya, shaking her head. "I merely came down here because I was told that Prince Malock, the Crown Prince of Carnag and my future husband, has returned from his voyage to World's End."

"Ah," said Nimiko. "That does not surprise me. I was not involved in the situation, but I know he had Kano's protection. No mystery there."

"He did?" said Raya. "Interesting. That explains quite a bit."

"Why did you tell me that?" said Nimiko. "Who cares if Malock returned alive or not? How is this relevant to me?"

"It's relevant because Malock is the only mortal I know of who has been to World's End and returned alive," said Raya. "That means he has seen and heard things that the vast majority of mortals have never seen and heard. Including, perhaps, information or knowledge that could help us mortals defend ourselves from the gods."

Nimiko chuckled. "How naïve. Even if Malock did learn something, I doubt it's anything you mortals could put into practice. My brothers and sisters in the south would never have allowed

Malock to return alive if that was the case."

"Would they?" said Raya. "Malock is definitely an idiot, but on the few times I met him, he did show a glimmer of cleverness behind that party boy persona he puts on display. He probably could have figured out a way to get back here even if the gods did not want him to leave."

"Let's say I grant you that's true," said Nimiko. "That still doesn't mean Malock will tell you anything. I am not as familiar with the Carnagian Royal Family as Grinf is; however, I do know that they have a proper fear of and respect for all gods, not just Grinf. Even when you are married, do you think Malock will approve of your holding me prisoner, once he learns of it? I doubt it."

"I will have to be very careful about how I go about getting that information out of him," said Raya. "It's not a task I look forward to, partly because of what you said, but also because Malock and I have never gotten along very well. Still, I must do it, no matter the risks to my personal reputation."

Nimiko scratched the back of his left ear. "I have been down here for two months, kept away from the light of the sun, and still you haven't told me why you're doing this. You keep saying you can't trust the gods, but you have no reason to believe that. We gods have never shown the slightest indication of wanting to destroy or harm you mortals."

Raya shrugged. "I guess that's true. You gods have never actively sought to wipe us all out, even though you have never been particularly merciful or kind to us. But have you ever heard of Hanyu the Prophet?"

Nimiko frowned, as if trying his best to remember. "No, I have not."

"He was a Tinkarian prophet who lived five hundred years ago," said Raya. "He wasn't very popular at the time, mostly due to his insistent prediction that the Red Empire—at that point in history the largest and strongest human empire ever created—was going to fall, despite the Empire's apparent strength and prosperity. Everyone laughed at him, especially when it was learned that he was a half-breed."

"A what?"

"Half-human, half-aquarian," said Raya. "Back then, half-breeds were regularly killed or, if their parents were kind, simply left in the wilderness as babies to die. The situation for them has improved since then, but it's still quite poor."

"Absolutely vicious," said Nimiko, looking down at his feet. "Killing babies just because they do not come out looking as you wish. And you say we gods are the cruel ones?"

Raya chuckled herself now. "Coming from the god who once blinded an entire village of Shikans who refused to worship you so that my grandfather's army could raze it to the ground, that is quite the statement."

Nimiko grunted and then stared at his feet, as if hoping he could break the chains binding his ankles to the floor.

"Where was I?" said Raya. "Oh, yes. Hanyu's prediction came true a mere year later. The Red Emperor and his wife were assassinated by political enemies. Since the Red Emperor didn't have children or a chosen successor to take his place in the event that he died, the government turned into a free-for-all, every-man-for-himself brawl, causing the entire Empire to shatter into dozens of individual warring states, spurred on by rebel factions that had up until this point been waiting for the perfect opportunity to strike. The situation was not helped in the slightest when the Aquarian Federation—the largest conglomerate of aquarian countries ever—attempted to attack the weakened Empire at the same time, though they were later driven back into the Crystal Sea by the new Skull Empire that arose from the ashes of the Red Empire."

"What does this have to do with the gods?" said Nimiko. "I remember most of that, as I was chosen to be the Skull Empire's patron god when it was formed. Beyond that, this seems like a boring, irrelevant history lesson."

"I'm getting there, don't worry," said Raya. "So Hanyu is mostly remembered nowadays for correctly predicting the fall of the Red Empire in a time of unprecedented prosperity. The Tinkarians revere him as the best prophet of all, though they tend to gloss over the fact that he was a half-breed. But that's not all Hanyu did; in fact, I would argue that his prediction of the Red Empire's fall was pedestrian in comparison to the other predictions he made."

"What other predictions?" said Nimiko.

"Hanyu wrote books," Raya continued. "Lots and lots of books, mostly about his visions of the future that he claimed to have received from Tinkar. The vast majority of those books are lost to history, thanks in no small part to their having been burned or destroyed by Hanyu's enemies after his death, but a few survived. One of those books is simply titled *Prophecies*, which my father—an avid book collector—bought from a merchant in the capital one day about ten years ago, though I don't think my father ever actually read it."

Nimiko grunted. "Get to the point."

"As a little girl, I was a voracious reader," said Raya. "When my tutor taught me how to read, I started reading every book I could get my hands on, even the ones written for adults. I didn't understand most of what I read—I was, after all, just a young girl—but my parents approved of it, as they believed the desire to learn was an important part of any successful ruler. I ended up reading Hanyu's *Prophecies*, which is where I discovered the real reason Hanyu's enemies despised and persecuted him."

"What was that reason?"

"In *Prophecies*, Hanyu makes a very strange prediction in the last chapter, in the last few paragraphs actually. He claimed that the Day of the Gods was coming, that a force known as 'Kasrath' would emerge from the Void and devour all of creation. He said the gods would not last forever; that someday, they would all die. He also made the claim that the Powers showed him this vision, though he offered no proof of that claim."

"Impossible," said Nimiko. "We gods cannot die. I mean, gods can kill other gods, but that has not occurred since the end of the Godly War. What does *Kasrath* even mean? It sounds like nonsense."

"I had to do some etymological research on it," said Raya. "The word is apparently derived from the Old Shikan prefix *kas-*, meaning 'beauty,' combined with the Old Aqua root *-rath*, meaning 'terror.' Therefore, 'Kasrath' roughly translates to 'Beautiful Terror' or 'Terrible Beauty,' depending on how you decide to translate it. I imagine Hanyu must have coined the term, as I can't find the word in any other book and he was known for coining words from the prefixes and roots of human and aquarian languages."

"A beautiful terror will destroy the gods?" said Nimiko with a snort. "You mortals certainly have wild imaginations. It didn't even happen, so it's obvious that he was wrong."

"Maybe," said Raya. "Hanyu certainly thought it was going to happen, but he never got to live long enough to see it. He committed suicide not long after writing that book, mostly because of the intense persecution he faced for his mixed heritage."

"A sad story, I suppose, but a pointless one, too," said Nimiko. "I still do not see what this has to do with anything."

"Don't you get it?" said Raya. "In that same prophecy, Hanyu reported that he felt intense pressure from the gods—specifically Tinkar—to kill himself. He said the gods were afraid of his prediction, afraid that other mortals would listen to and take seriously his message. He didn't actually want to die, but with the pressure from the gods and the discrimination from his fellow mortals, he hanged himself in the privacy of his home."

Nimiko sat up. "Hanyu was obviously delusional. Why would we gods ever be afraid of the clearly false words of a mortal? It's just another example of mortal arrogance, that's all."

"You aren't getting it," said Raya. "Why would Hanyu—who up until that point had been a firm supporter of the gods—make that prediction even if he was arrogant? It is especially notable that he claims that Tinkar, of all of the gods, encouraged his suicide. As the God of Fate, I think Tinkar would have a better idea about the future than most. I can only conclude, therefore, that he suspected Hanyu's vision was legitimate and that it frightened him—and by extension, the rest of the gods—greatly."

"I don't know much about what Tinkar has or hasn't done to his followers," Nimiko admitted. "But I do know that we gods are not afraid of obviously false prophecies like the kind that Hanyu regularly made."

"If that was true, then Tinkar would have ignored Hanyu," said Raya. "Because he didn't, it got me thinking: Why are the gods so afraid of losing control? Why do they treat us mortals like volatile beasts? There have been other instances throughout history of the gods destroying the lives of mortals they do not approve of, but this was the first to make me think that the gods may not be entirely on our side."

"Paranoia will get you nowhere, Raya," said Nimiko. "Nothing you say changes the fact that you are a paranoid mortal woman, easily frightened by scary words, as most mortal women tend to be."

"Think of it from our point of view, Nimiko," said Raya, pointing at the paintings of Grinf and Nimiko on the walls. "This world is ruled by beings capable of sinking whole islands, beings by whose word empires rise and fall. In some ways, we mortals are like ants trying to avoid being squashed by the much larger beings all around us."

"When you put it that way, I suppose it does make us gods sound ... frightening," Nimiko said. "But it is still a senseless fear. We gods would never destroy you mortals. We are not mindless killing machines, as you seem to think we are. We may punish you, but that is far as we will go."

"Maybe not now, but what about in the future?" said Raya. "There is nothing stopping you gods from turning on us mortals. We are weak and defenseless. Even with our magic, we are still nothing in comparison to you gods. If even half the legends about your powers are true, then just by existing, every single god in the Northern Pantheon is a threat to all of humanity. It would be foolish for us humans to lack a backup plan to protect us from your powers, should you ever decide to destroy us."

"I know of no human nation that has such a backup plan," said Nimiko, "because it would be foolish and unnecessary. How could you possibly defend yourself from us gods, anyway, assuming your paranoid prediction comes true?"

"Why do you think I want to talk to Malock?" said Raya. "I'm going to find out what he saw and heard during his voyage south. He may be able to give me some information so I can construct a better plan I can use to defend my people, the Shikans, better."

"Good luck with that," said Nimiko. "Once my brothers and sisters find out what you are doing, however, they will crush you like an ant."

"Not if everything works out the way I planned it," said Raya. She put a hand over her chest and said, "Yet even if they do, I would gladly give my life to protect my people from you gods."

Nimiko tugged at his chains again. "Brave words from a paranoid woman."

"It's not paranoia," Raya said, brushing her hair out of her eyes. "It's prudence. When a giant is stomping around, you don't just stand there and hope he doesn't step on you."

"You are playing a dangerous game, Princess Raya," Nimiko warned. "A *dangerous* game."

"I know that," said Raya. "I know that very well."

"By the way, you haven't even explained what will happen if your fellow mortals find out what you're doing," said Nimiko. "Does your father even know I am down here, chained up like a lowly prisoner? I can't imagine he would approve of this."

"Father doesn't know and he wouldn't understand," said Raya. "So many other people still hold the belief that you gods would *never* turn against us. They are naïve, but even I can't openly argue against them, lest I destroy my reputation and possibly even lose my status as royalty."

"You have a very low opinion of your fellow mortals," said Nimiko. "But I suppose I shouldn't be surprised. You mortals who call yourselves 'royalty' tend to behave that way."

"Coming from a god, that's laughable," said Raya. "But in the end, it doesn't matter what everyone else thinks. Soon, I will devise the perfect plan to defend us Shikans from the wrath of the gods.

And there is nothing you can do to stop me."

Nimiko scowled. "Many mortals throughout history have tried to outwit the gods. And each one of them has failed. I would beware of considering yourself different."

Raya shrugged and turned around. "Those other mortals never learned how to capture a god, now did they?"

"Where did you even get this knowledge from?" said Nimiko. "I know of no other mortal who has ever even known this was possible."

"A long-forgotten book here, some rumors there, and a little bit of magic," said Raya. "Primarily, though, I learned about it from a rather obscure group who call themselves the Brotherhood of Heathens. Their leader happens to know a great deal about the obscure field of mortal self-defense against the gods."

"The Brotherhood of Heathens?" said Nimiko. "Who are they?"

"A group who will play a very important role in the fate of Martir very soon," said Raya. "At least, that's what their leader claims. Personally I'm just glad that their information turned out to be correct."

"If they are going to be so important, how come I've never heard of them before?" said Nimiko. "Who is their leader?"

Raya shook her head. "You sure do ask a lot of pointless questions. I'm getting tired. I need to go to bed and get ready to leave for Carnag tomorrow. No one has told me we're leaving, but I wouldn't put it past my father to be arranging transportation to the island even as we speak."

Nimiko was quiet, but his thoughts were clearly reflected on his face, so she said, "And don't even think about escaping while I'm away. The Void metal by itself should be enough to keep you down, but even so, I will have set up certain precautions to prevent you from escaping."

"Such as ...?"

Raya glanced over her shoulder at him just as she was leaving the room. "Do you honestly think I'll tell you? I can tell why you're not the God of Intelligence."

With that, Raya closed the door shut, locked it, and began making her way up the stairs, feeling satisfied with herself. She was honestly looking forward to meeting Malock. More than anything else, she wanted to know what he knew. That way, she could better protect her people from the unreliable gods.

Chapter Ten

THE DARK NIGHT ON Destan seemed different to Jenur than it normally did. Each step she took through the low growth seemed exceptionally loud to her ears, not helped in the least by Rint, who due to his inexperience sneaking around made a lot more noise than he should have. Only Quro walked with total silence, a trick Jenur had never learned during her time as a Dark Tiger. Sure, she could move quieter than most people, but when she compared herself to her father, it was like she was stomping her feet, rather than softly moving her feet across the ground. Part of her wished she could be that silent, but she supposed it would always be outside her skill set no matter how hard she practiced.

Occasionally, the trio stopped and listened for anyone following them. Quro would then disappear into the darkness for a few minutes and return, always confirming that they were alone. Prior to escaping Rimo, Rint had expressed worry that Ramufa might come after them, but Quro had shot down the idea because Ramufa had been hired for the sole purpose of capturing the assassin who killed Deber. Ramufa didn't seem like the kind of guy who would stick around after being paid, so Quro assumed they would be safe as long as they didn't draw any unnecessary attention to themselves. The only reason he would circle back was to make sure that no one was following them, even though they had done their best to cover their tracks.

Nonetheless, Jenur thought about how they had escaped the Temple, just to be sure she hadn't missed anything. Just a few hours earlier, the party of three had sneaked out of the Temple's dungeons, making their way through a back exit that Rint remembered. It had been a bit difficult at first, largely due to the patrolling Guards, but they managed to do it without being seen. Having to drag Rint around made it far more difficult than it should have been, but with some smart timing on their part, they succeeded.

The trio had been traveling for hours since leaving Rimo, taking only the occasional break so Rint could rest. Quro claimed to have landed his boat somewhere east of Rimo, hidden from view in a very obscure part on the beach. Ordinarily, it would have only taken them an hour, possibly less, to make it to the hiding place, but due to Rint's age and their need to remain unseen and unheard from everyone, their pace had slowed considerably. That was why they had failed to reach the boat before dark.

To make it far less likely they would be spotted, Quro led Jenur and Rint through the Destanian wilderness. They stayed off every path or road, even the smallest, most obscure ones, because they couldn't be sure that they wouldn't run into anyone. This also slowed their pace as they made their own pathway through the brush and trees and hills that were entirely untouched by human hands. Jenur was surprised that they made as much progress as they had when she considered all of the various obstacles standing in their way.

Rint, thankfully, didn't complain or whine about having to leave his home. He did glance over his shoulder very frequently, however, and more than once almost tripped over a fallen tree branch or some tall grass because of his lack of awareness of his surroundings. It was incredibly frustrating, not helped in the least because his absentminded behavior reminded Jenur so much of Kinker, which in turn made her feel even more awful than she already did.

As for where they would go when they departed Destan, Jenur had been thinking hard about that. On one hand, she knew she couldn't go with Quro back to Ruwa, not if she wanted to live a long, fulfilling life into ripe old age. On the other hand, she didn't know where else she could go. She had no friends or family anywhere in the Northern Isles, aside from Quro, and she certainly didn't have any job skills that she could use to get a good job somewhere. For that matter, she didn't know where Rint wanted to go, either.

Guess I'll cross that bridge when I get there, Jenur thought as she leaped quietly over a fallen tree. *Maybe I'll go to Carnag and see what old Malock's up to.*

As they drew closer to the shore, the sound of the waves crashing against the sand filled Jenur's ears. Just a few minutes after that, the trio emerged onto a small beach that was virtually empty, aside from a few seashells poking out of the sand here and there. Rint and Jenur stood on the shore, keeping a look out on both ends, as Quro tore apart the leaves and grass he had put over his boat.

"There we go," said Quro as he removed the last of the boat's covering. "This should be big enough to take all three of us off Destan."

Jenur looked at the boat. It was a basic speedster, with a small motor on the back. It was clearly a one-person boat; in fact, when Jenur looked at her, Quro, and Rint, she doubted the boat would be able to take them very far without completely sinking under their combined weight.

Rint apparently agreed, because when he saw the boat his face became even longer than it already was. "No way something that small will carry all three of us to Carnag."

"It will have to do," said Quro. "Unless you happen to have another motorboat with enough room for all of us, that is."

"My boat could probably carry all three of us," said Rint. "Unfortunately, I doubt we'll be able to get it because the Priestly Guard probably have my house under surveillance. Especially now that they know we escaped."

"I'm surprised they haven't caught up with us already," said Jenur. "You'd think they'd have tracked us down by now."

Rint looked back into the trees obscuring their view of the rest of the area. "That's not terribly surprising. This is a pretty obscure part of the island, after all, and we did a pretty good job covering our tracks. They probably think we're somewhere in Rimo or the surrounding countryside."

"And by the time it occurs to them to search the beach, we'll all be long gone," said Quro. "Now help me get the boat into the water.

We'll figure out how to fit everyone in afterward."

Rint and Jenur moved to help Quro drag the boat out of the sand and into the water. When they were about halfway down, however, a small splash in the water caused Quro to stop and gesture for them to do the same. He then pointed out into the ocean and Jenur and Rint followed his finger, though Jenur saw nothing but the crystalline surface of the sea stretching out into the darkness, illuminated only by the light of the moon.

"What?" said Rint. "Did you see something?"

"We're being watched," said Quro, his voice almost a whisper. "Someone or something is in the water."

"Who?" said Rint, his voice also lower now.

"Not sure," said Quro. "But we need to be careful. Don't make any sudden movements or sounds."

Quro began walking toward the water, his dragon shark scales dropped out of his sleeves into his hands, while Jenur and Rint watched anxiously from their position near the boat. The surface of the ocean seemed perfectly still tonight, aside from the occasional wind blowing across it. Jenur didn't see anything out of the ordinary, but she remembered hearing the splash sound and so she knew that there definitely was something out there, though she assumed that the splash had perhaps been a fish or something. But if Quro said they were being watched, then something sinister was definitely afoot.

When Quro was ankle-deep in the water, he stopped and looked around some more. Without warning, a large tentacle shot out of the water at him, moving too fast for Jenur's eyes to follow. Quro didn't even hesitate. He slashed at the tentacle with his scales, causing the tentacle to retract into the water. Quro immediately turned and began running back to the shore, saying as he did so, "Go! Get away from the water! Whatever it is, it's—"

Another tentacle, this one shiny as silver, shot out of the water toward Quro. It wrapped around his ankle and pulled, causing him to fall flat on his face. Rint gasped, while Jenur immediately ran forward and grabbed Quro's outstretched hand even as the tentacle started to drag him into the water. She dug her heels into the sand to keep herself from being pulled in, but it was no use because the tentacle kept pulling Quro in and, by extension, her, too. Quro slashed at the tentacle, cutting a deep gash through its slimy skin and causing it to let go again.

When the tentacle let go of Quro, Jenur went stumbling backwards, falling on her behind and getting water and sand all over her pants. She was immediately hauled to her feet by Quro, who had somehow gotten up to his feet quickly, and he dragged her further up the beach even as Rint—who had by now retreated to the treeline—shouted, "Watch out!"

Jenur looked over her shoulder in time to see another large tentacle coming toward her. She ripped Quro's dragon shark scale out of his hand and slashed at the tentacle when it got within her reach, knocking it off course and sending it back into the water. By now, Quro and Jenur were out of the water and were climbing up the beach, their boots weighed down by the water and sand that had collected in them. Nonetheless, they kept running until they reached the treeline, at which point they stopped and fell on their bottoms, panting, their clothes dripping and the sand already drying over their skin.

Rint stood above them, looking out into the Crystal Sea with shock. "What was that? Where did that thing come from?"

"Not sure," said Quro, panting as he put his dragon shark scales into his pocket. "Do giant squids live in the waters around here or something?"

"I've never seen anything like it in my life," Rint said. "You're lucky Jenur is smart on her feet. Otherwise, you would have been dragged into the sea and we'd be stuck here."

Jenur, panting as she dusted the sand off her pants, shrugged. "You kind of have to be if you're going to be a Dark Tiger."

Quro stood up and glanced over his shoulder. The waves crashed against the shore, but there was no sign of the tentacles. "Perhaps we should take my boat to some other part of the island. If that thing is willing to attack us now, it would surely not hesitate to attack us while we're on the sea itself."

Rint shook his head. "No way am I going out on the ocean if that thing is out there. I'd rather take my chances with the Priestly Guard than risk taking on that thing."

"Well, I have to return to Ruwa, whether you want to leave or not," said Quro. "So we can't just stand here and let that creature keep us from leaving."

"Then what do you suggest we do to get past it?" said Rint.

"I am not sure," Quro admitted. "But I am sure that we can do something about it."

"Why don't you just jump into the water and kill it yourself?" Rint said. "You're an aquarian. You freaks love the water. You probably fight better underwater than you do on land, I bet."

Quro shook his head. "My clothes would weigh me down. Besides, it's too dark and I have no idea what we're up against. Going into the water after it would be foolishness, if not outright suicide."

Rint threw up his arms and sat down on the sand. "Great. Just great. We managed to sneak out of the Temple and Rimo without anyone noticing, made it halfway across the island without anyone seeing us, and then—just when we were about to escape—a giant squid comes out of nowhere and stops us. I would be cursing Kano's very name right now if I wasn't as devoted to her as I was."

"Your devotion to your goddess is quite admirable," came a voice from the treetops above them, "though I've wondered how it is possible, considering that it is your goddess's Priests who tried to kill you and your two assassin friends."

Jenur and Rint looked up, but Quro reacted a little differently. He drew his dragon shark scales out of his pocket again and hurled them into the treetops above them. A small "Eek!" was the only sound they heard before the branches above them shivered and someone fell out of the treetops. The small man landed on his feet and held up his hands as if to pacify them.

Jenur scowled. "Ramufa. What are you doing here?"

"He was obviously sent by the Priests to get us," said Rint.

"Quro, Jenur, kill him now."

"With pleasure," said Quro as he held up his other dragon shark scale and took a step forward.

Ramufa clasped his hands together like he was holding onto a rope and didn't want to let go. "Hear me out, assassins. I'm not here to capture you; in fact, the Priests don't even know I'm here. They have already paid me to do what I was supposed to do; namely, capture Deber's assassins, which are you."

"Then what are you doing here?" said Jenur. "Trying to scare us?"

"I wanted to see where you were going," said Ramufa. "I would never think of telling any of the Guards or Priests of your whereabouts. I would only do that if I was being paid and I am not being paid one cent by anyone right now."

"Of course you aren't," said Quro. "How can we trust you on that?"

Ramufa looked around the area, scratching his chin as he did so. "Well, I suppose the entirety of the Priestly Guard would have already jumped you three if I was actually trying to capture you again. Right now, they have no idea where any of you are and I have no intention of telling any of them, seeing as I have nothing to gain from it."

"He has a point," Rint said. "The Priestly Guard aren't exactly known for simply allowing wanted criminals to walk about freely."

"Well, we still don't want you anywhere around here," said Jenur, poking Ramufa in the chest with her finger. "After all the crap you put us through, you must have a very tiny brain to think we'd be happy to see you."

"I never said I'd thought you'd be happy to see me," said Ramufa. "As I said, it was mostly to satisfy my own curiosity. But I also have an offer to make to you."

"An offer?" said Quro. "What offer?"

Ramufa stood up to his not-very-tall full height and bowed. "My services, obviously. The same services that put you three behind bars and have caused you to react to me the way a child reacts to a bee sting."

"There's nothing you can do for us," said Rint, before either Jenur or Quro could speak. "Unlike a certain Priestess I once knew, we have no enemies we'd like to see imprisoned."

"You think all I do is mercenary work?" said Ramufa. "No wonder. You three obviously have never seen me before. Very well. Perhaps a demonstration of my true abilities is in order."

Ramufa turned and, in the blink of an eye, was gone.

"Where did he go?" said Rint, looking around wildly. "How did he—"

"The Thief's Way," said Quro. "He mentioned being an initiate of that discipline, remember?"

Jenur frowned. "Didn't he also say that he was personally trained by Hollech?"

"He was probably lying," said Quro, shaking his head. "I've never heard of any gods personally training any humans in any magical discipline before. I imagine it's something he tells his clients to make his services seem more worth it."

"Yeah, probably," said Jenur, nodding. "But that still doesn't explain where he went."

"I'm right here," said Ramufa's voice above them, once again causing the trio to look up into the branches above.

Due to the thick darkness, it was impossible to see Ramufa, at least until a beam of moonlight suddenly shone through the branches, revealing the monkey man, whose robes were dripping wet. He carried what appeared to be a sagging, silver pipe over his shoulder. At least, that's what Jenur assumed it was until Rint said, "By the gods, he's got one of that monster's tentacles."

Ramufa smiled and dropped the tentacle to the ground, forcing Jenur, Quro, and Rint to scatter to avoid being hit by it. It fell to the ground with a quiet *crunch* and Jenur looked at it. It had to be at least as thick as a tree limb and appeared to have been severed cleanly through using surgical tools, but as far as Jenur could tell, Ramufa didn't have any surgical tools on him.

The monkey man dropped to the ground as Rint said, in utter disbelief, "How did you do that?"

"Very easily," Ramufa said, smoothing the strands of hair over his head. "That's how."

"No, you don't understand," said Rint. "I mean, how did you get that monster's tentacle so easily?"

"Master Hollech taught me a lot of tricks," said Ramufa. "Such as how to easily remove the tentacle from a yuroyo squid."

"A what?" said Jenur.

"Yuroyo squid," Ramufa repeated, looking at Jenur as if she were a bit dense. "A very rare kind of giant squid. They're usually found in the southern seas, but this one was obviously ordered to come north."

"Hold on," said Rint, holding up a hand. "Ordered? You make it sound like the squid has a master."

"Of course it does," said Ramufa, giving Rint a look that said he was clearly concerned for the elderly man's sanity. "It was naturally the Mistress of the Sea Creatures who ordered it to come this north, probably to get the young lady."

"You mean Kano?" said Rint. "But why would Kano—"

"Kano?" said Ramufa with a chuckle. "Don't be silly. Kano has no real control over the creatures of the sea. True, she does have quite a bit of power over the water itself, but when it comes to the control of the sea creatures themselves, she has about as much power over them as I do over that tree I was just standing on."

"I don't get it," said Rint. "Who is the Mistress of the Sea Creatures, then?"

"The Kraken Goddess, naturally," said Ramufa. "The Goddess of Kraken, Fish, and the Storm."

"I have never heard of such a goddess before," Rint said, folding his arms and glaring at Ramufa. "How do I know you aren't lying?"

"No surprise there," said Ramufa. "The Kraken Goddess is a southern goddess. Most mortals don't know anything about the southern gods."

"That still doesn't explain why the Kraken Goddess is after us," said Quro. "Assuming, of course, this 'Kraken Goddess' even exists."

Ramufa shrugged. "Who can understand the minds of the gods? Even I have a hard time understanding Master Hollech and I have known him my whole life. If I were you, I'd stay off the seas for now."

"You know we can't do that," said Jenur. "The Priestly Guard will find us eventually. We have to leave tonight."

Ramufa stroked his chin. "Well, if you really need to leave right away, I can offer you my services at a special discount. For a mere three hundred coins—half down, half to be paid when I finish the job —I can get all three of you and your boat off Destan without having to go through the yuroyo squid."

"Why don't you just kill the monster?" said Rint. "You already proved you could remove one of its limbs."

"Quite true, but that was very difficult," said Ramufa as he squeezed the water out of his robes. "And I got wet. Very wet. Besides, if I was going to do that, I'd have to charge at least three thousand coins and since all three of you combined are probably worth only about half of that, it would be unfair of me to charge that much."

"Hey," Jenur said. "Are you insinuating that we're all worthless?"

"Not worthless," said Ramufa, shaking his head. "Just inexpensive. But teleporting you three and your boat should prove no problem. Just tell me what direction you want to go in and I can take you there."

"Now I know you are lying," said Quro. "I'm not knowledgeable about the Thief's Way, but I do know that initiates of that path cannot use it to teleport anyone except for themselves and what objects they carry with them."

"Most Thief's Way's initiates cannot do that," said Ramufa,

nodding. "But Master Hollech taught me a lot of things that most normal initiates don't know. Just trust me."

"We do need to leave," said Rint. "But I'm not so sure we trust you, even if you can do what you claim."

"You don't need to trust me," said Ramufa. He held out his wide hands and said, "Just pay me."

Quro pulled his pockets inside out. "We don't have three hundred coins on us."

"No worries," said Ramufa. "You can just pay me in monthly installments of thirty-three coins per person over the next year. I've set up similar payment methods with clients before, so don't worry, I know exactly what I'm doing."

"This is ridiculous," said Jenur. "You're trying to get our money for something we could do ourselves very easily; namely, get off this island."

"But you can't get off very easily," said Ramufa, gesturing at the squid tentacle at his feet. "That's the point. The yuroyo squid will eat you three alive or drag you to the bottom of the sea if you try. I'm not at all concerned for your safety, but I feel that I must point out that I am offering you a valuable service, especially for the low price I am offering you."

"He has a point," Rint said. "I'd rather he didn't, but he does."

"All right," said Quro. "Ramufa, we'll pay you later. For now, just get us out of here."

"What?" said Jenur. "But—"

"Excellent," said Ramufa. "Everyone hop in the boat. It's going to be a bumpy ride."

Rint and Quro were already climbing in. Seeing that arguing would get her nowhere, Jenur sighed and climbed in with them. She sat in the back of the boat, but even then had to pull her legs up to her chest to make room for Quro and Rint. There wasn't much room for any of them to stretch, leading to a very cramped feeling all around.

"Everyone in?" said Ramufa. "Excellent. Now hold on tight."

Ramufa grabbed the boat, smiled one last monkey grin, and then everything went completely black. The wind rushed through Jenur's hair, the entire world felt like it was spinning in circles, and Jenur's breath was stolen from her. She felt like she was going to throw up even though she knew that she couldn't, at least not here and, oh, she just wanted it all to end.

And then, it did. A splash of cold water up the back of her shirt caused her to gasp. Shivering, Jenur looked around and realized that they were now in the middle of the ocean. The moonlight revealed no sign of land for miles in every direction. That included the yuroyo squid; at least, if there were any sea creatures in the area, they were keeping well beneath the surface.

Before her, Rint was gripping his stomach, his face green, while Quro simply sat looking slightly confused. Ramufa stood on the bow of the small boat, somehow balancing on one foot. With his back to the moonlight, his face was shrouded in darkness, but Jenur knew he must be smiling.

"How was the ride?" said Ramufa. "You all look very sick."

"Guh," was all Rint could say.

"Guh is good," said Ramufa. He pulled out a notepad from his pocket and said, "Now, let's see: Quro, Jenur Takren, and Rint Dolan."

"What are you writing our names down for?" said Quro, shaking his head as if to regain his composure.

"Quite simple," said Ramufa. "I need to know your names in order to track you down for the money you owe me. You promised to pay me later, didn't you?"

"Oh," said Quro. "That's right."

"But don't worry," said Ramufa as he stuffed the book back into his jacket pocket. "I'm not mercenary, unlike some freelancers I know. I will give all three of you one month to come up with the one hundred coins each of you owe me for my service."

"I thought we were doing monthly payments of thirty-three each?" said Jenur.

"I changed it," said Ramufa. "This was a tricky thing for me to do, very unusual and a bit more difficult than I originally estimated, so I want to be compensated as soon as possible. Now I must go. Remember: One month. One hundred coins each. Bye!"

With that, Ramufa once again turned around and disappeared into thin air. His disappearance caused the boat to rock slightly, making Rint moan in sickness, while Quro stood up, putting one hand on the back of his head, and walked over to the boat's steering wheel. Jenur just sat there as Quro turned on the engine and soon the boat was racing off north to Carnag, though Jenur wasn't sure that was such a good thing now that she owed a crazy monkey man one hundred coins.

Chapter Eleven

MALOCK AWOKE MUCH EARLIER than he normally did. The large round clock hanging on the left wall said it was early in the morning, at least three hours earlier than when Malock's servants usually came by to wake him. He wondered for a moment why he had awoken so early when he remembered that this was the schedule he had taken up on the *Iron Wind*. He tried to go back to sleep, but it was impossible, thanks in no small part to the burning sensation rippling through his face like a burst of hot wind.

Sitting up, Malock tossed the covers off his legs and groggily walked over to the window next to his bed. He pushed aside the crimson curtains and stared out into the city of Port Blasan. The first rays of the sun were just beginning to stream over the tops of the buildings of the capital of Carnag, though they were slightly distorted by the Protection, a massive magical barrier that separated Carnag Hall from the rest of the city. It had been designed by a group of teichomancers, known as the Protectors, and was designed to allow members of the Carnagian Royal Family or people who worked for them to come and go as they pleased, though it was impossible for anyone else to enter without permission from a member of the Carnagian Royal Family.

Because it had been so long since Malock had last been in Port Blasan, he took this time to look over his hometown. In the east, the boot factories continued to belch smoke, barely visible from here but nonetheless obvious, while the Carnagian Stadium in the west rose over almost every other building. Dozens and dozens of buildings—most not nearly as large as Carnag Hall—spread out into in every direction, most beautiful and magnificent, as ugly buildings were not allowed near Carnag Hall. The top of the Temple of Grinf peaked out above a few buildings in the north.

As it was early morning, Malock saw very few people out in the streets. At the gates below, he saw the night guard changing shifts with the morning guard. He also spotted a homeless man—at least, he assumed the man was homeless, because he could not think of any other reason that a person would wear such ugly, ratty clothing—sleeping in the alleyway between two nearby buildings. Besides that, the city was still asleep.

The burn in his face itched terribly, causing him to scratch at it. He continued to look out over the city, but now he was comparing it to the Throne of the Gods, the massive city on World's End where Vashnas and Kinker had died. He remembered how he had always believed Port Blasan to be the most magnificent city in the entirety of the Northern Isles, how none of the other cities anywhere could even come close to its beauty.

But when he compared it to the Throne of the Gods, he found it lacking. The brick and mortar buildings here, while considered big by most inhabitants of the Northern Isles, might as well have been tiny mud huts with thatched roofs in comparison to the skyscrapers that dominated World's End. The Temple of Grinf was little more than a bunch of stones stacked on top of each other in comparison to the Temple of the Gods that had its home in the center of the Throne. Furthermore, he found the city's stone streets drab in comparison to the soft, yet firm white substance that had made up the pavement of the Throne's streets. Even the people—his own people—looked less-than-ideal when compared to the katabans inhabitants of the city on the edge of the world.

Malock shut the curtains and turned away, scowling. What was he doing, comparing his city to a city built by the gods themselves? He was still the Prince of Carnag, despite all that had happened, and had no right to be denigrating his own people and home. It was not right nor fair. Still, Malock had a difficult time not comparing the two and feeling quite disappointed at the disparity that existed between the two cities.

I know what I need to do, Malock thought. *I need to fall in love with my home again. And I can't do that while brooding in my room. I will need to go out and be among the people, but I can't let any of them recognize me.*

Malock walked over to his huge walk-in closet, which was filled with dozens of shirts and pants and shoes, many of which Malock had forgotten about, and he began looking for the dirtiest, rattiest clothes he could find. After a few minutes, he found an old white shirt with

142

wine stains on it that his servants had apparently forgotten to clean (which he found strange, as the servants of the Carnagian Royal Family were usually meticulous about this sort of thing) and a pair of simple brown pants with worn out knees (how *those* got there, he didn't know, as he spent little time on his knees). He pulled out his old boots from his voyage to World's End and found a hood that would hide his face quite well.

After getting dressed, Malock took a moment to look at himself in the mirror. With his ratty clothing, he thought he looked just like any one of the hundreds of homeless beggars that lived on the streets of Port Blasan. No one would ever look at him and realize who he really was. He felt proud of his disguise and then left his room, but quietly, opening the door without making a sound.

Getting out of Carnag Hall was easy. The walls of Carnag Hall were actually hollow, despite how thick they appeared on the outside. This was to give the servants a way to travel through Carnag Hall without being seen, which was useful whenever Malock or his parents had guests over and didn't want the servants underfoot. More than once over the years, Malock had used the servant passageways to sneak out of Carnag Hall whenever he wanted to, usually when he was going to go see some girls or do something else he knew his parents would never approve of. It had been one of his former servants who had taught Malock how to navigate the passageways and, though it had been a while since Malock had last used them, his memory of their layout was still accurate and he soon found himself in the streets of Port Blasan, with Carnag Hall behind him.

Malock had no particular destination in mind at first. He walked through the dirty alleyways of the city, trying to see the beauty in the place that he had always seen before. That, and he was also trying to avoid thinking about his upcoming marriage to Princess Raya. He knew that sooner or later he would have to meet her, maybe even today, and so decided that he would enjoy his freedom before the day's insanity began. Of course, he made a mental note to return as soon as he could, before any of the servants came to wake him up, because he had told no one he was leaving and if any of the people in Carnag Hall saw his empty bed ... well, he couldn't allow himself to be gone for very long.

So Malock decided that his first stop would be to the Fountain of Justice. It was not far from his current position, so he could get back home quickly if he had to. Additionally, unless his memory was playing tricks on him, he recalled the Fountain being a very beautiful piece of architecture. Maybe it wasn't as beautiful as the Throne of the Gods, but surely it would help Malock fall in love with his home again.

By navigating the backstreets of Port Blasan, Malock arrived at the Fountain of Justice in less than ten minutes. The Fountain of Justice was located in a wide open square about five blocks away from Carnag Hall. It was home to the famed Fountain itself, which was a statue of Grinf spouting water from his mouth. The Fountain of Justice had been built by members of the famous Divine Carvers, a group of lithomancers known throughout the Northern Isles for their magnificent stone statues of the gods. The Fountain—made of pure white cast stone, though not nearly as white as the pavement of the Throne of the Gods—still stood where it always did, right in the center of the square. Due to the early morning, there were few people out, mostly shopkeepers opening the doors of their stores or merchants setting up their stands to sell their wares. The Fountain of Justice was also a popular tourist attraction; hence the various merchants and shopkeepers setting up shop for the day.

But as Malock entered the open square, he spotted an unusual sight: A dozen or so aquarians, all wearing the same green bandanna around their heads, sitting outside a restaurant that Malock recognized as Justice Served, a restaurant that Malock had originally frequented during his teenage years due to its excellent service and delicious cooked horian falcon wings. It was always an early opener, which explained why the aquarians were sitting at the tables outside already eating breakfast, but that didn't explain who the aquarians were.

Aquarians made up a minority in Carnag, largely working in the docks or on the ships. It was not unusual to see a few aquarians among the general crowd of people who made their way through the Fountain of Justice, but seeing so many together in one place so early in the morning set off alarm bells in Malock's head. Unlike some humans, he didn't automatically equate the presence of so many aquarians with trouble-making; however, he was curious, especially about the green bandannas they all wore. He wondered if they were tourists.

The aquarians were all laughing and talking, not very loudly, but due to the quietness of the streets, they sounded much louder than they normally would. That was when Malock noticed a bunch of boxes, signs, and pots and pans piled on top of each other near the Fountain itself. None of the aquarians seemed to be paying attention to the signs and boxes, so Malock made his way over to them to inspect them.

The signs in particular interested him. Most of them were too big for him to move without making a lot of noise, but he did find one sign that looked like it might fit in his hand. He picked it up and turned it over. Written in big red letters was this simple phrase:

THE DAY OF THE GODS IS COMING. PREPARE.

"Interested in our signs, brother?" said a gurgling voice behind him, causing Malock to drop the sign and whirl around to see who it was.

The owner of the voice was one of the aquarians eating at Justice Served, his hands on his hips. He had a hammerhead shark-like head, his green bandanna just barely fitting over it. With his thick arms and rough skin, he looked like he was used to outdoor work. While he didn't look frightening—in fact, he seemed quite friendly, smiling as he looked at Malock—something about the way he stood made Malock apprehensive.

"Yes, I am," said Malock, deepening his voice to avoid being recognized. He pointed at the sign and said, "Just what is the 'Day of the Gods,' if I may ask?"

The aquarian chuckled. "I'm not sure I should tell you that right now. In just a few minutes, however, you and everyone in Port Blasan will know, when all of the usual tourists and commuters make their way through here. It's why we picked this spot to make our debut."

Malock didn't look the aquarian directly in the eyes, as he didn't want the aquarian to recognize him. "Your debut? Are you guys a new group or something?"

"We've only existed a few months," said the aquarian. "In that time, we've grown quite a bit, but in order for our movement to be truly successful, I have felt called to spread our message to the entirety of the Northern Isles."

"And your message is—?"

"You will hear it soon," said the aquarian. "Just stick around for a few more minutes and you will hear it all."

Malock frowned. "What is your name, if I may ask?"

"Skimif," said the aquarian without the slightest hesitation. "What is your name?"

Malock couldn't think of a good fake name, so he changed the subject. "So, Skimif, where are you from?"

"I hail from a tiny little aquarian town that is hundreds of miles southeast of this island," said Skimif. "It's called Tunya. Ever heard of it?"

Malock shook his head.

"Thought so," said Skimif. "Very few have. It's largely a farming community, but even so, most of the people who live there are quite poor, myself included." He hesitated, then asked, "Tell me, hood, is fifty coins a night an unreasonable rate for inns on Carnag?"

Malock shrugged. "I don't know. I've never stayed in any of the inns around here, seeing as I am homeless."

Skimif sighed. "I see. Well, that's how much the inn that I and my brothers and sisters are staying at is charging us. The innkeeper is human, so I suspect he may be overcharging us due to his prejudice against aquarians, but it doesn't matter. Not when this gives us the opportunity to preach our message to the world."

Malock looked around Skimif at the other aquarians sitting outside Justice Served. "Those are all your siblings? You have a big family."

Skimif laughed. "They are not my literal brothers and sisters. It's just that we mortals are all related, which gives us a kinship that we cannot easily dismiss. Because you are a mortal, I consider you a brother, even though we just met."

"Right," said Malock. "Sure. Are they all from Tunya, too?"

"Most of them are," said Skimif. "But they are not all of my followers. I have several dozen more making their way to the other islands in the Northern Isles. Most of them are aquarians, but I have a few trusted humans also dedicated to spreading the message. If we are going to survive the Day of the Gods, I feel we need both humans and aquarians on our side, which is why I am personally leading this mission."

"You make the Day of the Gods sound like a bad thing," said Malock.

Skimif smiled, revealing his sharp shark teeth. "Bad for the gods, maybe, but not for us."

"Bad for the gods? What do you—"

"Why do you wear a hood?" said Skimif, cutting Malock off. "It makes you look like a thief. Are you a thief?"

"O-Of course not," said Malock, stumbling over his words as he did so. "I just suffered a terrible burn as a child. It is common for burn victims to wear hoods to hide their ugliness from everyone else here on Carnag."

"I am sorry to hear that," said Skimif. "At least you are not wearing it because some god told you so. Otherwise, I wouldn't have felt sorry for you. I would have thought you were an idiot."

"You don't seem to have a very high opinion of the gods," said Malock.

Skimif shrugged. "Why should I? Their days are numbered. A new day will rise, one much better than any before, and the gods will not be there to witness it."

Malock raised an eyebrow. "Those are some pretty big words. What do you mean?"

"I've said too much already," said Skimif, putting one hand over his mouth. "Know this: If you at all care about the future, I suggest you stick around and listen to our message. It will transform not only your own life, but that of every mortal society on Martir. I can guarantee it."

"Who are you guys?" said Malock. "What's with the green bandannas?"

Skimif looked around, then leaned in closer and said, "I will tell you this much: We call ourselves the Brotherhood of Heathens."

Malock felt a chill go up his spine at the name. "Heathens? Why would you—"

"That is all I am telling you," said Skimif, pulling back and straightening up. "As I said, if you will just stick around for a little while longer, you will find out all you want to know, and far more."

With that, Skimif turned and walked back to join his fellow Heathens. Uncertain about what was to come, Malock made his way out of the square over to the restaurant next to Justice Served, which was not yet open. He took a seat at one of its outdoor tables as the first of the Fountain's tourists entered the area.

In just a few minutes, the entire square was full of people. A Nikon couple—recognizable thanks to their long red hair—was bargaining with a Carnagian merchant over a pair of obviously very cheap boots. An aquarian street musician had set up on the corner of a street, with an empty bucket at his feet and a guitar in his hands. A couple of factory workers walked past Malock, loudly complaining about their idiotic boss and his neurotic tendencies. A couple of children in clothes that were even dirtier than Malock's played near the Fountain, but they immediately ran away when the Brotherhood of Heathens gathered near it.

Through the throngs of people, Malock watched as the Heathens set up a solid wooden box, which Skimif immediately stood on, putting him about a head above everyone else in the area. No one took notice of Skimif, however, which didn't seem to bother the aquarian leader much because he was now rapidly shuffling through a stack of note cards in his hands. He reminded Malock of how the Prince felt whenever he had to make a speech.

The other Heathens, meanwhile, picked up the various signs they had gathered. Yet they did not lift up the signs, not just yet. One of the Heathens picked up the *THE DAY OF THE GODS IS COMING. PREPARE* sign that Malock had seen earlier and spun it in her hand nervously. She was the only one who appeared nervous; the others all wore looks of determination on their faces, as if they were preparing for war.

By now, a few other people had stopped to look at them, but it wasn't until Skimif and his Heathens started banging a bunch of pots and pans together that most people stopped to look at them. Malock felt secondhand embarrassment for Skimif because most of the people were looking at him like he was being childishly annoying. One person even shouted, "What the hell do you think you're doing, fish-face?"

That seemed to be exactly the reaction that Skimif was waiting for because he and his Heathens immediately stopped banging their pots and pans together. Skimif closed his eyes and took a deep breath for a moment before his eyes snapped open again, showing a much more confident self than Malock had ever seen before. In fact, Skimif almost looked like a different person entirely now, as if his spirit had been replaced with someone else's.

"I was trying to get your attention, sir," said Skimif, raising his voice to be heard over the entire area. "In fact, I was trying to get the attention of every man, woman, and child in this area. Yes, I wish for everyone to hear the message that I and my siblings have preached to many other people in the past."

Malock looked around. The entire crowd seemed to focus on

Skimif now, as if mesmerized by his words. Either Skimif was a great public speaker or he had such a powerful presence that people simply had to listen to him. Either way, Malock knew that getting such a busy crowd to stand still and listen for longer than a couple of minutes was a feat in itself.

"Oh yeah?" said the man from before with a sneer. "What's your 'message'? Are you trying to sell us some crap from some aquarian town or something?"

"We are not selling anything," said Skimif. "Money and wealth are the last things we desire. Our message is one we will not ask anyone to pay for because it would be criminal for us to charge for it."

"Yeah, right," said the man with a snort. "Last time someone told me that, they asked for a hundred coins after I agreed to take their course that would teach me the 'secret' to successful business."

"This message has nothing to do with business," said Skimif, though he didn't appear to be looking at the man specifically anymore. Instead, he was addressing the whole crowd. "Instead, it is a message that will shape the future of every man, woman, and child in the Northern Isles, humans, aquarians, and even half-breeds alike. Indeed, I can guarantee to all of you today that this is a day in history that people will be talking about for decades, perhaps even centuries, afterward."

The Nikon couple Malock noticed earlier was now chattering excitedly to one another in the Nikon language. Other people in the crowd were murmuring various noises of disgust or interest, but no one seemed to want to contradict Skimif. Perhaps it was because everyone wanted to find out what Skimif's message was. Malock leaned forward on his chair, remembering what Skimif had said to him earlier: "*A new day will rise, one much better than any before, and the gods will not be there to witness it.*"

"Since the beginning of time, since the day the first human stepped foot on the surface of the earth and the first aquarian swam through the deepest trenches of the earliest oceans, mortals have always worshiped the gods," said Skimif. "Though various civilizations, empires, and federations have risen and fallen throughout Martir's long history, worship of the gods has been the one feature that has consistently defined mortal experience. Indeed, one might even be able to say that 'to be mortal is to worship the gods,' as the human philosopher Katrom once wrote, though that is of course a debatable point.

"But not all mortals have always worshiped the gods. Running parallel to the worship to the gods have been mortals who historians and Priests have always referred to as 'heathens,' even though these people existed in many times, places, and cultures and often didn't know about each other. They were Eokina Warana, a former Priestess of Ghatmos who denied that god's sovereignty and was executed for it; Ghuna, the aquarian senator of the former nation of Jirin who dared to question the Old Kanonites' barbaric practices and was assassinated at the beginning of his second term in office for it; and many, many others, human and aquarian alike, who have refused to worship the gods even when everyone around them did."

The murmurs of the crowd became far more agitated now, yet

there was no rioting or yelling. This surprised Malock, as Skimif spoke of the heathens admirably, almost like he considered them heroes. That was quite risky because heathens were despised on Carnag by most people. In fact, it was just last year that a leading Carnagian intellectual had been outed as a heathen and executed by the government. Malock had even seen the execution himself. Whether Skimif knew that or not, the aquarian was quite brave for speaking as he was.

"Because of the intense persecution they have faced, heathens have always been scattered and disorganized, often operating as individuals or in small groups," Skimif continued. "Despite that, heathens have managed to pass down certain knowledge and information about how to protect themselves from the gods to their descendents. My own grandfather was a heathen, but he never knew any other heathens in his lifetime because of the secrecy most live in. And this is not that shocking; when most known heathens are arrested, beaten, tossed into jail, and even murdered for their beliefs, it is understandable that few would ever willingly announce their beliefs to the world at large, even if they are not ashamed of those beliefs.

"But today, we heathens will hide in fear no longer. Today, I am pleased to announce that a new organization bringing all heathens together has arisen: The Brotherhood of Heathens."

A collective gasp erupted from the crowd and there was more murmuring, except this time far more negative than before. Still, most of the people weren't in riot mode yet, although Malock spotted a few people on the edges of the crowd shake their heads and leave.

"But that is not even the meat of our *real* message," said Skimif, "the message that we believe will reverberate throughout the history of Martir, the one that will shake the foundation of every civilization in the Northern Isles, whether human or aquarian. It is a dangerously radical message, one that could very well get I and my followers killed, but it is the truth and if there is one thing I have always believed, it is that it is better to die for the truth than to live for a lie."

Just then, someone in the crowd shouted, "Oh, yeah? What's your so-called 'truth'? I didn't even know you Heathens had any truth."

Skimif actually looked taken aback by the person. He shook his head and continued, "That is a very, uh, good question, sir. I am pleased to see that you are paying attention. So I suppose I should just get straight to the point: The Day of the Gods is coming."

As soon as those words left Skimif's mouth, the rest of the Heathens lifted up their signs, revealing a whole host of slogans and words written in large print. Some of the signs were written in Divina, others in Aqua, and a few in a couple of languages that Malock didn't recognize. On the ones he could read, they read like this:

THE DAY OF THE GODS IS COMING. PREPARE.
A NEW DAY IS DAWNING.
DON'T LOOK BACK AT THE PAST.
THE FUTURE BELONGS TO THE MORTALS.
THE GODS' TIME IS UP.

Another person in the crowd shouted, "What the hell does all of that even mean? What's the Day of the Gods?"

"Another excellent question," said Skimif. "The Day of the Gods is a day coming in the future when all of the gods will die."

That last word—"die"—set off a storm of gasps of fear and shock from the crowd. An elderly lady nearly fainted, but was caught by a young man who appeared to be her grandson. A mother put her hands over the ears of her youngest child. Malock himself leaned forward some more until his upper body was almost entirely over the table he sat at.

"What foolish blasphemy!" A man dressed in the red robes of a Grinfian Priest stepped forward, glaring at Skimif. "Pure nonsense. The gods cannot die. Everyone knows this."

"It is not nonsense," said Skimif. "It is the truth. The gods have done their best to convince us mortals that they are eternal, but in reality, they have an end just like the rest of us. And that end is just around the corner. I and my brothers and sisters in the Brotherhood know this to be true."

"You are wrong," the Priest said. "Where is your proof of this 'truth,' as you call it? You expect us to believe your assertions mindlessly?"

"No, I do not," said Skimif. "The proof I have to offer is this: the Powers that Be told me."

More gasps, but the Priest said, "That is yet another baseless assertion. Besides, we all know that the Powers never contact mortals. They remain forever separate from the world. It is the gods who contact mortals, and even then only rarely."

"You want proof?" said Skimif. "I offer the proof primarily in the truth of the words themselves. Search your soul and you will find that you can sense it. I did not found the Brotherhood for no reason. I am not the only mortal to have felt this truth. Everywhere, this idea is spoken of in secret and in whispers. But if you desire more proof, I can offer it to you. Just be warned that you may not like it."

Skimif held out a hand and a small black energy orb appeared in it. It was unlike anything Malock had ever seen, although when he thought about it, he realized that it resembled a small black ball he had once owned as a child. The orb was not threatening to him in the least, but the rest of the crowd must have been afraid of it because they took a collective step back, as if afraid it would explode in their faces.

Then Skimif closed his scaly fist over the orb. Without warning Malock saw dozens of images fly through his mind. The images passed by so fast that he could barely comprehend even half of them. He saw humans, aquarians, gods; he saw land animals, sea creatures, and the world at large; and many, many other things that he couldn't even understand (including one image that appeared to show a large winged creature crouching on top of a building in some distant land he could not recognize).

Then the images stopped and Malock blinked and shook his head. At the same time, he heard a lot of screaming and shouting, and when he looked up, he saw that the crowd was in chaos. Some lay on the street, looking just as stunned as Malock felt, while others were running around with their hands over their eyes, shouting, "Make it stop!" Others—mostly younger children—were sitting on the street crying. Only a handful of people seemed unaffected by ... whatever had just happened, and most of them were the Heathens, who still stood carrying their signs from earlier.

One of the few people still standing was the Grinfian Priest, whose eyes were now bugged out. He looked between the crazed crowd and Skimif before saying, "What ... what was ..."

Skimif shoved the black orb into the pocket of his vest and said, "That was the vision the Powers showed me. I was told to show it to others if anyone doubted my word."

The Priest was speechless for a moment. His mouth opened and closed before he turned around and shouted, "Enforcers! Enforcers! Arrest these aquarians for causing a public disturbance!"

While the Priest shouted for any nearby Justice Enforcers, the Heathens immediately packed up their signs, boxes, and pots and pans, and ran off toward one of the alleyways, weaving through the disoriented crowd without much effort. Malock immediately stood up and ran after them, though he was briefly held up by the female Nikon tourist, who was babbling in Nikon and pointing at her husband who lay on the streets quite still. Malock apologized to her as best as he could, not sure if she could understand what he was saying, and then dashed off in the direction the Heathens left just as the last Heathen disappeared into the dark alley.

Malock dashed through the narrow alleyway until he ended up at a dead end. He looked down to the left and to the right, trying to spot the Heathens, but he could not see them or even hear them anywhere. He wondered how a dozen full-grown aquarians could disappear so quickly, especially since he didn't see anywhere they could have disappeared to. It seemed like they had vanished into thin air, but Malock was determined to find them anyway (although he was acutely aware that he had little time in which to do that, as his servants back in Carnag Hall were most likely already awakening and getting ready to wake him).

Biting his lower lip, Malock noticed a green bandanna on the street to his right. He picked it up and looked to the right, wondering if perhaps the Heathens had ran that way. With this piece of evidence, Malock ran down the street in that particular direction, jumping over a turned over trashcan as he hoped to catch up with the Heathens. He had to hold down his hood, however, to keep it from flying off.

The street turned sharply to the left, but before he could turn, someone nearby whispered, "Hey!"

Malock skid to a stop in the street and looked around before spotting two eyes peeking out from the front door of a nearby dilapidated building. The eyes glowed green and looked at him pointedly, causing Malock to point at himself.

"Yes, you. Get over here. Quickly, now, before the Enforcers come by."

Malock walked over to the door, which opened just enough for him to slip through. He did so, entering a dark hallway briefly illuminated by the light outside before the door shut closed behind him, plunging him into darkness. He stood in a narrow, foul-smelling hallway, which felt even narrower by the presence of other beings nearby. He almost panicked, but then a light shone nearby and he found himself standing face-to-face with Skimif, who was not wearing his green bandanna anymore. Another aquarian, this one with tentacles for arms and a very squid-like face, stood in front of the door behind Malock, looking at him with suspicion in her green eyes.

Skimif held out his hand. "That is my bandanna, I believe."

Malock placed the bandanna in Skimif's hand, but the Heathen leader didn't tie it around his head. Instead, he stuffed the bandanna back into his pocket and said, "Thank you for retrieving it for me. It fell off my head when we were running away and I was afraid it was lost forever."

"No problem," said Malock. Then he looked around and frowned. "I thought you said you were staying in an inn."

"That was a lie," Skimif said, scratching the back of his neck. "I only said it because I did not know if I could trust you with that much information. We're actually based in this building, largely because no one lives in it."

A chunk of plaster fell from the ceiling and landed on the floor at Malock's feet. Then a green rat scurried past their feet into a hole into the wall, followed by another dozen or so smaller rats that must have been its children. On the left wall hung a large painting covered in a thick layer of grim that looked decidedly unhealthy. Neither Skimif nor the female aquarian blinked at that.

"I see," Malock said. "I don't understand why you ran, though."

"Because we're not interested in picking a fight with the Justice Enforcers," said the female aquarian as she walked past him. "We're not a terrorist group, even though some people might be afraid of our message."

Then the female aquarian turned and pointed an accusing tentacle at Malock. "And just who are *you*, anyway? How do we know if we can trust you or not?"

"He's fine, Aqur," said Skimif, putting one hand on her pointing tentacle. "At least, I think he is. He was the homeless man I was talking to earlier, before our demonstration. Did you see him?"

The female aquarian named Aqur shook Skimif's hand off her arm and said, "Yeah, I saw you talking to him. I am just surprised that you are letting him in here and you don't even know what his face looks like."

"Trust me," said Malock, pulling his hood further down his face. "You don't want to see my face."

"See?" said Aqur. "He's trying to hide something. I know he is."

"Actually, he has a burned face," said Skimif. "That's what he told me. So he's probably not hiding anything at all."

"In truth, Aqur's accusation is not entirely inaccurate," said Malock. "But my intentions are not malicious. It's just that I want to find out more about you Heathens before I commit to anything."

"Then tell us your name and show us your face," said Aqur. "Or else I'll personally kick you out of here."

"No need to threaten him with violence," said Skimif. "He's a reasonable guy. And if he merely wants to know what we Heathens are all about, then I see no harm in telling him. It is our goal to gather as many Heathens as possible, after all, for the coming Day."

Aqur scowled and sighed. "Your belief in the trustworthiness of other beings will be the end of us all someday, Skim."

With that, Aqur turned and left, walking down the narrow hallway and disappearing into a side door. She slammed the door behind her as she did so, making Malock start and causing the painting on the left wall to shake.

"Aqur can be quite, er, temperamental, as you can no doubt tell," said Skimif. "For good reason, mind you, as she has been burned by people she thought she could trust before. Hell, I'm not even sure she trusts me completely."

"So why is she even in the Brotherhood at all?" said Malock. "She sounds more like a liability than anything."

"Because she is just as passionate about spreading the news about the Day as I am," said Skimif. "In fact, I'd say that she is even more passionate about it than I am. Probably the only reason she lets me lead is because of my vision from the Powers."

He said that as casually as one discussed the weather. Malock wondered exactly how stable the Brotherhood was.

"So you actually were contacted by the Powers?" said Malock.

Skimif nodded. "It was an ... experience. An experience that even surpasses the visions of the great Rundya."

"Who?"

"An aquarian mage who lived hundreds of years ago," said Skimif. "He is said to have received traumatic visions from the gods, though he never described them to anyone because he did not want to spread the trauma around."

"Never heard of him," said Malock. "Was he famous?"

"Where I come from, he is," said Skimif. "He came from Tunya. It's about all that my humble hometown is known for."

"That sounds very interesting," said Malock. "Will you tell me more about the Brotherhood?"

"Not here," said Skimif, gesturing at the cramped hallway. "Let's go to the living room, where the others are. There I will introduce you to the rest of the Brotherhood and answer whatever questions you may have about us and our mission."

Malock followed Skimif down the hallway before they turned to the right, entering a wide-open living room. The signs from earlier were propped against the walls, a work table in the northeast corner had paintbrushes, wooden boards, nails, and other carpentry supplies scattered on top, a single sofa stood in the center of the room, sagging heavily in the middle, looking quite old, and the pots and pans appeared to have been dumped in the northwest corner. If the other members of the Brotherhood (not counting Aqur) had not been sitting in the center of the room talking to each other, Malock would have assumed that this was purely a work room. Painted on the ceiling was a strange flaming circle with a metal pole sticking through it, which was obviously a symbol, but of what, Malock didn't know.

Skimif spoke to the other Heathens, who had turned to look at Malock when he entered the room. For whatever reason, Skimif spoke in Aqua, that weird screeching language of the aquarians that Malock had always wanted to learn but had simply never had the time to do so. He tried his best to figure out what Skimif was saying, but then the Heathen leader abruptly stopped and said in Divina, "I was just telling them who you are and what you are here to do."

"Do they trust me?" said Malock.

Skimif shrugged. "They don't even know you, but don't worry. Most of them aren't as rude as Aqur, so feel free to take a seat anywhere you like and we can start talking."

"I'll stand right here, thanks," said Malock, after glancing at the obviously wary Heathens.

"Suits me just fine," said Skimif. "Now, what were you going to ask me?"

Seeing no reason to beat around the bush, Malock said, "The Day of the Gods. Is it really coming?"

Skimif frowned. "You saw the vision I gave to the crowd, didn't you? I thought its meaning was obvious."

"But I didn't understand even half of what I saw," said Malock. "I saw the gods, aquarians, humans, and Martir, but none of it made any sense."

"It was opaque to me at first, too," Skimif admitted. "And it did require some interpretation on my part to understand it, but I think it's meaning is obvious once you get past the unorthodox way it is delivered: Someday soon, in the future, the gods' reign will end and it will be we mortals who control the world."

"Darn right we will," said one of the Heathens, a large male who resembled a crab in the face. "No more groveling at the gods' feet, no more living in fear that we'll offend them and their delicate divine sensibilities. I can already taste it."

"But ... how?" said Malock, looking between Skimif and the other

Heathen. "The gods cannot be killed except by other gods. Trust me. I know this."

"I am not sure," said Skimif. "The Powers did not specify how the gods will meet their end, but I can sense it. The gods' days are numbered. A new age is upon us. For the first time in the history of Martir, we mortals will be on our own."

Skimif's voice became more excited and higher the more he spoke. In fact, all of the Heathens seemed to get excited by Skimif's words. Though none of them spoke a word, Malock had no trouble understanding that every Heathen in the room was a firm believer in Skimif's promise; in fact, they might even be willing to die for it for all he knew. He could certainly spot fanaticism in the eyes of at least a few Heathens.

"When did that vision happen?" said Malock. "And how do you even know it was the Powers who gave it to you? What if it was one of the gods, trying to play a trick on you or something?"

Skimif scratched his left arm. "It was months ago, when I was working on my old farm. As for how I know it was the Powers ... well, that is something I am just certain of. I've read a lot of accounts of visions other mortals have received from the gods and they are nothing like the one I had. Nothing at all."

"But why you?" said Malock. "No offense, but why would the Powers choose to deliver their vision to you? Why not someone else?"

Skimif shook his head. "That is still a mystery to me. All I know for sure is that the Powers have chosen me and that I must obey them."

Malock raised an eyebrow. "You sound just like the people who follow the gods."

"The Powers are better than the gods," Skimif said. "Besides, you don't understand. When an otherworldly force gives you an order, you can't resist it no matter how much you want to."

"No, I understand perfectly," said Malock, remembering how he had felt drawn to World's End. "But why did it take you so long to tell others about this vision? You said it occurred months ago."

"It was a highly traumatic experience," said Skimif. "I was terribly confused at first. I spent the first few weeks after it sitting alone in my house, not doing anything, not even tending to my farm. I was trying to make sense of the images I saw. It was only a month later that I finally understood its meaning."

"What did you do after that?" said Malock.

"I traveled around the various aquarian nations," said Skimif. "Nemo, Idro, West and East Yura, and many others. In fact, it is only recently that I have started to spread this message to the surface world, where you humans live."

"And you haven't face any resistance to your message, at least until today?" said Malock.

"Oh, it hasn't been an easy journey," said Skimif, waving one of his hands. "Aquarians in general are a lot less loyal to the gods than humans are, but there is quite the vocal minority who try to squash dissent wherever it crops up. In fact, for a while there, a group of such people followed us from town to town and city to city, constantly disrupting our speeches and gatherings and spreading false rumors about us."

"Said we were terrorists," said the other male aquarian from earlier. "Terrorists! Can you believe that?"

"What happened to them?" said Malock. "Why did they finally give up?"

Skimif must not have heard Malock's question because he said, "But it was worth it in the end. Many of my fellow aquarians are now Heathens and are spreading the news of the coming Day to the furthest corners of the aquarian world. Hence why I am leading my team up here. I am hoping to replicate the success I had below."

"So that's your plan, then?" said Malock. "Try to get as many people on your side as possible before the coming Day?"

"Yes," said Skimif, nodding. "The Powers' vision made it clear that I had to make sure the message got out to as many people as possible, both human and aquarian. I don't know why, but they want me to make sure that there is not a single man, woman, or child on this world who does not know about it."

"Interesting," said Malock, scratching his chin under his hood. "Tell me, have you met any resistance from the gods themselves?"

"Not so far," said Skimif. "Just their followers."

"They can't possibly ignore this forever," said Malock. "Sooner or later they will try to crush you, won't they? Especially if they start losing followers in big numbers."

"That is a very real possibility that I think about every day," said Skimif. "It is odd, really, because the gods are subordinate to the Powers. I would think they would not try to do anything to stop me from spreading news that was given to me by the Powers themselves."

"I'm not so sure about that," said Malock. "The gods are insecure, to say the least. If they ever feel threatened by you—and so far they don't—I have no doubt in my mind they will make sure to strike you dead where you stand."

"And I accept that," said Skimif. "Hood, you may not understand, but this isn't just me. I have been given a purpose by the Powers, a reason to live. I was not exaggerating back there when I said that today would change the shape of history. I honestly believe that we are on the cusp of a new era, one superior to every era prior. And I am willing to die for that new era, if I have to."

Malock looked around at the assembled Heathens. There was no mistaking it now; each one of them was just as willing to die for the cause as Skimif was.

"I think that is all I feel comfortable telling you now, Hood," said Skimif. "The choice, now, is yours: Either join us Heathens as we march into the future or stand against us and support the gods. There is no third way."

Malock knew Skimif truly meant what he said. When Malock thought about it, he saw no reason to stand against the Heathens. After Kano, after Tinkar, after Grinf, and after all of the other gods and goddesses who had made Malock's life a living hell over the last few months, Malock didn't see any reason to support the gods anymore. More than most, Malock understood just how terrible the gods could be.

But Malock hesitated. He looked up at the ceiling, expecting

Grinf or one of the other gods to strike him down where he stood for even thinking these thoughts. He thought about his parents, who still believed in the goodness of Grinf and the other gods even after seeing Grinf punish their own son before their eyes. All his life, Malock had been taught to honor and revere the gods, even when they acted in ways he didn't understand. A large part of him was still afraid of going against the gods. He felt guilty for even considering joining the Heathens. Joining the Heathens would seal his fate for certain. He knew that if the gods ever decided to take direct action against the Brotherhood, then he would fall with them.

In spite of all of that, Malock looked Skimif directly in the eyes and said, "I'm in."

A wide, toothy grin spread across Skimif's face. "Excellent. I suppose you can remove your hood now and tell us your real name."

Malock nodded and lowered his hood, allowing the others to see him. One of the Heathens peered at him closely and said, "You look kind of like Prince Malock."

Brushing a few stray strands of hair out of his face, Malock said, "That's because I *am* Prince Tojas Malock, son of Queen Markinia and King Halock, Crown Prince of Carnag, and former Chosen One of Kano."

Skimif actually took a step back, as if afraid while the other Heathens gasped. One of them even reached for a pistol in his belt, but Malock held up his hand and said, "Fear not, my fellow Heathens. I'm not your—"

The click of a gun's hammer behind him caused Malock to stop mid-sentence. He looked over his shoulder and saw Aqur standing just a few feet behind him, the barrel of her gun only a few inches from the back of his head. He hadn't heard her come up, but that didn't change the fact that she looked more than willing to blow his brains out.

"See?" Aqur said, addressing Skimif, who seemed too shocked to speak. "I knew he was a spy. He's trying to infiltrate our ranks. Just like the son of Senator Auma back in Undersea City."

Malock bit his lower lip, thinking fast. He would have to choose his words carefully. He did not want to get his brains splattered all over the place.

So he said, in the diplomatic tone Father had taught him to use during heated negotiations with enemy nations, "I am not a spy. Think about it. Would a spy come out and reveal his true identity to his enemies, especially when this spy has no way to escape?"

"You're the Crown Prince of Carnag," said Aqur. "You probably think we won't kill you, that maybe we'll hold you hostage or something. I bet your parents have a topomancer searching for you and once he finds you, they'll find us, too."

Malock raised an eyebrow. "You really don't know how the Royal Family works, I see. We only have topomancers seek us out when it is an emergency. No one in Carnag Hall even knows I'm out. They all think I'm still in bed."

Skimif rubbed his eyes, almost like he was sleepy, and said, "Aqur, put the gun down. Malock is on our side."

"He hasn't proved that yet," said Aqur. "Besides, why else would the Crown Prince of Carnag be out so early, if not to infiltrate our ranks and destroy us from within?"

Malock tried not to sigh at her accusations, as he knew from experience that sighing at someone's paranoia rarely helped matters. "I didn't even know you guys existed until I saw your little demonstration today. And if I didn't know of your existence, then I doubt my parents or anyone else in the government does, either."

"He makes a good point," said Skimif.

"Not good enough for me," said Aqur. "He could still be lying."

Malock felt his temper rising, but he hid his anger behind an impassive face. "Consider this, then, Aqur. If I truly was here to infiltrate your ranks, why have the Justice Enforcers not arrived yet? Why are you and your fellow Heathens still free?"

"Because ... because you didn't plan for this," said Aqur, although Malock noted with satisfaction that even she didn't seem to believe her own words. "You're just trying to trick us."

"He makes another good point," said Skimif. "I may not know the Justice Enforcers as well as he does, but based on what I've seen of them, I doubt they'd stand by and wait if they knew that their Prince was in trouble."

Malock wanted to say to Aqur, *See? Even your leader agrees with me.*

But he kept his mouth shut and waited for her response.

After what seemed like forever, Malock heard Aqur make a sigh of disgust and lower her gun. He then looked over his shoulder. Aqur still stood there, but she had lowered her gun and was putting it back in the holster tied around her waist.

"All right," said Aqur. "I guess you're legitimate. But I'll have my eye on you, and if you do anything to jeopardize the Brotherhood—anything at all—you'll have lead in your head."

She said that while staring him directly in the eyes. Malock kept up his impassive face, but nonetheless had to use all of his willpower to keep from looking away or showing any sign of fear.

Skimif stepped forward again and said, "Thank you for your concern, Aqur. I am certain that Malock will never do anything to harm the Brotherhood. Right, Malock?"

"Yes, of course," said Malock, nodding.

"Sure," said Aqur, still looking at him like she didn't believe a word he said.

Skimif put an arm around Malock's shoulders and said, "All right, then, brother. Allow me to welcome you to the Brotherhood of Heathens."

Malock nodded, feeling uncomfortable with Skimif's arm around his shoulders, and said, "I would love to stay and chat, but I must leave soon. Like I said, no one knows I am missing, so if the servants come and see that my bed is empty, well—"

"I understand," said Skimif as he took his arm off Malock's shoulders. "But come back when you can. There is much about the Brotherhood that we should tell you about and much you can tell us about Carnag."

"Of course," said Malock as he pulled his hood back over his face. "By the way, don't tell anyone outside the Brotherhood about this. I want my affiliation here to remain a secret, at least for now."

"Are you ashamed to be a Heathen?" said Aqur. Her hand rested casually on the gun in her holster.

"No," said Malock, shaking his head. "The fact is, my family is very loyal to the gods, to Grinf in particular, and coming out as a Heathen, there's no guarantee I won't be punished or interrogated by the Justice Enforcers to find out more about you guys."

"You can work behind the scenes," said Skimif. "When your parents decide to do something about us—and I imagine at some point they will—you can use your influence to prevent them from harming us badly."

Malock nodded. "I'll try my best and see what I can do. Now I really must go, but I will return as soon as possible."

With that, Malock brushed past Aqur and walked down the hall to the exit. As he opened the door and peered out onto the streets to make sure they were deserted, he wondered what he had gotten himself into and whether he would ever regret this, especially if the gods decided to do something about the Brotherhood.

I doubt it, he thought as he slipped out the door and began walking back to Carnag Hall. *After everything else the gods have done to me, I can't ever go back to worshiping them. I will simply have to take the consequences of my actions, whatever they may be.*

Chapter Twelve

PRINCESS RAYA ALWAYS DISLIKED visiting Carnag. It wasn't necessarily a horrible island, per se. Crime rate was extremely low, thanks in no small part to the universal presence of the Justice Enforcers—which, as she understood it, was a group of Grinfian mages who enforced the law. In fact, Carnag had the lowest crime rate of any island in the Northern Isles, even lower than the crime rate of her home island of Shika, and that was not something she would ever admit to lightly. She supposed that her actual reason for disliking Carnag was because of the way she had been raised.

As a child, Raya had always been taught—at least implicitly—that the Carnagians were essentially inferior to the Shikans. Sure, the Carnagians could make some darn good boots, and yes, they had a powerful and effective Navy, but their brutal insistence on punishing all criminals and their focus more on the practical, brute parts of life meant that their intellectual underpinnings were always lacking, to put it lightly.

"They have no culture," Raya's father, King Fabadi, once told her many years ago, when she asked him why he didn't like the

Carnagians. "They never cultivate the kind of intellectual and philosophical ideals that have made Shika the nation it is today."

Raya at first didn't believe that until many years later, during the last Northern Summit on the island of Rane, when she first met Prince Tojas Malock. Rather than engage her in a thoughtful discussion about the political issues facing their respective nations, he hit on her like he would any girl. He seemed to care only about her outer beauty, which did little to raise Raya's opinion of his people. She knew that Malock probably wasn't stupid, seeing as he was a Prince, but that first meeting between the two of them left a bad impression on her that she had never quite gotten over.

That was why Raya wasn't actually looking forward to meeting Malock today. It had been exactly one week since the Prince of Carnag had returned from his voyage to the end of the world and Raya was following one of the Carnagian Royal Family's servants—a young, round-faced man named Orel—through the hallways of Carnag Hall. She had arrived on Carnag the day before, along with her father, King Fabadi, but had not been allowed to see Prince Malock until this morning. An ancient Shikan tradition about marriage was that the bride and groom must be allowed to have a private discussion together without the parents or anyone else involved. It was supposed to be a way to help the bride and groom get to know each other better, though that didn't mean Raya was looking forward to it.

"And on the left here, you can see a wonderful self-portrait of King Iryu the Second Most Just," said Orel, gesturing to a painting on the wall as they walked. "He was Prince Malock's great-grandfather and gained his title by instituting many fair and just laws that continue to govern Carnag's justice system. He was so just that Grinf himself was said to have blessed Iryu with a longer lifespan so he could continue punishing guilty criminals for the crimes they committed."

Raya looked up at the self-portrait. King Iryu vaguely resembled Malock, especially with the dark hair, but he otherwise looked quite different. He more closely resembled a stern judge who had no time for the excuses that obviously guilty criminals made to him.

"But why was he called the *Second* Most Just?" Raya asked. "Why not the Most Just?"

Orel's dark face suddenly became pale. "Princess Raya, you may not understand this, but the title of Most Just belongs to Lord Grinf and to Lord Grinf only. While King Iryu was a very just king, his justness was nowhere near that of Grinf's."

"Oh," said Raya. "How did Iryu die?"

"He fell off the balcony of Carnag Hall," said Orel, his face going back to its normal shade fairly quickly. "Some say he was pushed off by one of his servants, other say it was an accident; however it happened, he was a great king who is still greatly missed today, generations after his unfortunate death."

Raya nodded but said nothing. Throughout their walk through Carnag Hall, Orel had been pointing out the various interesting artifacts—mostly paintings and statues—scattered throughout the palace and explaining their history to Raya. Raya had not asked for him to do this, but her father had. He had said that it was vitally important for Raya to know as much about Carnag as she could before she married Malock, since she would someday be the Queen of Carnag herself. Not that she was complaining about this; after all, Raya always loved knowledge and learning new things, even if it was about Carnag.

While Orel continued talking about King Iryu's greatest accomplishments, Raya's mind wandered back to Shika. She knew Nimiko could not escape his chains, but it didn't stop her from worrying about him anyway. Another reason she had wanted to stay on Shika was to keep an eye on Nimiko. After all, it would not take much for Nimiko to kill her if he escaped.

Take your mind off him, Raya thought. *He's not going anywhere and it's unlikely that any of the gods will try to free him. Everything is going according to plan. As long as you don't act suspicious, no one will ask you about it.*

"We're here!" said Orel suddenly, his bright voice snapping Raya out of her thoughts.

"What?" said Raya, looking at Orel.

"The Royal Garden, of course," said Orel, "where you will meet your future husband."

Orel was right. The two of them had emerged from the back of Carnag Hall into the Royal Garden, a place that Raya had heard much about but had never visited before. Stretched out before her was a large garden filled with every kind of flower imaginable: The oddly-shaped black dollops, the short flowers with fiery orange petals known as Grinf's Eyes, silver stems, and many others Raya couldn't even name. Several large trees ran through the center of the Garden, with a narrow stream of clear water flowing through the gaps in their roots. A clean path of stone wound its way through the Garden. She even spotted a few benders, a special type of plant that was a favorite of Shikan children, primarily because it grew everywhere and was easy to bend in whatever shape one desired. A tall gazebo stood in the center of the Garden, though there was no one in it.

The Garden itself, however, was not void of people. About a dozen yards away was a table set for two, standing next to a clear blue pond whose surface sparkled in the mid-morning sunshine. A tall, strapping young man sat at the table, his head bent down as if in prayer, both hands wrapped tightly around a cup of tea. Three older people stood nearby, talking among each other. One of them was Raya's own father, King Fabadi, whose pale skin and silver-blonde hair contrasted sharply with the dark skin and graying hair of King Halock and Queen Markinia. A handful of servants stood by as well, looking quite dignified in their red servant clothes (although one, a woman, was clearly sweating in the hot sun).

Orel marched up to the table, with Raya following closely behind. Raya's father and Malock's parents ceased talking when they approached. Malock, for some reason, kept his head down, almost as if he didn't hear their approach.

"There you are," said King Halock, smiling at Raya. "How did you enjoy your stay in the guest room?"

"It was fine," said Raya. "The sheets were clean and the mattress was soft. I got more sleep than I usually do."

"Wonderful," said Halock. "Of course, we would only ever provide the best for our future daughter-in-law. Indeed, you probably slept better than even I and my wife, heh."

Raya merely nodded, but in reality, she had been up much of the night worrying about Nimiko. She hadn't been lying about the softness of the sheets and the comfortableness of the mattress, though.

Her father, King Fabadi, cleared his throat just then and said, "Well, Raya, now that you are here, I and Malock's parents will leave you two alone to talk and get to know each other better, as per tradition. We will leave some of the servants here to attend to your every need."

He gestured at the servants, three in all, who stood not far from him. Two of them were Shikans, who had come with Raya and her father to Carnag, while the other one was a Carnagian. All three stood erect and at attention, their faces impassive, as if showing any sort of expression was a crime around here. Then again, Raya did recall seeing one of the Justice Enforcers apprehend a man for littering on her way to Carnag Hall yesterday, so that thought may not have been quite as far-fetched as she thought it was.

"You will have two hours in which to talk," said Halock. "After that, we'll come get you two and have a fine time together becoming closer and getting to know each other. Just like a real family."

Again, Raya nodded, but she said nothing. She was still thinking about Nimiko, even though she knew she shouldn't. She had to keep her mind in the present at all times; otherwise she risked appearing disrespectful to King Halock and Queen Markinia. And while the King and Queen of Carnag both seemed jovial and friendly, Raya well remembered the heated argument that her father and King Halock had gotten into during the Norther Summit a year ago. As that fight had resulted in her father getting his nose broken, Raya knew exactly what Halock could do when he was angry.

Malock still wasn't looking up at Raya. Earlier that morning, Orel had informed Raya that Malock had suffered a terrible burn to the face on the day he got home. When Raya pressed him for details, Orel explained—in a very unconvincing tone—that a pyromancer had accidentally burned Malock's face while entertaining the Royal Family. Raya didn't argue with the story, but the fact that Malock had not been healed by a panamancer told her that he had been burned by something else, but by what, she didn't know.

"Tojas, dear," said Queen Markinia, looking over her shoulder at her son. "Your bride-to-be is here. Why don't you say hello?"

Malock looked up, and when he did, Raya felt her stomach lurch. While Raya had never found Malock a particularly attractive man (mostly due to his womanizing behavior), she had at least understood how other women could find him attractive. She remembered quite well his well-sculpted nose, his high cheek bones, and his charming eyes.

But, even though she had been warned about his face's disfigurement, she had a hard time believing that this was the same Malock she had met a year ago. His eyes were almost melted shut; his cheeks looked like little more than dried paste; and his lips were almost gone. His face resembled a squashed frog she had seen once in the streets of Port Hiji back on Shika, but even that had been more attractive than this.

"Good day, Raya," said Malock, his voice slightly distorted through his burned lips. "As beautiful as ever, I see."

Raya would have glared at Malock for his tone, but knowing the sensitive nature of this meeting, she merely bowed her head and said, "And you, Malock, are as amicable as ever."

Malock's expression was hard to read, in part because of his melted face. Halock clapped his hands together and said, "Already off to a great start. Princess, if you may take a seat."

Halock stepped aside and gestured for Raya to sit in the empty chair opposite Malock. Raya complied, walking past the King and sitting down on the soft-backed chair. After adjusting her seat, she looked directly at Malock. Now that she got a better look at him, he looked a lot more tired than she had first assumed. Had he gotten little sleep, too?

Her father's hand landing on her shoulder caused her to look up at him. King Fabadi had a smile on his face, but she understood his expression quite well: *If you mess this up, I will blame you.* And she understood that sentiment. She had no right to cause any unnecessary problems for her or her father or her people. She would have to be on her best behavior while talking with Malock, no matter how she felt about the situation (and to be frank, she wasn't very excited about it).

"Now, then," said her father. "We will be in Carnag Hall. Once you are done, simply order one of the servants to come and get us."

He gestured at the three servants who stood nearby as he spoke.

Raya and Malock nodded. A few minutes later, her father and his parents were gone, the backs of their robes disappearing into Carnag Hall's back exit. Only the three servants her father had indicated before still stood at attention, but they were so still and quiet that they might as well not have been there at all.

Turning back to face Malock, Raya opened her mouth to say something, but she then noticed that his head had drooped onto his chest. He was staring at his cup of tea, which looked quite cold by now, almost as if he was afraid to make eye contact with her. Either he was remembering how coldly their first meeting went or he was distracted by something. Maybe by his memories of World's End?

Because Malock seemed unlikely to start, Raya took the initiative. "So. Malock. How is your face?"

Malock looked up at her, a startled look in his eyes. "What?"

"Your face," Raya repeated. She felt like she was talking to a dumb person. "Does it still hurt?"

Malock shrugged. "You get used to it. I was told it will always hurt. Honestly, it was a lot worse when I first got it."

"Ah," said Raya. "Of course."

Awkward silence reigned between them again. Raya wanted to pick at her blouse's cuffs—it was what she usually did whenever she became fidgety—but she remembered how her father always scolded her for doing that and so she didn't. Malock, for his part, occasionally sipped from his tea. A cool breeze blew through, sending the branches of a nearby tree swaying and causing the Protection just outside of the

Garden to shimmer visibly for a moment before fading again.

Raya had no idea what to talk with Malock about. It wasn't like they had been good friends. Since that Northern Summit, they had only met a few times, and even then it had only been for political purposes. They never exchanged letters and, as far as she knew, they had no common interests between them. Malock was a party-loving socialite and she was a book-loving intellectual. Under ordinary circumstances, the two of them would never even be friends, yet they were going to be married and so they had to get to know each other.

Raya fished around for any topics of conversation she could come up with. Her eyes scanned the Garden for any unusual or interesting plants that Malock might have been able to tell her about. But frankly, despite her great interest in books and knowledge, botany was one of her weaker areas and so she couldn't think of any good questions to ask the Prince.

Then she remembered what she had intended to talk with Malock about in the first place. It might be a risky topic to explore, but she figured it would at least give her a little bit of conversation with him, even if he was reluctant to talk about it.

So Raya leaned forward slightly—enough to show she was interested, but not enough to make her seem threatening or rude—and asked, "How was your voyage to World's End?"

Malock froze like a pond in a flash freeze. He even seemed to stop breathing, which made Raya worry that she had gone too far when he said, without warning, "A complete disaster, all things considered."

Raya raised an eyebrow in interest. "Oh? And what do you mean by that?"

Malock looked up at her with obvious reluctance. "I started the voyage with five ships. I only came back with one."

Raya bit her lower lip and sat back. "Oh. I'm sorry to hear about the loss of so many men."

"Thanks," said Malock.

Despite Malock's tone making it abundantly clear that he didn't want to talk about it, Raya had to ask more questions. "Can you tell me about some of the things you and your men saw? I mean, surely you must have seen a lot of interesting things, right?"

Malock's burned face looked even uglier when he scowled. "Deadly, lethal, dangerous, life-threatening ... sure. But interesting? If you had been through even half of what I was, you wouldn't even think about calling it 'interesting.'"

His tone was as sharp as a knife, but Raya didn't allow him to cow her.

She said, "Can't you at least tell me a little about what you saw and experienced? I'm not asking for the whole story. Just the most interesting parts."

Malock rolled his eyes; at least, she thought he did. With his eyelids as melted as they were, it was hard to tell what his eyes were doing.

"You wouldn't want to know," said Malock. "All you need to know is that the gods ... well, I'm not going to say one word about them."

Malock said all of that while looking over Raya's head at Carnag

Hall. Raya didn't understand why he did that. It was almost as if he was afraid that she would find out something that she shouldn't if she pressed him. That made her all the more curious to find out what he knew and what he experienced.

"So you ran into problems with the gods?" said Raya. "Did you actually meet some gods in the southern seas? I heard it was Kano who had summoned you. Did you get to meet her?"

Malock's fingers tightened around the tea cup so much that Raya thought he was going to break it. "Yes. I did meet Kano."

"Interesting," said Raya. "What was she like?"

"Wet," said Malock.

Raya wanted to roll her eyes, but she kept her cool. "I mean, did she look like how you thought she would? What did she sound like?"

"Like every other god in the world," said Malock. "In charge, bossy, and dismissive of anything that didn't directly affect her. Nothing much to talk about, to be honest."

Malock was clearly hiding something from her. Raya didn't know what, but she could tell he was trying to get her to stop asking those questions. She was not about to give him that satisfaction, at least not until she found out everything she wanted to know.

So she said, "Why did she summon you to World's End in the first place?"

"That's a secret," said Malock. "I am under no obligation to tell you or anyone else why she summoned me. It's nothing personal; it's just I'm not supposed to tell anyone."

That was an obvious lie, but Raya figured it would be fruitless to get him to tell her the truth, so she changed the subject.

"Then tell me about World's End," she said. "I've only ever heard legends about the place; in fact, I used to believe it was just a myth myself. But clearly, since you've been there, it's as real as any other island in the world."

Malock sighed and scratched his right cheek. "It's more beautiful, amazing, and brilliant than any city we mortals have ever—and perhaps will ever—build. There is nothing quite like it anywhere in the world."

"Wow," said Raya. "Were there other gods there or—"

Malock was now glaring at her with the kind of fierceness she had seen captains of ships show to their insubordinate sailors. It actually made her shut herself up, even though she was still burning with questions that she desperately needed the answers to.

"I liked you better when you didn't talk to me," said Malock. "You asked a lot less questions."

Feeling a little flustered, Raya said, "Well, what am I supposed to say? You went to an island no one really thought existed and came back to tell the tale. You shouldn't be so surprised."

"I don't want to talk about it because I just spent the last week being interrogated day and night by our playwright," said Malock. "He's writing a play based off my adventures for posterity. He's currently calling it *The Mad Voyage of Prince Malock*, which I think is a stupid name. So if I seem a little less-than-enthusiastic about answering your questions, it's because I've had to relive my memories more than I would like to over the past week."

He said all of that in one burst, like he had been holding it all in. The servants nearby shuffled their feet, almost like they were worried, but they didn't move.

"Then why didn't you say so in the first place?" said Raya. "Could have avoided wasting a lot of time if we had done that."

Malock scowled at her and sipped his tea. Then he looked away and sighed. "I am sorry for the outburst. It's just I've been under so much stress over the last week, and this is after coming back from my voyage to World's End, which was no pleasure cruise, no matter what anyone else says."

"Oh, I get it," said Raya. "All of the wedding preparations have been bothering me, too. That's actually why I wanted to ask you about your voyage. I was hoping we could take our minds off the wedding for a while."

"I appreciate the thought, but it was severely misguided," said Malock. "You really don't want to know what happened on that voyage."

Yes, I do, Raya thought. *Especially if it will help me figure out how to protect my people from the gods more effectively.*

But she didn't dare say that thought aloud. She could sense that Malock was not happy about the gods, but she wasn't going to be quite so candid about her own feelings about them. She would have to be far more subtle.

So Raya said, "Did you hear about that one group a week ago? The Brotherhood of Heathens, I think they called themselves?"

To her surprise, Malock started, almost like she had shouted at him. It was only for a brief moment, however, because then Malock resumed his normal hard-to-read self (or perhaps it made more sense to call it his unusual hard-to-read self, as he was normally much more jollier and candid than he currently was).

"Yes, I heard about them," said Malock. "It's hard not to when they are on the streets every day, preaching a message about this whole 'Day of the Gods' nonsense. They're not going anywhere, I'm sure."

Malock didn't look at her as he spoke, but Raya observed that he sat far more erect than he normally did. Admittedly, Raya wasn't always the best reader of body language (she was too cerebral for that), but something about the way Malock moved told her that she had hit upon something important.

Raya thus continued. "I don't know. I've heard that their leader— I think his name is Skimif—draws a larger and larger crowd with every public demonstration."

Malock looked at her suspiciously. "How did you know that? You've only been here for a day."

Raya bit her lip. She couldn't let Malock know that she herself was allied with the Brotherhood, nor that she knew as much as she did about them because Skimif often sent her messages updating her about the Brotherhood's progress. At least, she couldn't tell him that here, with the servants standing nearby listening to every word.

So Raya said in a more casual voice, "Oh, it's just that I've been paying a lot of attention to the news and rumors for a while. We get a lot of Carnagian merchants on Shika trying to sell us their wares and they usually bring news with them."

"Oh," said Malock. "Of course."

Malock then sat back in his chair, bringing his teacup closer to his mouth as he said, "It's actually very frustrating. The Justice Enforcers have been doing their best to arrest the Heathens, but no one knows where their hideout is. Even our topomancers are having no luck in tracking them down. It doesn't help that their numbers actually have been growing, meaning that even if we succeed in arresting a few Heathens, it will not be enough to even slow the movement's growth."

"You speak rather candidly about all of this," said Raya. "You don't sound very sad about it."

Malock shrugged. "I am very upset about it. Trying to get people to stop worshiping the gods ... it's outrageous, I tell you, completely blasphemous. They are risking bringing the wrath of the gods down upon us all."

Raya tilted her head. Though Malock sounded quite bitter about that, she saw right through his behavior and tone. He clearly wasn't nearly as critical of the Brotherhood as he was trying to make himself out to be. In fact, he might have even been sympathetic to them, but again she couldn't be sure about that yet. She would have to tread carefully.

"Have you ever actually heard anything they've said?" said Raya. "I've heard they're saying the gods are all going to die soon."

"As I said, it's all nonsense," said Malock. "The gods are eternal. I was taught that and you were taught that and every mortal who has ever lived was taught that. Pretending any differently isn't going to change anything."

Again, Raya noted a hint of falseness in Malock's tone. It seemed like Malock was denouncing the Heathens because that was what he was 'supposed' to do, not because he actually felt that way. Raya had to dig deeper.

"But they're attracting a rather large following," said Raya. "I've heard their membership is close to three hundred. That's pretty impressive for a group that announced its existence a mere week ago."

"So what?" said Malock. "It's purely because Skimif is a good public speaker. It won't last. People will realize how silly the whole thing is or remember that the gods aren't kind to heathens and leave just as quickly as they joined."

"So the reason you aren't worried about your Enforcers arresting them is because you think the movement will die out on its own?"

"Of course," said Malock. "The Grinfian monks have been publishing pamphlets and giving speeches debunking the Brotherhood's arguments. Once people hear the Grinfian monks' arguments, the entire movement will collapse."

Every word Malock spoke sounded totally insincere to Raya. She had no doubt in her mind now: Malock was sympathetic to the Brotherhood. Why that was so, she didn't know, but she did know that she needed to let him know that she was, too. But she couldn't just say it. She could only imagine what her father and Malock's parents would say if they found out that she and Malock were sympathetic to heathens.

Raya cast her eyes about the Garden, looking for some way she could communicate with Malock without anyone else hearing. She wished that telemancy had been part of her education because then she could have communicated it to him directly into his mind and no one would be the wiser.

That was when her eyes landed on the Shikan benders growing out of the nearby pond not too far away. Tall and stiff, the green plants were ubiquitous on Shika. She wondered why the Royal Garden had any, considering that it was on Carnag, but she decided it didn't matter because the benders' presence gave her a great idea.

"Malock, would you like to see something I can do?" said Raya. "It will be very entertaining, I can assure you."

Malock looked at her warily. "What is it?"

"You'll see," said Raya. She turned to the three servants standing behind them and said, "One of you, go get me four of those benders. Bring them to me without delay."

One of the servants, a Shikan man, immediately dashed over to the benders, picked out exactly as much as she ordered, and was back by Raya's side in an instant. The servant gave the benders to her and then returned to stand by his fellow servants. Raya turned the benders over in her hands. She caressed the plants' smooth surface, but carefully because they also had small, bumpy ridges that could cut her fingers if she was reckless with them.

Malock eyed the benders like they might explode. "What are those?"

"Shikan benders," said Raya, placing them in her lap. They were quite light. "Very common back home. They're popular among children of all classes because of how easy they are to bend into different shapes and forms. You can even tie them together to make better creations."

Malock raised an eyebrow. "And what does that have to do with anything?"

"When I was a girl, I used to play with these all the time," Raya continued. "Whenever I wasn't doing any of my studies, I would spend hours at a time just twisting them in a variety of different shapes. Once I even made a fairly complicated horian falcon, though it ended up decaying after a while because benders just don't last long after you pick them."

"I still don't see what a child's toy has anything to do with this situation," said Malock.

Raya smiled. "I still remember how to do it, even though it has been a while since I last played with these. Why don't I make you something? It can be my gift to you, my future husband."

Malock was now looking at her like she had lost her mind. "Since when did you have a playful side?"

Raya shrugged. "Just because I happen to be smarter than you doesn't mean I can't have a little fun, too. You just hold on. It shouldn't take me long at all."

Ignoring Malock's disbelieving mutterings, Raya began to twist and bend the plants. It was a bit awkward at first, as she had not done it in a while, but soon her muscle memory kicked in and she felt like a kid again. She actually enjoyed the challenge of bending the plants together in just the right way, of trying to achieve the shape she saw in her head. In fact, she enjoyed it so much that when she finished creating her work, she was genuinely disappointed. She created under the table so Malock couldn't guess what it was. But she was confident that once he saw its final shape, he—and not any of the servants, who were surely watching her as Malock was—would understand its meaning immediately.

"Done," said Raya as she lifted her creation out from under the table and placed it before Malock. "How do you like it?"

Her creation was simple. It was three of the benders woven together in a circle, with the fourth in the center of the circle. It was supposed to be a representation of the symbol used by members of the Brotherhood to identify one another; in fact, the reason she chose the symbol was precisely because only members of the Brotherhood would even recognize it for what it was. Admittedly, it was a highly simplistic representation of it, but she figured Malock was smart enough to recognize it for what it was, assuming he had any sort of association with the Heathens at all.

Malock took the symbol and examined it. At first, his burned face made his expression hard to read, but then Raya saw the telltale signs of realization dawning on Malock's features. He looked up at her, his mouth gaping. Raya simply nodded, which was the only way she could get the idea across to him without any of the servants understanding.

"Well?" said Raya. "How do you like it?"

Thankfully, Malock was smarter than Raya remembered. He changed his expression to a less shocked one and said, "Why, it is very, er, nice, Raya. Simple, but elegant. I see you have far more talents and knowledge than I originally believed."

Raya smiled again. "As Princess of Shika, I must be talented in a variety of areas. Although that particular thing is not my best work."

"I will make sure to put it in a safe spot," said Malock, placing it back on the table. "Maybe I will even have it framed so it will not decay. A symbol of our marriage, of the unification of two islands that were formerly enemies."

"That sounds good to me," said Raya. "I can show you how to do it in private later, if you want."

She gave Malock a significant look as she said that. She hoped to communicate her real message to him through facial expressions alone: *If you want to know more about what I know about the Brotherhood, we can talk about it later.*

To her relief, Malock seemed to get it, for he said, "Certainly. I would love to learn more about how to do that sort of thing. It might be an interesting hobby to take up in my spare time."

Sitting back in her chair, Raya said, "It is a very soothing hobby, though admittedly not one practiced by adults very often."

"I've always been a bit of a big kid," said Malock. "Learning how to bend benders should be fun."

The two continued to talk about various things until Raya's father and Malock's parents emerged from Carnag Hall to fetch them for lunch, which was to take place in the grand dining hall of Carnag Hall. Raya stood and walked by her father's side, while Malock walked between his own parents. When they got to the entrance, Raya and Malock allowed their parents to go through first. Before they followed, the two exchanged a quick look, a look that told Raya all she needed to know:

Prince Malock was indeed a member of the Brotherhood of Heathens. And he knew that she was, too.

Chapter Thirteen

O F ALL THE THINGS that could have happened," said Jenur, wrapping her arms around her legs as Quro flipped the motor's lid open, "the engine just *had* to die, didn't it?"

"It's happened before," said Quro as he examined the dead motor's innards. "That's why I always keep my toolbox on board. Jen, could you hand it to me? It's under the steering wheel."

Jenur crawled over the bottom of the boat to the toolbox. She had to crawl over Rint's legs to reach it, as the old man had stuck his legs out to stretch them and he didn't have much room to pull them back in. The toolbox itself was easy to find, however, but it weighed a ton. With some effort she managed to drag it across the bottom of the boat to Quro (though she had to have Rint lift his legs to do it right), prompting Quro to say, "Thanks," as he bent down to pick up the tool he needed.

While Quro worked on that, Jenur returned to her spot and pulled her legs up to her chest. Her dark hair clung to her head thanks to the water of the ocean splashing her earlier, and she had already had to dump out a few gallons of water from her boots today. With her stomach growling and her throat dry, Jenur was starting to think that maybe she would have been better off staying on Destan, even if it meant risking the wrath of the Priestly Guard.

Jenur, Quro, and Rint had been traveling north for at least a week now. They had been traveling almost nonstop, stopping about once a day to eat and drink, among other things. They had stopped by a few islands—tiny little spits of land that weren't on any map—but the islands themselves lacked much edible food or drinkable water. In fact, it had been such a long time since Jenur had had a good meal that she would have even been happy to have a meal like the kind she used to have on the *Iron Wind*.

Nor did it help that Quro's boat—which he called the *Lucky*, though Jenur didn't see what was so lucky about it—was tiny. It had clearly been designed for one person. Rint and Jenur only fit by making themselves as small as possible, but it was worse for Jenur, as Rint's old joints forced him to stretch more often, leaving even less room for Jenur to move in. Only Quro appeared unaffected by this, but she figured he had to be at least as pissed off about the lack of room as she and Rint were. She knew Quro well enough to know that he didn't always express his thoughts or feelings aloud.

To take her mind off things, Jenur decided to look out over the ocean. She looked out over the port, but saw nothing except water for miles in every direction. But she didn't even see that much because a thick fog had descended upon the area a few minutes ago, which just made the situation even worse.

About the only good thing about this is that there isn't a giant sea

197

monster trying to eat us, Jenur thought, turning her attention back to the boat. *Or pirates trying to raid us or anything else like that.*

She avoided making eye contact with Rint, who was now muttering under his breath some foul curses about the *Lucky*'s motor and the progress they had made so far. She didn't hate Rint. It was just ... well, he wasn't Kinker. Despite the obvious similarities in how they looked and even talked, the two brothers couldn't have been more different. Rint treated Jenur like a child, demeaning her intelligence and maturity. He complained far more often about the hardships they had gone through than Kinker ever had and more than once displayed his less-than-tolerant thoughts regarding aquarians (although he kept his bigoted comments to a minimum, perhaps because he didn't want to be thrown overboard by Quro). The old man seemed far bitterer to Jenur than Kinker had, which Jenur supposed was understandable when she considered Rint's current situation, but it still made him unpleasant to be around, especially on a small boat in the middle of nowhere.

In fact, at times Jenur even regretted saving Rint. He certainly didn't seem thankful that she and Quro had gone out of their way to save his life. Between his bigoted comments toward Quro and his general lack of respect for her, Rint was proving himself to be a far less kind person than his younger brother. Jenur tried to reassure herself that Rint was probably just extremely stressed by learning about the truth of his brother's death, as well as being forced to leave the only home he had ever known. That still didn't stop her from wanting to slap him upside the head with the heel of her shoe, though, whenever he said something that ticked her off.

She remembered well how he had responded when she told him the full story of Kinker's death. He didn't cry—he claimed to have already done all of his mourning months ago, when he first thought his younger brother was dead—but he did show even less respect to Quro than before. Jenur didn't understand that until she remembered that it had been Vashnas, an aquarian, who had killed Kinker. Considering how most Destanians were already fairly bigoted toward aquarians, it was not surprising that Rint's opinion of Quro would dramatically decrease the way it did.

She wondered what Rint would do once they got to Carnag. For that matter, she wondered what *she* was going to do when she got to Carnag. She had an idea of heading even further north—perhaps all the way to the Great Berg, as few Dark Tigers ever went that far and not many people lived up there anyway, which would make it easier to hide—but her ideas were still quite vague and largely dependent on whatever Rint chose to do. She knew it was irrational, but she felt responsible for the old man and she wasn't going to let him out of her sight until she was certain he was going to be okay.

That's why Kinker died, Jenur thought, leaning away from Quro as he dug through his toolbox for something. *If I had been there, I could have stopped Vashnas. Could have killed that evil witch before she even thought about killing Kinker.*

Her grief and guilt rose up in her again like a geyser. She had thought she had grown out of it, but there it was again, making her feel horrible. She thought that killing Deber might have gotten rid of it, but now that Deber was dead, Jenur still felt guilty for not protecting Kinker when he needed it the most.

Never again, Jenur thought. *I will never allow another person close to me to die, at least not while I'm around. Even if one of the gods tries to kill that person, I won't let them.*

If she said that aloud to Rint or Quro, they likely would have scoffed. At least Rint would have. He was quite cynical in that regard. He didn't seem to believe in anything except his own survival. It was a promise Jenur intended to keep just the same, however, if only to herself.

"That's quite strange," said Quro, his tone—unusually worried—breaking Jenur out of her thoughts.

"What's strange?" said Rint, looking up in alarm.

"The engine," said Quro, scratching the back of his head. "I can't figure out what's wrong with it."

Scowling, Rint said, "Then look at it more. It's your boat. You should be able to figure it out."

"Perhaps I should have phrased it differently," said Quro. "The engine is completely fine, as far as I can see. The motor is not damaged, the fuel lines are still in one piece, and the power switch is still on. It appears that the engine simply stopped working."

"That doesn't make any sense," said Rint. "Machines don't 'just stop working.' I'm not much of a mechanic, but even I know that there is usually a reason for malfunctions in the damn things."

"If there is, I can't find it," said Quro. "And trust me when I say that I examined the engine thoroughly and checked all the usual spots where it might have broken down or been damaged. The entire engine appears to be in one piece."

"If you can't fix it, does that mean we're stuck out here in the middle of the Crystal Sea?" Rint asked.

Quro nodded as he slapped down the lid on the engine. "It would appear so."

Rint groaned. "Wonderful. What's next, a pirate ship comes out of the blue and sinks our boat?"

"Doubtful," said Quro as he looked around the foggy sea. "This is a rarely traveled section of the Crystal Sea, mostly due to the heavy fog that is present year round. Most likely we'll be stuck floating here for however long it takes for me to figure out why the motor quit on us."

Rint groaned even louder. "As if that makes it any better. What if a storm comes through? Giant waves sink us?"

"What am I supposed to do about any of that?" said Quro in annoyance. "I'm not a mage or a god. You'll just have to be patient and hope for the best."

"I should have stayed on Destan," said Rint, looking down at his feet. "At least there I wouldn't be stuck in the middle of the ocean with you two."

"Maybe we should have left you there," said Jenur, glaring at him. "For such an old man, you don't seem to have much wisdom or patience."

Rint opened his mouth to say something (probably something very rude) when Quro raised his hand and said, "Quiet, both of you."

Rint and Jenur looked up at the aquarian. He appeared intently focused on something that neither of them could see. But Jenur understood that look well, for she had seen it before: It meant Quro heard something.

"What is it?" said Jenur. "Dad, what do you hear?"

"Something cutting through the water," said Quro. He frowned and leaned slightly to starboard. "It's huge, but I don't know what—"

At that moment, a loud, earsplitting horn echoed through the fog, so loud and so close that it made Jenur temporarily deaf. Rint slapped his hands over his ears, while Quro dropped down to the boat's floor like he had been punched out by a boxer. The horn kept blaring so loud that it sounded like it was coming from every direction.

Knowing that shouting would be useless, Jenur looked around through the thick fog, trying to spot the source of the horn. Her heart failed her when she saw a massive glowing red eye peering at her through the fog hundreds of feet away. It reminded her of the red eyes of the entity known as Messenger-and-Punisher; in fact, for a moment, she thought that it *was* Messenger-and-Punisher, perhaps coming to take her away for good.

But then a burst of smoke and fire exploded out of the top of the red eye. Rint and Quro seemed to have noticed it, too, because Rint was staring at it and clearly shouting obscenities that were drowned out by the blaring horn, while Quro simply gazed upon it with horror and curiosity etched onto his face.

The red eye that belched smoke and fire was coming closer and closer, prompting Jenur to look for any paddles or anything she could use to move the boat out of the way. But she didn't see anything, nor did she try to use her arms to move the boat because she knew it would be useless unless she could get Quro and Rint to help. Seeing as they were currently frozen in shock at the sight of the incoming monster, that meant they were all pretty much screwed.

Just as Jenur was wondering what the afterlife was going to be like, the fog obscuring the red-eyed, smoke-belching monster lifted. As it did so, the horn suddenly went silent, but that didn't make Jenur feel better because she now recognized the massive ship that was coming toward them, even though she wished she didn't.

"What in the name of every god in the Northern Pantheon is *that*?" said Rint, gazing upon the hull of the ship before them as it slowed to a crawl.

"The *Clockwork Heart*," Jenur said.

Quro looked at her in surprise. "You mean you know what that ... *thing* is?"

Jenur nodded. "Long story short, that's the ship that took me and my fellow sailors back north after we reached World's End."

"That's a *ship*?" said Rint in utter disbelief. "She looks like a floating fortress."

"Technically, she's also a goddess," said Jenur with a shrug.

"A *goddess*?" Rint looked like he was going to faint any minute now.

"It's slowing down," Quro said. "Jenur, who is on board that ship?"

"You don't want to kn—" Jenur was interrupted by a loud voice coming from the bow of the ship.

"Yoohoo!" the voice rang out, unnaturally loud in the quiet fog.

"Jenur, is that you down there in that box?"

The *Clockwork Heart* was much closer to them now, enough that Jenur could see a young woman standing at the bow, waving down at her with mock cheerfulness. Jenur didn't wave back.

"Who is that woman up there?" said Quro, staring up at the woman. "Friend of yours?"

"More like annoying acquaintance," said Jenur. "Her name is Hanarova."

"Jenur!" came Hana's shrill voice. "You look lost! Why don't you come up on board and we'll help you? The automatons might be able to fix your motor for you!"

"How does she know that our engine is not working?" said Quro, looking at Jenur suspiciously.

"I have no idea," said Jenur. "And that's what worries me."

"Does it matter?" said Rint, whose pale face contrasted sharply with his practical voice. "She's right. Why not accept her help?"

"You got over your fear pretty quickly," Jenur observed.

"Because I am a practical man, Jenur," said Rint, "and practical men do not allow their fear to immobilize them. She can't be that bad if she helped you get back north, can she?"

Remembering how Hana had nearly fed her to some of the southern gods, Jenur said, "Yes, she can be. But I guess you have a point because our only option right now is to float endlessly on the ocean and hope we don't get sunk by pirates or by bad weather or something."

"You are finally seeing the light," said Rint. "I was getting worried there for a while. I thought you were just a stubborn girl, like most girls your age."

Ignoring him, Jenur turned to face the *Clockwork Heart* and shouted, "Pull her up close, Hana! We'll accept your help!"

"Okay!" said Hana's voice. "Just hold on there!"

As the *Clockwork Heart* drew closer to the *Lucky*, Jenur wished she still had her knife with her. She thought she was going to need it.

Once aboard the *Clockwork Heart*, the trio were met by Hanarova. She looked exactly the same as Jenur had seen her last, wearing a practical sailor's uniform that made her look a lot more human than she really was. She brought with her a dozen or so of the automatons, all of them holding sharp-tipped metal spears, standing silently behind her like soldiers ready to march into battle. Their presence made Jenur uneasy.

"Long time no see, Jenur," said Hana, walking up to her with a smile on her face. "Who are your new friends?"

"I'm her father," said Quro. "And this is Rint Dolan."

"Dolan," Hana repeated. "That name sounds familiar. Where have I heard it before?"

"I had a younger brother," said Rint. He was staring at the automatons, like he couldn't quite believe his eyes. "Named Kinker. Ever met him?"

"Nope," said Hana. "But I do recall someone telling me about a Kinker Dolan once. He died or something on World's End, right?"

"Yes, he did," said Jenur. She folded her arms and said, "I didn't know you were still here, Hana. I thought you and the Mechanical Goddess had already returned to Stalf."

"Of course not," said Hana. "We still haven't done the thing we came here to do. So we probably won't be heading back south until the end of the month, at least."

"I don't understand," said Rint, his eyes still locked on the automatons. "Are they wearing metal armor or something?"

Hana ignored him. "So how did that little assassination thing go on Destan, Jenur? Did you kill anyone?"

"Why do you want to know?" said Jenur. "And why should I tell you?"

Hana held up her hands. "Geez. I was just trying to be friendly. You humans can be very touchy sometimes, you know that?"

"Only because I know you," said Jenur. "Cut the crap, Hana. What's the real reason you saved us? And why did the Mechanical Goddess shut down the boat's motor?"

Hana laughed. "You think the Mechanical Goddess did that? That's a very silly thought. The Mechanical Goddess would never do such a thing."

"Of course she wouldn't," said Jenur. "It's just a coincidence that the boat's motor failed at the same time you showed up, isn't it?"

Hana frowned. "When you put it that way, it does sound like we planned it to happen that way, doesn't it?"

"You're avoiding the question," said Jenur. She turned around and said, "Rint, Quro, let's go. Whatever these two are planning is

THE RETURN OF PRINCE MALOCK

probably not good."

"What?" said Rint, looking back at Jenur in alarm. "But the motor is still broken, and even if they let us leave, we'll just be stuck in the middle of nowhere."

"Better that than getting involved in whatever these two are up to," said Jenur as she walked over to the davit, where the *Lucky* hung.

Before she could get very far, one of the automatons appeared in front of her. It literally just appeared out of nowhere, as if it had teleported there somehow. Unlike its fellow automatons, it carried a large blade and wore a thick red scarf around its neck. The automaton raised the blade and pointed it at Jenur's chest, causing Jenur to back up to avoid getting impaled.

"Leaving already?" said Hana. "You just got here. Why don't we sit down and have a good, long talk about everything that's been happening recently?"

After making sure the sword-wielding automaton wouldn't stab her, Jenur turned around and pointed at Hana. "What are you trying to do here? What's your plan?"

Hana put her arms behind her back as the smokestacks of the *Clockwork Heart* blew tons of smoke into the air. It might have just been the normal exhaust from the ship's engines, but Jenur figured that the smoke was the Mechanical Goddess's way of speaking, though what she was saying, Jenur didn't know.

"I guess there's no point in lying anymore," said Hana with a shrug. "But just to be safe ... automatons? Restrain them."

The automatons raised the spears they held and surrounded

Jenur, Quro, and Rint in an instant. Rint, as usual, cowered like a frightened monkey, while Quro reached for the dragon shark scales in his belt. Unfortunately, before he could grab them, one of the automatons launched its hands through the air, seized the scales, and retracted its hands back into its arms. The automaton in question then popped open its chest like a treasure box and dropped the scales inside there. The automaton with the sword stood just outside of the circle, but he looked more than ready to take Jenur or the others down if they tried anything.

"There we go," said Hana. "Now I don't have to worry about any of you trying to get away."

Jenur tried not to show any fear as she faced Hana, but it was difficult to do because the automatons had brought the tips of their spears close to her body. "So what are you trying to do, then? Going to feed us to some of the Mechanical Goddess's other siblings?"

"Don't be silly," said Hana. "After what happened last time, the rest of the southern gods wouldn't eat any mortals we caught even if we offered them free of charge. We have a different job for you, one we hope you will gladly accept."

"A job?" said Rint. "What kind of job?"

Hana began circling the automatons, her hands still behind her back as she said, "You may not know it, but just recently, an aquarian farmer named Skimif has been going all over the mortal world claiming that the 'Day of the Gods' is coming."

"The Day of the Gods?" said Jenur. "What's that?"

"According to him, the Day of the Gods is supposedly a day in the future when all of the gods will die," said Hana, her tone highly skeptical. "And when I say *all* of the gods, I mean all of them. Northern and southern alike."

The deck beneath their feet shuddered, but whether that was simply the normal movement of the ship or the Mechanical Goddess communicating her unease, Jenur didn't know.

"How is that possible?" said Quro. "The gods can't die. It sounds to me like this Skimif fellow is merely making stuff up."

"He probably is," said Hana, nodding as she kept walking around the circle of automatons. "But here's the thing: Mortals—humans and aquarians—are starting to believe his words. They're starting to think that he's right. He even started a new group, called the Brotherhood of Heathens, whose sole purpose is to spread the news about the coming Day and to convince as many mortals as possible to stop worshiping the gods."

"What?" said Rint. "Why would anyone ever proudly call themselves a Heathen? This Skimif guy sounds like a moron."

"Doesn't sound so bad to me," said Jenur. "I don't see any reason to worship the gods, even if they aren't actually going to die."

"Well, Jenur, you're not one of the gods, so your opinion doesn't matter," said Hana. "What does matter is that Skimif is seeing success. The Brotherhood is gaining new members every day, on almost every island and city in the Northern Isles. Now it hasn't spread to every single island yet, but the gods believe that at its current growth it will not be long before the Brotherhood's membership numbers in the hundreds of thousands."

"Again, what's so bad about that?" said Jenur. "Who cares?"

"The gods care," said Hana. "Mostly the northern ones, but even some of the southern gods are concerned about this so-called 'Day.' The northern gods don't want to lose all of their followers, but unless someone does something soon, it would appear that the Heathens will soon become the majority."

"Still don't see what this has to do with us," said Jenur, scratching the back of her head. "Sounds to me like the gods are just getting scared."

Hana stopped circling the automatons now. She was back where she started, standing opposite Jenur. "You still don't see where I'm going with this? I guess I should explain some more. You see, the two most important members of the Brotherhood are Princess Raya Kabadi, of Shika, and Prince Tojas Malock, of Carnag."

"Malock?" said Jenur. "He's a Heathen now? You're pulling my leg. He was a god worshiper through and through when I last saw him."

"Yes, well, his opinion of the gods has soured quite a bit since you saw him last," said Hana, shaking her head. "Anyway, both Raya and Malock have yet to reveal their true beliefs about the gods to the public. But the northern gods know that those two idiots are already working behind the scenes, trying to make their respective islands' governments far less hostile to the Heathens. If the Heathens seize the governments of both Shika and Carnag, they could extend their influence even farther, as Shika and Carnag do a lot of trade with other islands."

"I know what you want us to do," said Quro. "You want us to kill Prince Malock and Princess Raya."

Jenur gasped and looked at Quro as Hana said, "You are only partly correct, Quro."

"B-But I'm not an assassin," said Rint, trembling in his boots. "I'm just a normal fisherman, ma'am. I mean, sure, I hired Quro to kill Deber, but that's because I couldn't do it myself."

"Didn't you just hear what I said, old man?" said Hana. "I said Quro is only partly correct. There is still more to the job than that."

"What is it, then?" said Jenur, turning back to face Hana. "Why do the gods want us to kill Malock and Raya?"

"It's a bit complicated, but let me explain," said Hana. "You see, the Heathens are right now making claims about the northern gods. How they're unfair, how they're cruel, how they only care about themselves and no one else, how they squish all freedom of thought, and so on and so forth. You know, the usual criticism that heathens in general have lobbed at the gods over the centuries. Essentially nothing new."

Hana listed all of those criticisms like they were obviously false. Jenur disagreed, but she knew better than to open her mouth right now.

"The northern gods don't want to prove their criticism correct by openly smiting Skimif or Malock or any of the other prominent Heathens," said Hana. "Mortals love martyrs, after all. If a god like, say, Grinf were to smite Malock in public, then the other mortals would rally behind the Heathens' banner. It would make the whole situation that much more complicated for the gods."

"Let me guess," said Quro. "By having us do it, it will appear like the northern gods had nothing to do with it."

Hana smiled. "Now you're catching on. Yes, indeed. Jenur here will go to Carnag and assassinate both Malock and Raya. She will do it without being caught, of course, but shortly thereafter the assassin's identity will come to light, as well as her 'reason' for killing Malock."

"And what reason could I have for killing Malock?" said Jenur. "Yeah, he can be a pompous brat sometimes, but I would never kill him for it. He's a friend."

"Would you?" said Hana. "I guess you forgot how he nearly handed you over to Messenger-and-Punisher under the mistaken belief that you were the Tinkarian spy? If news of that betrayal got out to the general population, most people would immediately understand that you assassinated Malock because you wanted revenge."

"You're assuming I'm going through with this at all," said Jenur. "What about Quro and Rint? Aren't they going to help?"

"Three assassins are far more likely to be caught than one," said Hana, shaking her head. "Therefore, Quro and Rint will be staying here on this ship while you head to Carnag to kill Malock and Raya. They'll be kept below deck in their own personal cabins, where they will have all of their personal needs taken care of."

"You mean we'll be your prisoners," said Quro. "Right?"

"That's another word for it, I suppose," said Hana with a shrug. "But I'm in no mood to debate semantics, frankly."

"Semantics?" said Jenur. "This is more than semantics. You're blackmailing me."

"We're not blackmailing you," Hana pointed out. "After all, we technically haven't yet taken Quro and Rint prisoner yet."

"We might as well be prisoners," Rint muttered. "No way we can escape this ship, right?"

"True," said Hana. "But you are at least free to try to escape, although I don't think you will get very far to be honest."

"Is this what you came up north to do?" said Jenur, gesturing at the deck of the *Clockwork Heart* under their feet. "Hold my friends prisoner while I go and kill another friend, because the gods told you to?"

"That wasn't the exact plan," said Hana with a yawn, almost as if she was getting bored. "But yes, we did come this far north to deal with the Brotherhood. It was Grinf, actually, who asked us to do this, mostly because few outside of the Northern Pantheon know who the Mechanical Goddess is, so even if she's discovered as the culprit behind the assassinations, no one will ever link her to the northern gods."

"Why didn't you just kill Malock when you had him on board?" said Jenur. "He was practically defenseless, even with the rest of the crew protecting him."

"The Mechanical Goddess didn't know he would join the Brotherhood," Hana explained. "She's not Tinkar. She can't possibly predict every little move you mortals will make. He wasn't a threat at the time, but now he is, which means he must be eliminated for the good of the gods."

Jenur stepped forward, but was forced to step back when the automatons dug the points of their spears a little deeper into her chest. They didn't quite pierce her clothing, but Jenur could sense that it would not take much effort on the part of the automatons to stab her through.

"I knew we couldn't trust you," said Jenur. "Just knew it. Malock —"

"Will never know we are behind this," Hana finished. "Because you, Jenur, will kill him without him knowing your identity. He won't even have to know that he was killed by a friend."

"You're utterly insane," said Jenur. "What if I refuse to do it?"

Hana shrugged. "Easy. We'll kill you."

"But the southern gods can't kill mortals when they're in the north," Jenur said. "So you can't kill us."

"The Mechanical Goddess can't hurt you, that's true," said Hana. "But I'm a katabans, not a goddess, and these automatons certainly aren't deities either. So we're exempt from that particular clause in the Treaty."

"Loopholes," said Quro. "I don't even know what this 'Treaty' is, but I do know a loophole when I hear one."

"So you only have two options now, Jenur Takren," said Hana. "Either you agree to the offer and assassinate Malock and Raya, or you die."

"What happens if I accept this offer?" said Jenur.

"If you accept and succeed, then we'll let you and your friends go," said Hana. "If you fail ... well, if you fail, then that means you're probably going to die. Or at least be captured by the Brotherhood and in all likelihood tortured for your attempted assassination."

Jenur gulped. "The Brotherhood can't be that bad. I mean, Malock is a member of it."

"I was just laying out possible consequences of your failure," said Hana, again shrugging. "All I know is that, if I were you, I'd accept this offer. It's the only way you and your friends could possibly get out of this alive."

Biting her lower lip, Jenur thought hard about the offer. She didn't want to take it. She wasn't going to be the hand of the gods, striking down mortals who were too arrogant to bow down to them. She was an independent human being. Her first instinct was to tell Hana to jump off the ship, regardless of the consequences of saying that.

Yet, when Jenur looked at Quro and Rint, she hesitated. Quro remained cool and impassive, as though he was confident Jenur would make the right decision. Rint, on the other hand, looked close to collapsing. His knees shook and he was grabbing at his beard nervously. His resemblance to Kinker was uncanny and for a moment Jenur had a vision of Rint's corpse lying on the deck of the *Clockwork Heart* along with Quro's and hers.

Then Jenur sighed, prayed a silent curse to all of the gods, and said to Hana, "All right. Fine. You win. I'll assassinate Malock and Raya. Just as you ordered."

Hana put her hands together, her smile widening. "I knew you weren't an idiot. But of course, we're going to need to make sure you do what you're supposed to do."

Hana snapped her fingers and the automaton with the sword sheathed its weapon. It then pushed past its fellow automatons until it came up to Jenur. Jenur turned to face it. Its expression was cold and unreadable, which made Jenur wish, once again, that her knife hadn't been taken away from her.

"I call this machine Calir," said Hana. "As you can tell, he's a bit different from his siblings. He's the first in a new line of automatons that the Mechanical Goddess is creating, automatons who are much stronger and faster than the current models."

"Is that all he can do?" said Jenur, taking a step back from Calir.

"Nope," said Hana. "He can do a lot more than that. Calir?"

The automaton grabbed Jenur's right arm and forced her sleeve above her elbow. Calir moved its heavy hand down onto her elbow, its cold grip tightening as Jenur tried to break free, but it was no use. Then Jenur felt a sharp pain shoot up her arm, starting from where Calir had grabbed her elbow and making its way up to her shoulder. Then Calir let go, causing Jenur to look down at her elbow. A small red dot of blood stood out against her pale skin, while the spot itself burned with pain the longer she looked at it.

"There you go," said Hana. "All better."

Jenur whirled around and showed the dot to Hana. "What the heck is this? What did Calir do to me?"

"He injected you with a tracker," said Hana. "This way, the Mechanical Goddess will know where you are and what you are doing at all times."

Jenur looked down at her arm in horror. "But ... how does that ..."

"Don't worry," said Hana. "It won't last forever. Once you complete your job, the tracker will deactivate and eventually leave your system through your back end."

"This is insane," Rint said. "She's just a young girl, not older than eighteen, and yet you're asking her to assassinate a prince and a princess, knowing that she could fail?"

Rint's words of concern actually shocked Jenur, but Hana, apparently, wasn't surprised. She just yawned and said, "This 'young girl,' as you call her, has a history as a professional assassin working for the most well-known assassins' guild in the entire Northern Isles. She's probably killed people of far higher rank than Malock or Raya. Nice try for sympathy points, though."

"T-This is still wrong," said Rint. He was speaking fast now, as if afraid that he might not get his words out if he didn't. "Despicable. If the gods truly want Malock and Raya dead, why not do it themselves? It is cowardly to act through someone else."

Hana stroked her pointed chin. "Now I don't have all the facts, but unless I'm wrong, didn't you hire this aquarian here to assassinate your enemies? Doesn't your criticizing the northern gods for doing the exact same thing as you make you, you know, a huge hypocrite?"

"At least I didn't threaten to kill Quro's friends if he didn't do what I wanted," said Rint. "I don't know very much about this Treaty and southern gods and stuff—in fact, I have a feeling I am missing out on quite a bit—but I do know scum when I see them.

And your 'Mechanical Goddess' is nothing but."

Those stinging words made Jenur actually feel some measure of respect for the old man. Even Hana was staring at him like she had not expected him to speak so forthrightly. The ship shuddered beneath their feet, almost as if the Mechanical Goddess had said something.

"I agree with Rint," said Quro. "I've never been a fan of the gods, but this is low even for them. It's even worse for me because Jenur is my daughter. I won't stand by as my daughter is forced to kill one of her friends."

Quro stepped forward, but before he could do anything, Calir seemingly slid across the deck toward him. The automaton smashed its fist into the back of Quro's head, causing him to fall face first onto the deck. He landed hard on the deck, his crash echoing loudly into the air. He didn't get up.

"Dad!" said Jenur, but she couldn't go to check on him because of the automatons surrounding her. "No!"

"Thank you, Calir," said Hana, smiling at the automaton. "Hopefully that taught him a lesson."

Jenur's hands balled into fists as she said, "You monster."

Hana gave a short chuckle. "Me, a monster? It was Calir who knocked out your 'father.' But he'll live, don't worry. Unlike a certain someone I know, I don't kill my enemies' family members for no reason."

Jenur looked at Hana, not sure what she meant. "What?"

Hana stared at Jenur with an emotion Jenur had never seen in the katabans's eyes before: Hate. "I still remember how you killed Bet, Jenur, but I guess I can't ask a professional assassin to remember the name of every person she's ever killed, now can I?"

Before Jenur could respond to that, Hana snapped at the automatons, "Take the prisoners below deck. Lock them up in separate rooms. Also, check their bodies and clothes very thoroughly. I don't want either of them even to think of escaping."

The automatons obeyed Hana's orders without question. Four of them picked up Quro and carried him away, while another four herded Rint after them. Calir stood by with the remaining four automatons, blocking Jenur's way, making it impossible for Jenur to rescue her friends. Not that she even planned to try. She knew she wouldn't live longer than a minute, if that, if she tried to save them.

"All right, then," said Hana, putting her hands together. "Let's talk about what you'll need to pull this off, Jenur, as well as how we're going to get you to Carnag without anyone seeing you. Don't you worry; we've already got a few ideas in place."

Chapter Fourteen

Three weeks later ...

BEFORE THE SUN ROSE over the horizon; indeed, before its rays even began to creep over the rooftops of the buildings of Port Blasan, Malock awoke, tossed off the covers of his bed, walked over to his closet, picked out his usual ratty street outfit, and in another minute or two was out on the streets again, keeping his head down, doing his best not to draw attention to himself.

As he walked, Malock looked around at his surroundings. The city had drastically changed over the past few weeks, and even now, he found it hard to get used to them. The streets were so clean they practically sparkled, many of the buildings had received fresh coats of paint, and no homeless people lay in stoops or doorways of nearby buildings. A Justice Enforcer passed by Malock and the Prince couldn't help but notice that the officer's uniform—dark red leather jacket, with short boots designed to allow for swift movement, and the Hammer of Grinf stitched into the chest and back—was freshly cleaned and pressed. That was no surprise. Over the past few weeks,

King Halock had ordered all Justice Enforcers to wear immaculately clean clothes at all times in order to make themselves look better for the wedding. The Justice Enforcers, from what Malock had gathered, were not fans of this decision, but they nonetheless obeyed their King's demands.

As Malock turned a corner into an abandoned street, moving away from the nicer sections of the city, he thought about how much Port Blasan had changed over the past three weeks. Because his wedding with Raya was to take place on Carnag, Malock's parents had made it their life mission to make Port Blasan look more fabulous than ever. This was mostly to impress the visiting Shikan nobles, who no doubt would be looking for reasons to criticize the Carnagians. Frankly, Malock could care less how the city looked, if only because he knew that it would never be quite as beautiful or clean as the Throne of the Gods. He could care even less about what the Shikan nobles did or didn't think of it.

Just then, a young woman joined him as he walked. When he looked at her, he saw that she wore a tattered gray dress frayed at the hem, with ugly plain sleeves that looked tight around her arms. She didn't wear a hood like he did, but her blonde hair was so messy and hung so low over her face that it might as well have been one. From what little he could see of her face, it was filthy, covered in a thick layer of grime that almost looked like a mask.

"Mask," said Malock, returning his gaze to the streets. "Good morning. How did you sleep?"

The young woman simply said, in a voice that was shriller than her usual voice, "Oh, I slept so-so. I only got about four hours of sleep, though, because of the wedding preparations."

Malock grimaced. "I only got three and a half, if even that much. That wedding organizer is a pain, isn't he?"

Mask nodded. "I will never understand how he keeps coming up with new questions. 'What color do you want the carpeting to be?' 'Do you want the flowers slightly tilted to the right or to the left?' 'Do you want the Priest to introduce you as Princess Raya Kabadi, Princess of Shika, or Princess Raya Kabadi, daughter of King Fabadi?'"

Malock shook his head as they turned a corner together. "He asked you those questions, too? I sometimes wonder if that man ever sleeps."

"Probably doesn't," Mask—who was Raya—said. "The only reason he doesn't keep us awake twenty-four seven is because he knows you can't have a royal wedding with a sleep-deprived couple. Otherwise, there's no telling what he would try to get away with."

"True, true," said Malock. He looked around the street and said, "Let's continue this conversation later. I don't trust that these streets lack ears."

"Fine by me," said Raya. "Don't want to be late for our meeting with Skimif, now do we?"

As the pair walked, Malock reflected on how close he and Raya had gotten over the last few weeks. Ever since he learned that she was also a member of the Brotherhood, he had found her far more interesting than he originally had. He still didn't quite love her the way he loved Vashnas, but he no longer thought of her as the stuck-up intellectual downer he originally had.

Actually confirming that she was a member of the Brotherhood had been difficult, at first, because the two had not been afforded much privacy together after their discussion in the Garden. It was thanks to the Brotherhood itself staging a protest just outside Carnag Hall—which Malock had been anticipating—that Malock had been able to talk to her alone long enough to find out for sure.

After that, Malock taught Raya how to navigate the servants' passageways so she could sneak out of Carnag Hall with him. And once she got the hang of it, she became even better at it than him. She even discovered a new way out of Carnag Hall that he had never even known about. The two of them had been sneaking out of Carnag Hall every few days ever since, though always separately, just so they would not be easily caught or seen.

Frankly, Malock was glad for this. The wedding preparations were going at hyper speed, or so it seemed to him. The wedding organizer—a Carnagian man named Rire Kitan—seemed determined to make sure that neither Malock nor Raya ever had any alone time. In spite of the fact that Malock and Raya's marriage was political rather than romantic, their opinions on how the marriage should be done were still wanted (sometimes to an annoyingly meticulous degree, as they had discussed just a few seconds ago).

But that wasn't the full reason that he and Raya sneaked out of the palace as often as they could. Due to their concern over the future of the Brotherhood, Malock and Raya tried to visit Skimif and the rest of the Heathens as often and discreetly as they could, usually in the same building where Malock had first joined the Brotherhood itself. Despite their concern, the two had taken little concrete action to further the Brotherhood's cause.

It wasn't that Malock and Raya didn't care about their fellow Heathens. It was just that they had been so busy with the wedding preparations that they had had no time to help. That they had still not gone public with their Brotherhood membership had also restricted their ability to help, though Malock knew that one of these days they would have to. With the rapid growth and influence of the movement, circumstances might soon force them to do it even if they weren't ready.

Soon, the duo arrived at the front door to the building that acted as the Brotherhood's Carnagian headquarters/hideout. After checking the street to make sure that no one was watching them, Malock knocked on the door three times. A moment later, the door cracked open and he saw the familiar green eyes of Aqur looking out at him.

"Who's there?" said Aqur in a drowsy voice, like she had just gotten up.

"Hood and Mask," said Malock. "We're here to see Skimif."

Aqur yawned. "All right, all right, hold your horses, I'll undo the latches."

The door slammed shut, followed by the sounds of locks being undone, and then the door opened again, this time more widely. Aqur stood in the doorway, looking down at Malock and Raya with sleepy eyes.

"Come in," said Aqur, stepping aside and gesturing at the doorway. "Quickly. Before anyone sees you."

"No one's around, Aqur," said Raya as Malock and she stepped beyond the doorway. "We checked."

Aqur snorted as she closed the door behind them and redid all the locks. "Last time you said that was back on Shika. Only reason we didn't get caught was because the idiot who saw you didn't know the first thing about stealth."

Malock tossed Raya a curious look. "You mean they've already been to Shika?"

Raya looked away. "Oh, Aqur and Skimif visited me once. It was when the Brotherhood was still new. I heard about them from an aquarian friend of mine, who managed to arrange a meeting between us when I expressed interest. We met in a rundown bar, but I was almost found out because this pickpocket had followed me because I looked like I had a lot of money on me."

"No surprise there," said Aqur with a grunt. "You're the Princess of Shika. I'm surprised you don't go to sleep in lace made of gold."

Raya shrugged, like she didn't know how to respond to that.

"Is that when you first joined the Brotherhood?" said Malock.

"Yes," said Raya. "But let's not waste time talking about things that have already passed. We wanted to talk to Skimif, didn't we?"

"He's in the basement," said Aqur, pointing at the end of the hall. "He's awake. Been up all night."

"Why?" said Raya.

"Don't know," said Aqur, shaking her jellyfish head. "He hasn't come out of his room and doesn't want anyone in. He did say that he wanted to talk to you two if you ever showed up, though."

"Is he having another vision from the Powers?" said Malock.

"I don't know," said Aqur. "He's acting stranger than usual. I'd be careful, though, because he's got Pointy with him and—"

"Pointy?" said Raya. "Who's Pointy?"

"His sword," said Aqur with disgust. "He got the sword off a weapons merchant from Nikos a day ago and gave it that name because ... well, I probably shouldn't say this, seeing as I'm a Heathen and all, but only the gods know why."

Malock frowned. "Skimif *has* seemed more on edge recently. Last time I talked to him, he was really distracted. I wonder what's up."

"Go and ask him yourself," said Aqur. "Me, I'm going back to bed. Didn't get a lot of sleep last night because Skimif was up all night making a lot of noise. Mostly throwing stuff around, but he screamed a couple of times, too."

Malock and Raya exchanged concerned looks. Throwing stuff around? Screaming? Not allowing anyone else to see him? Skimif had always been a little strange, but this behavior sounded out there even for him. Malock wasn't sure that he wanted to see the ex-farmer anymore.

Nonetheless, he followed Raya down the hall, albeit reluctantly. They passed the living room on their way to the basement and a quick glance into it showed Malock that all of the Heathens who stayed here were sleeping in there, mostly on the floor or couch. None of them even stirred as Malock and Raya walked past, which was good because Malock was in no mood to talk to any of them right now, not when he was curious about Skimif's current condition.

Raya reached the door at the end of the hallway first. She put her ear to it, listening with a frown on her face, and then looked over her shoulder at Malock, who had folded his arms across his chest more because he needed something to do with them than out of impatience.

"Don't hear anything," Raya said. "He might be—"

A loud *thump* from the other side of the door caused Malock and Raya to jump. Then everything went quiet again.

"One of us should knock," said Malock. "You know, so Skimif can know we're here."

Raya stepped back, away from the door, and said, "You do it."

"Me?" said Malock. "Why me?"

"Because you suggested it," said Raya. "Didn't your parents ever teach you that the person who suggests a plan has to be the one to put it into action?"

"No," said Malock. "Is that what your dad taught you?"

"Yes," said Raya. "Besides, what's the worst that could happen? Skimif's a friend. He'd never harm you, even if he is undergoing some trouble right now."

This time, the sound of glass breaking and someone's muffled swearing made Malock start.

"Probably just dropped a plate or bowl," said Raya. "Knock."

Malock bit his lower lip, but as he didn't think he could get Raya to do it, he walked up to the door and knocked on it once. A loud voice on the other side shrieked, "Who's there?"

The shrieking voice caused Malock to jump back a good three or four feet, his heart hammering, but Raya—apparently unaffected— said to the door, "It's us, Malock and Raya. Remember?"

"Malock and Raya?" said Skimif's voice on the other side. "Oh, thank the Powers. Please hold on a minute while I tidy up things in here."

A moment later, Malock heard what sounded like Skimif kicking something under his bed, followed by a few choice curse words, possibly due to injuring himself. Another moment, and the door opened. Skimif stood in the doorway, but he looked terrible. Heavy bags hung under his eyes, which looked weird on his hammerhead shark head. He wore a simple white sleeveless shirt, with brown leather pants that looked like they hadn't been washed in weeks. He was completely barefoot, despite the cold wood under his feet. He smelled like fish that had been left out in the sun too long; in fact, his skin looked drier than it normally was, like he hadn't taken a shower or gone swimming in a while.

Nonetheless, Skimif managed to smile when he saw Malock and Raya. "Malock, Raya, so good to see you. Please come in."

Skimif turned and walked down the staircase to the basement. Once again, Malock and Raya exchanged concerned looks before following him down. Then Skimif stopped halfway down and said, in a far harsher voice than before, "Close the door."

"What?" said Malock, glancing over his shoulder at the door. "Why—"

"Just do it," Skimif said. The steps shook under them when he hissed, which sent all kinds of alarms off in Malock's mind.

Raya immediately closed the door, and for good measure, she locked it, too. Skimif breathed a sigh of relief when she did so.

"Thank you, Raya," said Skimif. He still hadn't turned to face them. "I just don't want to bother my brother and sister Heathens, who all had a very long day yesterday at the Temple of Grinf protest. You two heard about it, right?"

"Of course," said Malock. "Were twenty Heathens really arrested by the Justice ... Enforcers ..."

Skimif had begun walking down the stairs again without even waiting to hear what Malock had to say. When Skimif reached the bottom step, he must not have been paying attention to where he was going because he almost tripped and fell on his face.

"Would you two hurry it up?" said Skimif, again not looking at them. "Don't just stand there on the stairs looking like idiots."

His harsh tone shocked Malock greatly, but he and Raya nonetheless obeyed, making their way down the creaky wooden steps as rapidly as they could. It was more difficult than it normally might have been because the staircase didn't have any light to illuminate the way. They reached the bottom without tripping or falling, however, so it was all good.

Skimif's room was dark, so dark in fact that Malock couldn't see anything, though he could smell Skimif's body odor emanating from everywhere. He put a hand over his nose as he heard Skimif search for something. Then he heard a match being lit and not a moment later a small lamp shone, which Skimif hung from a steel chain on the ceiling.

Malock had to stifle a gasp when he saw Skimif's room. The basic layout remained the same; a cot in the northeast corner, a dresser in the other, with a mirror on top and a bowl of water for washing his face and arms. Yet many other things had changed, such as the pile of clothes haphazardly tossed in the northwest corner, the shattered shards of the mirror lying on the floor in front of the dresser, and a sword—a Nikon double-blade by the look of it—sticking hilt first out of the floor.

But the most shocking difference was along the walls. Written in what appeared to be blue paint were words; hundreds of thousands of words, going from the south end of the room to the north. They were written in an extremely small hand, far smaller than Malock could read, but they were nonetheless legible. And unless his eyes were playing tricks on him, the words formed images, including an image of what looked like the island of Carnag from a bird's eye view. He even thought one of them was the Throne of the Gods, though he couldn't be sure about that one.

"Skimif," said Raya, her voice slightly trembling. "What *is* all of this?"

Skimif sighed and turned around. Now that Malock got a closer look at him, he noticed that the Heathen leader had blue paint stains on his hands, like he had been writing with his fingers. A long frown ran from one corner of his mouth to the other and he looked close to collapsing.

"The Powers," said Skimif. "The Powers contacted me again last night, after I bought Pointy from that Nikon merchant."

Skimif pointed at the Nikon double-blade sticking out of the ground as if it were important that Malock and Raya know what he was talking about.

"Again?" said Raya. "Is this the second time they've contacted you?"

Looking close to tears, Skimif nodded. "Yes, yes it is. I was just sitting in here admiring Pointy when more images flooded my mind. Couldn't even grasp half of them, but I started writing anyway. Had to send Aqur out to buy a few buckets of blue paint. It's my favorite color, you know, and is easier to read against the red brick here."

Skimif's rambling concerned Malock, prompting him to say, "You look tired, Skim. Maybe you should go back to bed. We can come by some other time. We really ought to be back in Carnag Hall, anyway, because Rire is probably—"

Skimif jerked forward. "No! I mean, please stay. It's just been me and these words down here and I can't trust any of the other Heathens to see this. I don't want to destroy their trust in me."

"You think they'll abandon the Brotherhood if they find out you wrote a lot of words?" said Raya.

"No one wants to follow a crazy person," said Skimif. "Especially if they found out what all of this means." He looked at the writing all around him and muttered, "Why, Powers, why?"

"Well, what *does* it all mean, then?" said Malock. "You can trust us, Skim. We won't tell anyone if you don't want us to. We're good at keeping secrets, Raya and I are."

Skimif walked over to his cot and sank down onto the sagging mattress. He put his arms on his knees and stared at the floor. This was by far the most defeated Malock had ever seen Skimif, made even more disturbing by the flickering light of the lamp and strange writing on the walls. The light cast a shadow over Skimif's face like a hood.

"You know what I said earlier?" said Skimif, without looking up at them. "About only understanding half of what the Powers showed me?"

"Yes," said Malock. He stepped forward. "And?"

"I understand enough to know what's coming," said Skimif. "It's sickening, but I can't see any way out of it. You can't fight fate, after all."

"You still haven't explained what you're talking about," said Raya, a tinge of impatience coloring her voice. "Just tell us already."

Skimif's shoulders slumped. "I don't think you want to know."

"I already said you can trust us," said Malock. He was now starting to understand Raya's own impatience. "We're your friends."

With a sigh, Skimif gestured at the writing on the walls. "I wrote down everything I saw. A great cloud of destruction ... gigantic monsters flying in from the Void ... by the Powers, I can't even understand it ..."

"You're babbling," said Malock. "None of it makes sense. What great cloud of destruction? What gigantic monsters flying in from the Void?"

"It all adds up," said Skimif. He looked up at them, his face partially revealed by the light. "Don't you see? When you put it all together, it's obvious."

"No, Skim, it's not," said Raya. "At least to us. You obviously know more than we do. Mind telling us about it?"

Skimif hesitated, then pointed at the ceiling with one finger. "Look above you and tell me what you see."

Frowning, Malock and Raya looked up at the ceiling. At first, it looked like a bunch of random thick blue lines streaking in random directions, but the closer Malock looked, the more he realized that he was seeing large letters—indeed, whole words—painted on the ceiling. He had to step back a couple of times to take it all in and when he did, he wished he hadn't.

Written on the ceiling was a simple sentence: *THE END IS COMING.*

"The ending is coming?" said Raya, returning her gaze to Skimif's face. "What does that—"

"Don't you get it?" said Skimif, throwing up his arms in anger. "The end is coming! You know what the end is, right?"

"Yes," said Malock, nodding. "I think I do."

"Then what does it mean?" said Raya, glancing between Malock and Skimif. She seemed annoyed that she had yet to figure it out on her own.

"It's very simple, Raya," said Malock. "It means that the end of the world is near."

Raya gasped. "The end of the world? No way. That can't be true."

"It is," said Skimif. "I must have misinterpreted their original message. The Powers weren't just going to destroy the gods; they are going to destroy the entire world of Martir. They will kill us all."

"But why would they ever do that?" said Raya. "It makes no sense. They created the world, didn't they? Why would they ever want to destroy their own creation?"

"How am I supposed to know?" said Skimif, burying his face in his hands. "I'm just the messenger. All I know is that everything is at an end and that all is hopeless."

Malock ran a hand through his messy hair, trying his best not to panic. "Are you sure you understood the message right, Skim? I mean, what if you misunderstood it?"

"I don't think so," said Skimif. "Not this time. I wish to the Powers and beyond that I had, but this time I am very confident that I got it right. It was much clearer than the last one; in fact, I think it might have been a correction to the last vision."

"We need to tell everyone," said Raya. "Not just the Heathens, but the whole world."

Skimif stood up again and looked at Raya with wide, frightened eyes. "No way. The Brotherhood will become discouraged, maybe even fall apart entirely. As for everyone else, no one will believe us. Not even the gods will listen, I'm sure."

"I don't understand," said Malock. "Why did the Powers send you this message? Are they trying to prepare us for the end? Are they trying to scare us"

"I don't know," said Skimif again. "I don't know, I don't know, I don't know. Maybe they just want us to know what they are planning because they don't want us to die confused."

Raya was sweating profusely now, wiping the sweat out of her eyes as she said, "This can't be happening. We have to stop it somehow."

Skimif looked at Raya mournfully. "And how do you intend to do that? The Powers are stronger than the gods themselves. If they say they are going to destroy the world, then they will destroy the world. Might as well give up and wait for death to come."

"That's pessimistic," said Raya.

"It's the end of the world," said Skimif. "What else could it be?"

Raya tapped her chin. "I think I know what I should do. Did I ever tell either of you about how I caught Nimiko, the God of Light?"

Malock looked at her with all of the disbelief he could muster, while Skimif nodded and said, "Yes."

"Well, he's currently in Castle Shika," said Raya. "I don't think he's going to escape, but I've been thinking about him quite a—"

"When did you capture a *god*?" Malock interrupted. "Seriously, you never even mentioned that to me before. How long have you had him?"

"A couple of months now," said Raya, sounding annoyed by Malock's interruption. "It was actually Skimif who gave me the information I needed to capture Nimiko."

"That is true," said Skimif. "I learned the information from the vision the Powers gave me, as well as some research I did on my own into heathen studies. Other heathens have been gathering this sort of knowledge for centuries, though it was hard to find at first because other heathens tended to be secretive about their work to avoid having it destroyed by their enemies."

Malock shook his head, less out of disbelief and more out of shock. Privately, he wondered what other major secrets Raya and Skimif had been keeping from him. If they could hide a god from him, then he had no doubt they could hide something equally big if they had to.

"But why did you capture Nimiko?" said Malock to Raya. "What drove you to even try that?"

"The gods themselves," said Raya matter-of-factly. "I felt threatened by them. I felt that capturing one of them would be a good way to defend my people from them, should the gods ever turn on us."

"How did you even do that?" said Malock. "I've had quite a few firsthand encounters with the gods and let me tell you that they aren't a bunch of easily fooled pale deer you can capture with bait and a box."

"It was simple, really," said Raya. "Nimiko has always been closer to us Shikans than the other gods have been to their subjects. I simply requested a meeting with Nimiko and when he arrived, I fooled him into placing Void metal chains around his wrists and ankles. He's not nearly as clever as some gods, so it was easy to trick him."

"Void metal?" said Malock. "Isn't that supposed to be a legend?"

"It's very real," said Raya. "Rare—the rarest type of metal in all of

Martir—but real. There's no doubt about it."

"How come the other gods haven't noticed yet?" said Malock. "Surely they would notice if one of their own went missing."

Raya looked down at her feet just then, as if trying to avoid Malock's gaze. "I know how risky it is to keep him, but you know how the gods are, Tojas. All they ever care about is themselves. They probably either don't know about Nimiko's kidnapping or think he can take care of himself. Either way, I think I'm safe for now."

"None of us are safe," said Skimif in the most miserable voice Malock had ever heard. "The world will end no matter what we do. Every man, woman, and child on this planet—human, aquarian, and god alike—will die."

"Surely there must be something we can do," said Malock. "Raya, you said you knew what to do. Something about Nimiko, right?"

"I think so," said Raya. She hesitated. "It's a risky plan, the one that just came to mind. Not even sure it will work, to be honest. Could easily result in our deaths."

"And?" said Malock. "What is it?"

Raya began playing with the free strands of her hair. "So the Powers haven't yet come to destroy the world, yes? What if I had Nimiko take me to the Void so I could find the Powers and convince them to not destroy Martir?"

"Impossible," said Skimif. "Ridiculous. Won't work. All of the legends say that mortals cannot exist in the Void. Even if you could get Nimiko to do that, the Void itself would destroy you before you could get very far."

"Do you have a better plan?" said Malock, before Raya could defend herself. "Listen, Skimif, when I went to the southern seas, nearly every single legend I had heard about that part of the world turned out to be a complete lie. What if the Void is not lethal to mortals? What if that's just a myth the gods came up with to keep us from going beyond its boundaries to whatever lies out there?"

Skimif sank down onto his bed again. "It's still a foolish idea. The Powers are above and beyond anything any of us have ever seen. How could a mortal even communicate with them, much less convince them to spare the world?"

"You still haven't offered any helpful alternatives," Malock said. "Except, apparently, sitting down and whining about how pointless it all is."

"I know it might not work," said Raya. "But Malock has a point. We don't have any other alternatives. I have to try it, if only to save my own people."

"Very well," said Skimif. "But what about the wedding? It's today. When will you find the time to even try such a thing?"

"That's the only valid point you've made so far," said Raya. "I'll do it first thing after the wedding. I will probably go back to Shika to get some things, and while there I will make Nimiko take me to the Void."

"I want to come with you," said Malock. "I want to save Martir as much as you."

"No," said Raya, shaking her head. "You should stay here. It would look strange if both of us disappeared, don't you think?"

"I think either of you disappearing would cause a huge political problem that would erode the already fragile relations between Carnag and Shika," Skimif said. "Will you tell your father that you're leaving? I heard he's very protective of you, Raya."

Raya scowled. "Father wouldn't understand because he doesn't know about this or about Nimiko or anything. I'll just have to leave without explaining things to him. If I succeed, he'll understand eventually; if I don't, it doesn't matter because we're all gonna die anyway, right?"

"She has a point," said Malock. "Besides, I could probably come up with a good excuse for her disappearance if I had to."

"Could you?" said Skimif, eying them both skeptically. "I'm sorry if I sound pessimistic, but I just don't think either of you comprehend how serious this situation is."

"We get it, Skim," said Raya. "Yeah, maybe we're not as old as you, but that doesn't make us any less intelligent. It's our only chance."

Skimif snorted. "You haven't experienced what it's like to be consumed by the Powers. They do not communicate the way we do, or even the way the gods do. I just think it's a fool's errand."

"This is getting us nowhere," said Raya. "Skim, you don't have to support us if you don't want to. But we don't need your support or approval to save the world."

"What am I supposed to do, then?" said Skimif. "Sit here and wait while you go and save the world?"

"No," said Malock, shaking his head. "You continue leading the

Brotherhood as if nothing has changed. Keep spreading the message about the Day of the Gods. Even if the world is about to end, that doesn't mean we can or should let the gods continue to be worshiped like they deserve it."

"There's no way I can hide this knowledge forever, though," said Skimif. "Sooner or later the others will find out. And when they find out, there's nothing to stop the entire movement—indeed, the entire world—from falling apart."

He spoke so dejectedly that even Malock was starting to believe his words. Thankfully Raya folded her arms and said, "Then be strong, Skim. Pretend if you have to. At least pretend long enough for me to try to convince the Powers that they shouldn't kill us all."

Skimif sighed. "All right. I guess I'll just have to put on my confident face again, like I do whenever I have to give a speech."

"There you go," said Raya. "I know it will be hard, but you have to try. We've come too far for the movement to fall now. And until we know for sure that there's no hope, we have no excuse for falling into despair."

"She's right," said Malock, nodding. He then remembered something and started. "What time is it?"

Skimif shrugged. "I don't know. Why?"

"We have to head back to Carnag Hall," said Malock. "Before the servants come to wake us. If they find us missing from our beds on the day of the wedding ... by the Powers, I don't even want to think about what our parents will do."

"Right," said Raya. "We should leave now. Then tomorrow, I

will start the journey to the Void."

Skimif looked around his room as if this was the last time he would ever see it. "I wish I had a wedding gift to give to you two, but alas, I have nothing. Unless you want Pointy?"

He gestured at the sword sticking out of the floor. "I don't know how Pointy got there. I think I must have stabbed him into the floor while I had that vision. Don't remember."

"No, it's all right," said Malock, holding up his hands. "You don't need to get us anything. Just keep doing what you're doing. That will be gift enough."

"Very well," said Skimif. "Good bye, then. I hope that your wedding is happy and that your journey to the Void is successful. For all of us."

Malock and Raya nodded and then turned and climbed back up the stairs to the main hallway. When they got to the door, Raya found some extra keys hanging on the side wall, which she used to unlock the door. As she did so, Malock looked over his shoulder. Skimif stood at the bottom of the stairs, looking up at both of them, the lamp in his hand. The lamp died out at the same time Raya opened the door, making Malock feel uneasier than ever.

I hope that Skimif is wrong, Malock thought as he and Raya passed through the doorway. *But something tells me that he is not.*

Chapter Fifteen

Jenur tried not to look at her own body as she jumped from rooftop to rooftop, heading directly for Carnag Hall, where the wedding between Malock and Raya was soon to take place. That was because her body was completely invisible and, despite her weeks of practice, she knew she would freak out if she so much as glanced down and saw nothing where her body normally was. She had discovered that a couple weeks back when Hana had first given her the invisibility clothes that cloaked her body, clothes which had apparently belonged to Hana at one point. Jenur had been given the clothes to help her sneak around Port Blasan more effectively, and so far it had worked, as not one soul had seen her even once during the entire week that she had spent in the city.

But Jenur wished that someone had seen her. Wished that one of those Justice Enforcers had seen her. She wished that someone would stop her, but her instincts from her years of practice as a Dark Tiger kicked in every time she thought about bringing attention to herself and she didn't. And more than once over the past week, she had had to remind herself that the Quro and Rint's lives were on the line, which was always effective in stopping her from turning herself over to the Enforcers.

Because no one had stopped her, Jenur had spent the past week studying all of the security precautions put into place to make sure the wedding went off without a hitch. It was a long list. Justice Enforcers and Sun Guardians—the Shikan equivalent of the Justice Enforcers, though they weren't quite as ruthless as the Enforcers from what she had seen—were stationed in practically every corner of the city. Two whole squadrons of Enforcers and Guardians defended Carnag Hall itself, while dozens of others stood in place all along the parade route that Malock and Raya would take as per the traditional Carnagian marriage norms. Additionally, the Protection around Carnag Hall had been strengthened to the point where it was now visible even when no one was trying to break it down. In fact, Jenur could see the Protection now even from her current position, the sun shining off its crystalline surface, making it look like a giant crystal dome built around Carnag Hall.

Not only that, but it was nearly impossible to arrive on or depart from Carnag unseen today. More Justice Enforcers and Sun Guardians patrolled the ports, inspecting the crew and cargo of every ship that came in, even if it was a Carnagian ship. The only reason Jenur had managed to get to Carnag without being caught was because of her stealth outfit, but she knew that the constant, twenty-four hours a day monitoring of the ports meant that escaping Port Blasan would be difficult, if not impossible, once she performed the evil deed.

Just like on Destan, Jenur thought as she landed heavily on a rooftop and staggered before recovering and taking off again. *Except this time, there's a good chance I may not even get halfway to the docks before I'm captured.*

Of course, that was just self-effacement on Jenur's part. She figured she probably could escape before any of the Enforcers or Guardians found her. While the Enforcers and Guardians were highly efficient at capturing most criminals, they had never captured a Dark Tiger before, not even once. In fact, Jenur remembered Quro telling her a story once about how he easily evaded capture from the Justice Enforcers after completing an assignment on Carnag one time. He had tricked a bunch of Enforcers into arresting an aquarian who looked like him, but by the time the Enforcers realized their mistake, Quro was miles from Carnag on his way home to Ruwa.

The largest obstacle facing Jenur was the Protection itself. It was supposedly unbreakable by normal means. Even most magic could not pierce it. From what she gathered, the only beings who could destroy it were the teichomancers who built it, and all of them were on the inside of Carnag Hall for the wedding.

Of course, the Mechanical Goddess must have realized that, Jenur thought as she drew closer and closer to Carnag Hall. *Probably why she gave me this thing.*

Jenur felt her pocket as she jumped from rooftop to rooftop. Prior to leaving the *Clockwork Heart,* Jenur had been given a glass box that Hana said would be useful if Jenur ever found herself needed to get past a magical obstacle. Hana had not said any more about it after that, but Jenur assumed the box would somehow help her sneak through the Protection.

After a few more minutes of rooftop jumping, Jenur finally reached a building just outside the Protection, near the south end of Carnag Hall. It was a tall stone apartment complex, but thankfully the rooftop was empty when she got there. She did a quick check of the area to make sure there were no Justice Enforcers or Sun Guardians, and then climbed down the building's fire escape to reach the streets below.

Just as her feet touched the pavement, she heard multiple people walking in her direction. Startled, Jenur sidled against the wall as a dozen Justice Enforcers—plus a handful of Sun Guardians—walked past the fire escape. It was only after they passed that Jenur realized she didn't actually need to cling to the wall, as being invisible meant that the Enforcers and Guardians couldn't see her even if she had been standing right next to them. She supposed it was just her reflexes at work.

After checking the streets again, just to be sure there was no one nearby, Jenur walked across the street up to the Protection itself. The massive magical barrier was even more dazzling up front, but Jenur didn't let it overwhelm her. She patted her pockets, found the crystal box, and pulled it out of her pocket.

Remembering how Hana had told her how to use it, Jenur shoved the box against the Protection's surface. She didn't know what to expect, so she was a bit surprised—though pleased—when the box expanded until it was about her size and width. Then the box's interior dissipated, forming a doorway of sorts in the Protection itself.

She hesitated for a moment before stepping through it. As soon as she did, the box retracted back into its smaller form, which she grabbed and stuffed into her pockets to keep it safe for later. She would need it after she did what she was supposed to do.

Despite being invisible, Jenur still walked bent over to the outer walls of the Hall. The walls were made of a smooth white stone that she couldn't identify. There were no handholds or footholds in the walls, but that didn't bother her. She dug through her pack for a climbing rope, found it, and hurled it at the top of the wall. The hook flew over the top of the wall and landed with a *clunk* on the other side. She tugged on the rope twice to make sure it would hold, and when she was satisfied that it would, she began to climb up the wall.

Finally, she reached the top of the wall and crouched low to take in her surroundings. Spread out before her was the famed Royal Garden of Carnag Hall, with a dazzling variety of plants and trees in an even more dazzling variety of colors and shapes, including a large flower with pink-dotted petals. She scratched the back of her head when she saw that, but soon shifted her attention away from the flora because there was more going on in the Garden than some strange plants.

Standing in the center of the Garden was a tall, old-fashioned gazebo, with a white roof that shaded the interior area well. The gazebo was covered with flowers that were thankfully less garish than the hot pink one; mostly red, with some golden petals tossed in for good measure. It was obviously where the wedding ceremony itself was going to take place, as a red carpet ran from the gazebo's steps all the way to the back of Carnag Hall.

In the Garden itself stood dozens of people already, most of whom appeared to be Shikan or Carnagian nobility, all wearing fancy white or red robes, depending on their nationality, all probably awaiting Malock and Raya. Jenur didn't know who any of them were, however, because she didn't follow politics. Though the various minor royals talked among each other like old friends, even from a distance Jenur could sense an undercurrent of hostility in their body language. Why that was, she didn't really know or care. She just took note of the positions of various nobles, even though she didn't think any of them could pose a real threat to her mission.

What she did think could pose a threat to her mission, however, were two dozen or so men and women stationed mostly around the walls themselves. These men and women looked like servants, but when Jenur spotted a wand in the hands of one such man and noticed how most of them scanned the Garden with observant eyes, as if looking for signs of possible trouble, she immediately knew who they were: Justice Enforcers and Sun Guardians in disguise. She speculated they were not in uniform because they did not want any would-be assassins or troublemakers to see them, but it was a useless trick on their part that didn't fool Jenur one bit.

I'll still have to be careful, Jenur thought. *Can't let them catch me. Even though it would be better if they did.*

Jenur almost wanted to jump down, tear off her invisibility clothes, and let all of the guards see her. Then they could arrest her and put her in jail and Jenur wouldn't have to kill Malock or Raya.

Of course, if that happened, no doubt the Mechanical Goddess had a backup plan all figured out. Maybe one of the Goddess's automatons would come in and finish the job. Or maybe Calir's tracking device would actually cause Jenur to explode and kill everyone in the Garden. Whatever it was, Jenur didn't know and wasn't sure she wanted to find out.

Her mind turned to how she planned to kill Malock and Raya. It had been a difficult decision to make and she wasn't sure she could pull it off without being caught, but in the end, she decided on using the same blowgun that Quro had used on Deber. It wasn't exactly the same as Quro's blowgun, however, as Quro's had been confiscated back on Destan. The one Jenur had been given—and which currently lay in her pack, waiting to be used—was made of metal and, according to Hana, designed to fire with the exact same force as a normal gun. Hana had explained in detail how the metal blowgun's design took advantage of the blower's breath to send the dart flying farther than normal, but Jenur hadn't paid much attention at the time because she kept imagining the dart flying into Malock's neck and killing him, a distracting mental image if ever there was one.

Sitting cross-legged on the wall, Jenur watched King Halock— that had to be who it was, because he looked just like Malock, except older and with less hair—entertaining some Shikan nobles with a story of some sort. It must have been funny because the nobles laughed at certain points and sipped from their wine cups whenever there was a lull in the action. An older woman sat near Halock, who was probably Queen Markinia, and she, too, laughed with the nobles, occasionally interrupting to add something that would without fail win more laughter from the wedding guests.

Just seeing Halock reminded Jenur of Malock. Especially the way he smiled. It almost made Jenur get up and leave. There was no way she could possibly do this. She may have been a coldhearted assassin, raised and trained by a group of coldhearted assassins, but she didn't think she would be able to follow through with this one. Nor did she want to kill Princess Raya, either, even though she had never met her before.

Nonetheless, when a servant dashed out from Carnag Hall and announced, "Prince Tojas Malock, Crown Prince of Carnag, and Princess Raya Kabadi, Princess of Shika," Jenur stood up and drew the blowgun out of her bag even as the rest of the wedding attendants turned to watch as two people walked out of the palace. Jenur didn't look at the people until she had loaded the blowgun with an aerodynamic dart that she had been told could clear a thousand feet under the right conditions. She had a hard time believing that, but when she thought about all of the other things that the Mechanical Goddess had created, she supposed it was not that unbelievable.

Looking up, Jenur choked when she saw Malock. It wasn't his perfectly smooth, perfectly combed-back hair, with a gold crown with a stylized version of Grinf's hammer built into the crest that made her do that. Nor was it the red shirt he wore or the gold robes hanging off his shoulders. It was his face, which looked like he had slammed it against a burning hot furnace a couple dozen times and then slept on it for a few hours. His ugly face contrasted so sharply with the handsome face that Jenur remembered that, at first, she could hardly believe it was him.

Walking next to Malock was a young woman who looked to be around Jenur's age, perhaps older by a few years. Her skin was paler than Malock's, identifying the woman as Princess Raya Kabadi. Unlike Malock, Raya's face didn't look at all distorted or burned, though she didn't look very happy. The Princess wore a flowing white dress that looked far more expensive than it needed to be, though Jenur didn't focus too much on her appearance because she knew that all royals tended to wear extravagant, overpriced clothing even when they didn't need to.

The two walked down the red carpet, while the other royals watched in silence. The Enforcers and Guardians also watched, but as far as Jenur could tell, Malock and Raya were entirely defenseless. She could even kill them now if she wanted, but she wanted to wait for the right moment. If she attacked them now, she knew she would be caught. At least, that's what she told herself.

Neither of them looked happy. The soon-to-be-married couple more closely resembled soldiers marching to war than a couple about to be wed. For a moment, Jenur thought they might actually be happier dead and unmarried than alive and wed, though she banished the thought from her mind swiftly.

While those two continued to walk, Jenur calculated the distance between her current position and the gazebo. It had to be several hundred feet at least, which much to her disappointment would be no problem for her blowgun. As long as she stayed in her current position on the wall, she would be able to shoot Malock and Raya without much difficulty, even once they were in the gazebo. And she hated knowing that.

In just a few more seconds, Malock and Raya were now in the gazebo, along with a Priest of Grinf who was talking to them in low tones. The wedding guests had now gathered in front of the gazebo, all of them holding wineglasses filled to the brim with red wine. A few of the guards had made their way closer to the gazebo, but none of them were close enough to stop Jenur's darts from striking Malock and Raya.

Silently, Jenur raised her blowgun, aiming first for Raya. She only did that because she didn't know Raya as well as Malock. Killing her would be easier to do, even though Jenur bore no ill will toward the Shikan Princess. Besides, the dart's kenyo poison would be quick. Once the dart pierced Raya's skin and the poison entered her veins, the Princess would be dead in less than ten seconds. Then Malock would ... he would join her.

Jenur just stood there, blowgun held up to her mouth, as the Priest started talking. He was too far away and speaking too quietly for Jenur to understand him, but it didn't matter whether she understood him or not. All Jenur needed to do was blow the darts into Malock and Raya's necks and then run as fast as she could.

Her body froze at the very thought. The Priest now took Malock's right hand and Raya's left and put them together, probably as part of the ceremony. He then put his withered hands on their shoulders, as if assuring them of Grinf's blessing. Jenur noticed another Priest stood by, probably a Priestess of Nimiko based on the white robes she wore. She, too, stepped forward and placed her hands on the shoulders of the two royals.

You know what will happen if you don't do it, Jenur thought. *Hana will kill Quro and Rint. She wasn't joking around when she said that.*

Tears unexpectedly began to sneak out from Jenur's ducts, but she wiped them away. Crying would only make it harder to aim. She had to get this over with. The longer she waited, the longer it would take for her to do this and the more likely she was to be caught.

As she readjusted her aim, Jenur spotted an older man—a Carnagian noble, most likely, based on the gold hammers etched into his robe's shoulders—who, for whatever reason, reminded her of Kinker, even though the older man didn't look anything at all like Kinker. That made her hesitate again.

What would Kinker do? Jenur thought. *What would he say, if he saw what I was about to do? Would he support me in making this decision to save his brother's life or would he be against it?*

Just thinking of Kinker made her heart ache, but her aim didn't waver this time. As always whenever she was about to kill, her mind became clearer, more focused. She never knew why this always happened right before the kill, but it was a sign that she was going to go through with it no matter how she felt about it.

Now both Priests were speaking. They took turns reading from a book on a stand. Malock and Raya stood still, while some of the guests looked bored and restless. The older noble from before even yawned, though discreetly. The only guests who seemed intently interested in the wedding playing out before them were King Halock,

Queen Markinia, and a man who could only be King Fabadi of Shika. Halock looked like he was getting emotional, though to be fair, he wasn't crying quite as much as Markinia. Fabadi appeared impassive and disinterested, but with the way he sat forward, it was clear he was very much interested in seeing his daughter married.

It had never occurred to Jenur that Malock's parents cared for him so much. She was reminded of Quro, who, while perhaps not the perfect father, had nonetheless saved her life when she was just a little baby and had raised her the best he could. She remembered how frightened he had looked when he told her that he thought she had died, and she realized that Halock and Markinia would likely feel the same way about their own son's death, if Jenur went through with his assassination.

I can't do this, Jenur thought, starting to tremble where she stood. *Not Malock. Not even Raya. Malock's my friend. But if I don't kill him, then Hana will kill Quro and Rint. And Quro is more valuable to me than Malock, right? He's my father. Isn't his life worth more to me than Malock's?*

A sickening feeling rose in her stomach. By now the Priests had finished speaking. Malock and Raya faced each other. It was obvious they were going to kiss any second now. And when they did, they would immediately leave to go parading around Port Blasan to celebrate their marriage and Jenur would lose the perfect opportunity to kill them.

So Jenur took a deep breath, did a quick calculation to make sure her aim was still on target, put the tip of her blowgun up to her mouth, closed her eyes, and blew on it. She felt her breath pass through the metal tube, imagined the air pushing the dart through. In her mind's eyes, she saw the dart fly through the air and strike Raya in the neck. Saw Raya fall to the floor of the gazebo. Saw Malock and the wedding guests staring in shock before another dart struck Malock in the neck, causing him to fall on top of Raya.

That was why Jenur was puzzled when she heard none of that. Opening her eyes, Jenur saw the strangest thing she had yet seen: A single hand floating in midair, not connected to anything else, with the dart she had shot caught between its index and middle finger. Jenur just stared at the hand in disbelief.

"Now, now, now," said a quiet, yet familiar, voice to her left, "we can't have that, now can we, Jenur Takren?"

Almost too shocked to move, Jenur turned her head until she was face to face with a familiar monkey grinning man. His left hand was missing, but there was no blood. It was just a clean stump, totally smooth, at least until he pulled his arm back and the hand reappeared, the dart still between his fingers. He held his right hand behind his back, like he was hiding something.

"R-Ramufa?" said Jenur, keeping her voice as low as possible. "What are you—"

"Shhh," said Ramufa, holding one finger up to his mouth. "You don't want to ruin this beautiful ceremony, do you?"

Jenur glanced back at the gazebo. Malock and Raya were now kissing and the guests were clapping their approval. None of the guards seemed to notice her or Ramufa.

"How can you see me?" Jenur hissed, looking back at Ramufa.

"I'm invisible."

"So am I," said Ramufa, who seemed to have enough sense in his head to keep his voice low. "Temporary invisibility, of course, but invisibility nonetheless. Master Hollech taught me how to do it, and I am thankful for his personal instruction, as aoramancey is the most difficult aspect of the Thief's Way to learn on one's own."

"What are you even doing here?" Jenur said. "How did you know what I was trying to do?"

Ramufa's smile widened considerably. "Because Master Hollech told me to do it instead."

It took Jenur a second to process what Ramufa was saying, but when she did, she was too late. Shocked gasps and even screams filled the air, causing Jenur to snap her head to the wedding ceremony. Her heart failed her when she saw what had happened.

Malock was on his knees in the gazebo, but he didn't appear to be hurt. He held Princess Raya in his arms, shaking her and clearly trying to awake her. The wedding guests all stood looking shocked. The duke she had noted earlier had even dropped his wine, spilling it all over his leather boots.

Then King Fabadi ran up onto the gazebo. He shoved Malock out of the way and took his daughter's body into his arms. He was crying as he held her body close to his, his tears streaming down his face. The two Priests were calling for the guards, half of whom were running toward the gazebo, while the other half were searching the rest of the Garden for the assassin.

Jenur turned back to Ramufa. "What ... how ... why ..."

Ramufa chuckled. He pulled his right hand from his back and showed her a long, bloody knife that looked quite ancient.

"Did you really think that Master Hollech was going to stand by and let Malock and Raya and the rest of those Heathens go around free?" said Ramufa, his low voice far more threatening than before. "Master Hollech's not much interested in losing his followers, just like the rest of the northern gods."

"But why?" said Jenur. "I thought it was the Mechanical Goddess who had been asked to do it."

"Silly," said Ramufa as the knife dripped blood. "The Mechanical Goddess didn't send you to kill Malock and Raya. She sent you to *defend* them. From me. Wasn't it obvious?"

"No, no it wasn't," said Jenur, shaking her head. "Hana said—"

"You can't trust a katabans," said Ramufa with a snort. "She was just saying all of that to get you upset and into trouble. No, the Mechanical Goddess isn't the type to hire assassins. Especially to assassinate mortals that she has taken a liking to."

"But this doesn't make any sense," said Jenur. "Why would the Mechanical Goddess want me to defend them? I thought the southern gods hated mortals. I mean, the Kraken Goddess tried to kill me, my dad, and Rint for no reason."

Ramufa chuckled as the guards below shouted for order amid the chaos of the wedding. "Remember, the southern gods hate their northern siblings at least as much as they hate us. The southern gods, lest you forget, despise how we're protected by their northern siblings. Think of how angry the northern gods would be if us mortals stopped worshiping them and you can see why the Mechanical Goddess has a vested interest in making sure that the Brotherhood of Heathens succeeds in its mission to 'liberate' all mortals from the northern gods' control."

Then Ramufa leaned forward slightly, his sweaty body odor filling her nostrils. "As for the Kraken Goddess, she had nothing to do with that earlier attack. That squid that attacked you three was my pet. I had it attack you because at the time I was hoping to make some easy money from you and your friends, but now I see that that just isn't going to happen, sadly enough."

Jenur reached for her own knife, saying as she did so, "Well, if that is true, then the least I can do is catch you and let the guards arrest you before you escape."

Ramufa's hands moved as fast as lightning. He grabbed Jenur's hand that was reaching for her knife and shoved his own blade into hers. Before Jenur could even comprehend what he was doing, Ramufa shoved Jenur off the side of the wall into the Garden below. At the same time, he shouted, "Guards! Guards! I have found the assassin! Come quick!"

Jenur didn't have time to react. She fell for what seemed like forever and then landed with an abrupt *crunch* onto a thick bush. The fall stunned her and before she could recover, she heard the heavy footfalls of the guards coming to get her. She tried to sit up, but her invisibility clothes had gotten tangled up in the bush, so she spent precious seconds trying to untangle her clothes, but it was no use.

A few seconds later, Jenur was surrounded by at least a dozen tall, strong men wearing servant robes and wielding wands. They all pointed their wands at Jenur, as if daring her to make a move. Somehow they all saw her, perhaps because her invisibility clothes had gotten ripped and her hood had fallen off her head.

"Don't even breathe, killer," said one of the guards, a Shikan man with a sweaty forehead. "You are under arrest for the murder of Princess Raya Kabadi of Shika. Put the murder weapon down and hold out your hands."

Seeing no way out of this, Jenur dropped the bloody knife and held out her hands. The guard who had spoken waved his wand once and a pair of thick, heavy, tight metal manacles materialized around Jenur's wrists. She tugged at them experimentally, but found that she couldn't even move her wrists they were so tight.

"Take her into Carnag Hall," the guard snapped to his fellow guards. "Keep an eye on her and don't let her escape. I will inform Prince Malock and the others that we have caught the killer."

Jenur allowed the guards to haul her to her feet and half-drag, half-pull her across the Garden to the Hall. As they did so, Jenur glanced over her shoulder at the walls, but didn't see Ramufa anywhere. She also looked over at the gazebo, but with all of the people still crowding around it, she couldn't see Malock at all.

I wonder if he will save me, Jenur thought as the guards took her into Carnag Hall. *Will he even believe me when I say I didn't do it? Or will he think I killed her to get back at him?*

Whatever the case, Jenur knew—beyond a shadow of a doubt—that she hated Hana, Ramufa, and everyone else she had ever run into. Those monsters might as well burn in eternity for all she cared.

Chapter Sixteen

THOUGH PRINCE MALOCK WAS dripping wet from the rain, he didn't bother to dry off as he walked through the halls of Castle Shika. A stout man named Jingus—one of the servants of the Shikan Royal Family—was leading him, his voice quiet and his demeanor sober. Every now and then Jingus would sniff, which was no surprise to Malock, as Jingus appeared to have been very attached to Raya, more so than any of the other servants that lived in the castle.

Jenur walked by Malock's side. Unlike Malock, she now wore a hood and robes to hide her identity, mostly because no one outside of the Carnagian and Shikan Royal Families were even aware that she was still alive. When Malock had learned of the identity of Raya's 'killer,' he had been shocked to learn it was Jenur (though for whatever reason, Jenur had referred to herself as 'Gaharna Vicin' when the Justice Enforcers had interrogated her, perhaps to protect her real identity, which was why Malock had gone along with it at the time). He believed her, however, when she claimed that she hadn't done it, mostly because her story—about a servant of Hollech being the true culprit—fit in with what Malock knew about the gods. It had been easy to convince his parents to spare her life, but King Fabadi had been absolutely enraged and seemed to think Jenur was lying. The only reason Jenur was even here was because Malock had promised to punish Jenur at a later date for her 'crime,' even though he had no intention of ever carrying out such a punishment. He did have to keep Jenur under his watch at all times, however, to ensure she wouldn't run away, although she had already told him that she had no intention of going anywhere for the time being.

As they walked the Castle's brightly lit halls, Malock remembered Raya's funeral. Almost everybody who was anybody on Carnag or Shika had been invited to the funeral, which had taken place in the Royal Cemetery, despite the thick rain. Malock had brought along an umbrella, but that had done little to keep him dry from the torrential rains that seemed to plague Shika like a disease.

It had been a mere week since Raya had been assassinated, so when Malock saw her corpse being lowered into the ground, he could barely take it. He didn't break down during the funeral, however, because he knew that that type of behavior was looked down upon in Shikan funerals. Tradition allowed only King Fabadi, as Raya's father, to show any sort of emotion, and he had cried quite a bit over his daughter's death.

After the funeral, the rest of the guests had gone into Castle Shika's mourning room—technically the castle's ballroom—to exchange their memories of Raya and to give their condolences to King Fabadi. That was when Malock and Jenur took advantage of the opportunity to leave without anyone noticing. They had found a servant, named Jingus, who agreed to take them up to Raya's room. Malock had told Jingus he wanted to go there to mourn her privately, but in reality, Malock was looking for something that Raya had told him about before she died. He hoped it was still there, though he supposed if it wasn't, he surely would have known by now.

"Here we are, Prince Malock," said Jingus as they stopped in front of a large oak door, which was currently locked. "Normally, when someone dies on Shika, we don't let guests into the deceased's room. But as you were going to be Princess Raya's husband, I think we can allow an exception to that tradition just this once."

"Thank you, Jingus," said Malock as the servant undid the locks. "I appreciate it."

Jingus nodded as he stepped away from the undone locks. "No problem at all, Prince Malock. I am sure this is what the Princess would have wanted if she hadn't ... if she was still with us."

The servant looked close to tearing up, so Malock said to him, "You can go back to the mourning room. My friend and I will make sure to lock the room back up when we're done."

Jingus simply bowed as way of showing thanks and walked down the hall until he turned a corner and was out of sight. Then Malock pushed open the door to Raya's room and entered, with Jenur following closely behind.

Raya's room was about how Malock expected it to be. Tall bookshelves lined the walls, while a fancy, flowery bed stood in the center of it all. A large reading chair sat in one corner, while two large windows overlooked the courtyard of Castle Shika. It reminded Malock a lot of his own room back in Carnag Hall, although it was slightly smaller.

Malock heard the door close behind him and turned to see Jenur standing in front of it. She lowered her hood and frowned as she looked around the room.

"So," said Jenur, "where, exactly, is this super secret entrance Raya told you about, Mal? I don't see anything out of the ordinary here."

Malock remembered what Raya had told him and walked over to the bookshelf at the very end of the room. He ran his finger along the spines of the books until he came across a yellow book titled *A Short History of the Six Pillars of Magic*, by Rundya, that appeared quite old. As he saw no other yellow-spined books, he knew this had to be it.

He pulled the spine back, but it only came out partway. As soon as he let go out of the book, a portion of the bookshelf slid away, revealing an old door that had not been there a moment ago.

"A secret entrance?" said Jenur. "Where does it lead?"

"Let's find out," said Malock.

He found the key to the door behind the yellow book and then inserted it into the keyhole and turned. A small *click* told him that the door was now unlocked. He twisted the knob and opened the door, revealing a spiral staircase that went down around a corner. A dim light from somewhere at the bottom was the only source of illumination in the dark stairwell.

Malock gestured for Jenur to follow him and the two walked

down the steps carefully. While Malock knew what to expect, he was well aware of the risks that he and Jenur were taking. There was no telling whether Nimiko, the God of Light, was still down there or not, but the mere presence of the light made him hopeful that the god had not yet escaped or been rescued.

They eventually reached another door, this one much older than the one they had taken to get down here. Like the other door, however, it was locked, but Malock discovered that the key from before worked with this lock, too, so he unlocked and opened the door and entered with Jenur by his side.

They now stood in a small dungeon, roughly the size of Malock's captain's quarters back on the *Iron Wind*, that smelled like sweat and blood and rotten food. Along the walls were faded paintings, but Malock didn't bother to look at them. He was looking at the man at the other end of the room, the god whose wrists and ankles were chained to the wall.

Nimiko looked up when Malock and Jenur entered. His gaunt face and ragged, loose-fitting clothes made him look less than a beggar, but his expression belonged to an almighty being who would smite you from the face of the earth if you dared to disrespect him.

"Who are you?" said Nimiko. His voice was as weak as his body. "I thought only Princess Raya knew of me."

"Princess Raya is dead," said Malock, his tone as harsh as he could make it. "Killed by a servant of one of your brothers."

Nimiko raised an eyebrow. "Am I suppose to cry? If I had the energy, I would be leaping with joy. Are you here to free me?"

"No," said Malock, shaking his head. "Instead, we're here to make you an offer."

Nimiko sat up and scratched the back of his right ear. "An offer? Are you trying to sell me something?"

"It's not that kind of offer," said Jenur, rolling her eyes. "Geez, you really *are* slow."

Nimiko's eyes literally flashed. "If I wasn't chained up right now, why, I would—"

"Enough bickering," said Malock, holding up one hand. "Here's the offer, short and to the point: The Powers are intending to destroy Martir. We want you to take us beyond the Void to find the Powers and convince them to spare the world."

Nimiko stared at Malock for a moment before shaking his head and chuckling. "I don't believe it. The Powers would never destroy the world. You are trying to trick me."

"It's the truth," said Malock. "That is why your brothers and sisters haven't tried to free you, isn't it? They have left you here because they do not see a point in freeing you if all of existence is going to come to an end soon."

Nimiko scowled. "Don't pretend to understand how we gods think, mortal. Our thoughts are higher and finer than whatever goes through that pile of mush you call a brain in your skull."

Malock shook his head. "I understand how the gods think far better than you know, Nimiko, but that's irrelevant. The world is coming to an end and we need your help."

Nimiko snorted. "So you mortals think you can survive the Void and convince the *Powers*, of all beings, to not destroy the world? You are even more arrogant than I thought."

"Better to think we can save the world than to sit around and act like there's nothing we can do about it," said Malock. "You gods certainly aren't doing anything about it."

Nimiko shrugged, an awkward gesture in his current position if ever there was one. "If the Powers desire it, then it is not in our place to deny them it. Unless you want to die a painful death, that is."

"You sound just like Skimif," Malock said.

"Who?"

"Doesn't matter," said Malock. "You're going to take us whether you want to or not. Got it?"

"You can't force me to go," said Nimiko. He tugged at his manacles and said, "These Void metal chains have done a fine job holding me back, but if you are going to move me, you will have to free me first."

"Not necessarily," said Malock. "Raya told us about some extra Void metal chains and a collar that she found down here which she had her servants move into the castle's armory."

"A collar?" said Nimiko in disbelief. "Are you going to walk me around like a dog?"

"If you won't behave," said Jenur with a shrug. "Unless you've got a better suggestion for a way we could keep an eye on you?"

Nimiko slumped against the stone wall. "I suppose I don't have much of a choice, do I?"

"Indeed you don't," said Malock. He then looked over his

shoulder at Jenur and said, "Jen, could you fetch the chains and collar? Do it quickly and without being seen or heard. I want to leave as soon as possible without anyone seeing us."

"I'll be back in a flash," Jenur said as she stepped outside the open door and started climbing up the stairs.

Malock turned back to face Nimiko. The god was staring at Malock, his eyes glowing softly.

"What?" said Malock. He pointed at his face and said, "Wondering where I got this?"

Nimiko shook his head slowly. "No, but I can tell that you got it from Grinf."

"Then what are you staring at?" said Malock.

Nimiko chuckled. "Just imagining what your body will look like when it steps beyond the Void. I have only seen one mortal pass through the Void. The explosion was quite messy."

Malock folded his arms and turned away. He would not dignify that comment with a response.

Continued in:

The New Era of Prince Malock

Book Three in the Prince Malock World

Now available wherever books are sold!

About the Author

Timothy L. Cerepaka writes fantasy stories as an indie author. He is the author of the Mages of Martir fantasy novels, the Tournament of the Gods fantasy novels, and The War-Torn Kingdom fantasy novels.

Find out more at his website: www.timothylcerepaka.com

www.ingramcontent.com/pod-product-compliance
Lightning Source LLC
Chambersburg PA
CBHW022004010726
47494CB00003B/890